THE DROWNING ISLE

Simon McCleave is a million-selling crime novelist. His first book, *The Snowdonia Killings*, was released in January 2020 and soon became an Amazon bestseller, reaching No.1 in the UK Chart and selling over 400,000 copies. His fifteen subsequent novels in the DI Ruth Hunter Snowdonia series have all ranked in the Amazon top 20 and he has sold over two million books worldwide. *The Drowning Isle* is the fourth book in the Anglesey series.

Before he was an author, Simon worked as a script editor at the BBC and a producer at Channel 4 before working as a story analyst in Los Angeles. He then became a script writer, writing on series such as *Silent Witness*, *Murder In Suburbia*, *Teachers*, *The Bill*, *Eastenders* and many more. His Channel 4 film *Out of the Game* was critically acclaimed and described as 'an unflinching portrayal of male friendship' by *Time Out*.

Simon lives in North Wales with his wife and two children.

www.simonmccleave.com

Also by Simon McCleave:

To find out more visit **www.simonmccleave.com**

THE DROWNING ISLE

SIMON McCLEAVE

Published by AVON
A division of HarperCollins*Publishers*
1 London Bridge Street
London SE1 9GF

www.harpercollins.co.uk

HarperCollins*Publishers*
Macken House, 39/40 Mayor Street Upper
Dublin 1, D01 C9W8
Ireland

A Paperback Original 2024
1

First published in Great Britain by HarperCollins*Publishers* 2024

A catalogue copy of this book is available from the British Library.

ISBN: 978-0-00-862019-6

Set in Sabon LT Std by HarperCollins*Publishers* India

Printed and bound in the UK using 100% Renewable Electricity at
CPI Group (UK) Ltd

To Lee, Keilie, Lowri and Seren x

ANGLESEY

There is a word in Welsh that has no exact translation into English – Hiraeth. It is best defined as the bond you feel with a place – a mixture of pride, homesickness and a determination to return. Most people that have visited Anglesey leave with an understanding of Hiraeth.

YNYS LLANDDWYN

The small tidal island of Ynys Llanddwyn, just off the south-west coast of Anglesey, is named after the patron saint of Welsh lovers – Dwynwen. It is believed she lived in the fifth century and was the daughter of King Brychan Brycheiniog. She fell in love with a man called Maelon, whom she was forced by her father to reject. Dwynwen subsequently dedicated herself to helping those unhappy in their love lives, eventually building a home on this remote island.

The ruins of a medieval church dedicated to Dwynwen can still be seen today, and fourteenth-century poet Dafydd ap Gwilym claimed he saw a golden image of her at the site when he visited. Every year on the twenty-fifth of January, Wales celebrates St Dwynwen's Day, similar to St Valentine's Day in many places around the world.

Thomas Pennant's account from the 1770s mentions small ruins nearby being the prebendal house, which housed

Richard Kyffyn in the fifteenth century. He worked with Sir Rhys ap Thomas and other Welsh chieftains to plan for Henry Tudor's return from exile in Brittany, using fishing vessels to send intelligence to him.

At St Dwynwen's Well on Ynys Llanddwyn Island, a sacred fish is said to predict the fate of couples in love; while unsettled waters in the well signals good luck and contentment.

Nearby are two beacons: one that looks like a windmill tower but has been abandoned; the other a guide for ships passing through the perilous Menai Strait, with cottages built to house the pilots who boarded them. In December 1852, this lighthouse saved thirty-six people from three shipwrecks within seven days.

Rocks and geology from about 500 million years ago form the foundations of Ynys Llanddwyn Island – where pillow lavas gracing its beaches demonstrate the awesome underwater forces that shaped it, beginning south of New Zealand. The island has been named in the First 100 World Geological Heritage Sites list – key geological sites of international scientific relevance with a substantial contribution to the development of geological sciences through history.

This place also forms part of a National Nature Reserve, which includes Newborough Warren to the south and The Cefni saltmarsh to the north, all managed by Natural Resources Wales.

PROLOGUE

The teenage boy came out of the dense, Alpine-like Newborough Forest and glanced around. He then made his way through the grassy dunes of Newborough Beach, which was located on the south-west coast of Anglesey, an island off the coast of North Wales.

It looks different doesn't it? the boy thought in his confused state. Even though he'd been to Newborough dozens of times before, it looked different.

But there was a good reason why it looked different that afternoon.

He was hallucinating from the magic mushroom-laced chocolate that he'd eaten with his friends about an hour earlier. Plus a few slugs of vodka and a toke on some weed. He didn't know where his friends had gone. He didn't really care. They were probably still dancing and playing around in the forest, tripping the light fantastic. They were all camping overnight in Newborough to celebrate their eighteenth birthdays.

Ahead of him there were shallow pools, gullies and small channels that dissected the vast expanse of the sandy beach. The surface water shimmered in the glow of the sun. Colours were changing. Shards of pink, turquoise, purple and green. What was it that John Lennon had written? *Tangerine trees and marmalade skies.*

Wow, that looks amazing, he thought, even though he got the feeling that he'd been distracted from something that had frightened him.

He noticed he was out of breath but couldn't remember why. Someone or something had been chasing him in the forest. Was that right? The voice in his head seemed to echo, as if in a deep cave. It felt like he was walking around in his own dream.

God, I'm properly fucked…

His eyes rested back on the plethora of colours that emanated in a shimmering medley. It must have been what The Beatles had seen when they took LSD and wrote tracks for *Sgt. Pepper's. Cool.* He loved that album. His mates could keep Sam Fender.

Beyond the shallow pools lay the tidal island of Llanddwyn.

To the south, the spectacular landscape of Snowdonia, formed over 500 million years ago.

God, this is so beautiful.

To the east, the vast, dark expanse of Caernarfon Bay and then the Irish Sea. At low tide, a winding path lay across the neck of sand from the mainland to this isle.

The island itself was covered with crowberry, liverwort and hair lichen. Close to the church ruins was Dwynwen's

2

Well, where nuns had blessed visitors to the island with holy water 1,600 years ago. To the right of the ruins, a moss-covered memorial – a huge, stone Celtic cross – stood on the higher ground of the island's north-west tip with the inscription: *In memory of St Dwynwen, 25 January 465.*

Glancing back across the dunes from where he'd come, the boy spotted the dark figure that had been chasing him emerging from the darkness of the forest. It hadn't been a figment of his hallucination after all.

Oh shit! What do they want? Why are they chasing me?

For a moment, he wondered if it was one of his mates playing a trick on him.

But it wasn't.

Suddenly, the person ran towards him aggressively, shouting at him to listen.

Fuck, I'd better get out of here, he thought. *Is this even really happening?*

Now full of panic, the boy turned and sprinted away along the beach. The salty wind stung in his nostrils. The gulls cawed from the sky above him as if they were urging him on to escape. *Go on, go on, run, run away.*

His legs felt leaden, as if they didn't even belong to him. Every step was a struggle. His body felt drained of energy. All he wanted to do was lie down in the sand and look up at the sky.

Come on, you've got to bloody run!

The lethargic feeling cleared as quickly as it had come.

With a sudden clarity, the teenage boy darted along the sand, the sound of the footsteps behind him getting louder.

Just keep running, he told himself.

He tried to shout for help but his throat was dry and nothing more than a rasping sound came out.

Petrified with fear, he was trying to work out why they were chasing him. Or was this a dream? The drugs were playing havoc with his sense of reality.

Is this really happening, or am I imagining it?

Whoever was behind him was getting closer and closer.

They were gasping, panting, murmuring some kind of incantation.

The boy's heart pounded wildly in his chest.

Maybe he could just stop and reason with his pursuer?

No. *What if they attack you and kill you?*

His paranoia and fear were overwhelming.

Glancing back, he saw the figure behind. It looked like they were wearing some kind of mask. But then their face changed and morphed into something else.

Jesus. What the hell is going on? Is this just some horrible figment dragged up by my subconscious?

The drugs were hindering his ability to separate reality from hallucination.

The boy continued running, pumping his arms as he sucked for air. His lungs were now burning.

Please, don't let me die here.

Looking back over his shoulder again, the boy ran into a rock he didn't see ahead of him, which took his legs out from under him and sent him crashing face first into the sand.

He gasped as the wind was knocked out of his chest. 'Bloody hell!'

He tried to get his breath.

And then his pursuer was on him like a flash.

They were shouting something at him through gritted teeth.

'What the hell do you want? Just tell me!' the boy demanded as he looked up at a face that he suddenly realised he recognised.

The boy lashed out and punched his pursuer.

'You're pathetic!' the boy shouted angrily as he struggled. 'Pathetic and stupid.'

Then a vice-like grip seized his throat.

Choking, gasping, coughing.

CHAPTER 1

April 2022 – 48 Hours Earlier

It was 6.15 a.m. and Detective Inspector Laura Hart of the Anglesey Police Force stood on the flat, wet, sandy beach at Beaumaris and took a lungful of fresh sea air. This was Laura's morning routine – well, at least four or five times a week.

'Race you in?' said a voice.

It was her nineteen-year-old daughter, Rosie. She had blonde hair tied back off of her face, bright blue eyes and a fair complexion. She was on the tall side, with a small button nose and rosebud lips, and wore a nose ring and two earrings in the top of each ear. She was smart and good natured.

Laura pulled a face. 'Really? Let me just ready myself.'

'Wimp!' Rosie laughed as she ran forward, her feet patting noisily on the sand as she went. She gave a yelp as she hit the icy sea but didn't stop. Pushing on through the waves, she arched into a dive and then disappeared under the water for a few seconds before bursting through the surface with a victorious 'Woo hoo!'

That's my girl, Laura thought with a mixture of pride and relief, glad to see her daughter happy for once.

It had been just over a month since Rosie had been kidnapped and buried alive by serial killer Henry Marsh. It had left psychological scars, with Rosie experiencing night terrors and panic attacks, and even though she was receiving excellent trauma counselling, Rosie was still struggling.

Laura had read about the huge benefits on mental health of cold-water swimming. Apparently, immersion into the icy sea induced something called a 'cold shock response'. This was a gasp reflex, the constriction of blood vessels close to the surface of the skin as your body tries to conserve heat. This was combined with a raised heart rate and hyperventilation, though repeated exposure to this process diminished the trauma response. The cold-water therapy taught your body and its nervous system to adapt.

'Mum? Hello?' Rosie yelled from the sea. 'Today would be good.'

'You cheeky bugger,' Laura shouted back.

In that moment, the rhythmic whoosh of the waves and the salty fragrance of the sea seemed to intensify.

Looking across the Menai Strait towards the dark, jagged plum outline of Snowdonia, Laura took a deep breath and steeled herself.

Here we go.

Breaking into a run, she watched as the freezing water raced towards her feet and then covered them.

Her shins splashed the sea, spraying water over her hips and then her torso. The momentum of her run carried her forward as she dived into the next wave and disappeared under it. For a second or two, she could feel nothing – that slight delay between the nerve receptors in her skin and her brain connecting – then the sharp, uncomfortable shock of the cold rushed in. She broke the surface and gave an immense gasp.

Endorphins zipped through her. Adrenaline, dopamine and serotonin. The legal, natural highs provided by the miracle that is the human body. All the stress, anxiety and repetitive thinking that she had woken with that morning were simply blasted away.

Wow.

'Better?' Rosie asked with a grin as she bobbed around in the cold sea.

'Much,' Laura laughed as she pushed her own blonde hair back off her face. It was so lovely to see a smile on her daughter's face.

'I'm making fajitas tonight, if you fancy?' Rosie said as her teeth started to chatter.

'Are you indeed?' Laura smiled.

'Steak or chicken?' Rosie asked.

'Oh God, chicken,' Laura replied. 'You know what a fusspot Jake is. One tiny speck of red in his steak and he'll refuse to eat the lot… just like his dad.'

Rosie blinked, dipping her shoulders back under the water. 'Is he?'

'Your dad had to have everything cooked through. In fact, he preferred most things burned to a crisp,' Laura explained with a laugh.

'Isn't that really unhealthy? Like carcinogenic?'

'I did tell him that. All the time.'

'I don't think I knew that about him,' Rosie said, deep in thought. 'Am I like him?'

'Of course,' Laura replied. 'Stubborn, cheeky, untidy…'

'Hey!' Rosie laughed and splashed water at her.

Laura looked at her. 'You're like your dad in lots of lovely ways. For instance, you're kind and genuinely interested in helping other people.'

Rosie nodded and then pointed to her face. 'Yeah, and I've got his stupid thick eyebrows that I have to pluck on a daily basis.'

Laura smiled at Rosie. It wasn't just the eyebrows, she also had Sam's dark, hooded eyes and long eyelashes. She glanced out across the water and saw a shadowy outline bobbing around on the surface, distracting her from the conversation. It could have been nothing more than the light and early morning mist playing tricks, but it looked as if someone was swimming out there.

It had been nearly four years since Sam, her husband and Rosie's father, had been killed in the line of duty in Manchester. Laura had been at the warehouse where Sam had died that day – 12 August 2018. It was a date that would be etched in her memory forever. Sam, a uniformed officer in the Manchester Metropolitan Police (MMP), had been taken hostage by a notorious organised criminal gang (an OCG) called the Fallowfield Hill Gang. Laura was one of the top police hostage negotiators in the force but had failed to secure his release before the warehouse where he was being held exploded. The guilt and grief of that dark day had prompted her to leave the police force and return to her childhood home – Anglesey. She had bought a house in Beaumaris, a seaside town on the south-east coast of the island, and moved with her daughter, Rosie, and now twelve-year-old son, Jake.

For a while, Laura had worked teaching negotiating skills and strategies within the world of business. However, when Jake was caught up in a hostage situation and she was forced to come to his rescue, Laura realised that her yearning to return to police work was too overwhelming to ignore. She was now back working as a detective inspector at Beaumaris Police Station.

Rubbing the salty water from her eyes, Laura looked again at the shape.

'You okay, Mum?' Rosie asked. 'You look like you've seen a ghost.'

'Oh no, it's nothing.' Laura gave a forced laugh. 'I'm just miles away, darling.'

Laura could hardly tell Rosie that she wondered if it could be Sam out there swimming. But that was exactly what Laura was thinking.

Part of Laura's grieving process in the years since Sam's death had been regular conversations with him, as though he were standing right in front of her. He would pop up with no warning and though she didn't believe in ghosts, Sam's sudden appearances in her conscious often felt uncomfortably real and out of her control. She assumed they were her way of dealing with the trauma of losing him. An inability to really let him go.

However, in recent months, these visions had become less frequent. Laura knew that this was a good sign, as it meant that she was finally beginning to accept Sam's death, but it also made her sad.

'Were you thinking about Dad?' Rosie asked as they both started to traipse out of the water and head back to their towels and warm clothing.

Laura nodded. 'Yes.'

'Do you ever get scared that you'll forget what he looked like or sounded like?' Rosie asked as she grabbed a large blue towel from the sand.

'Sometimes, yes.' Laura didn't want to admit that it often terrified her that her memories of Sam were fading over time. His twinkly smile, his smell or the sound of his laugh. She then looked at her daughter. 'But it's okay. I can see him in you and Jake. And I also know that he's around and looking out for us whenever we need him.'

'Yeah,' Rosie said, looking a little teary. 'I get that feeling too.'

They hugged for a few seconds.

'Come on,' Laura said, trying to sound positive, 'I'll make us some porridge when we get back.'

CHAPTER 2

Detective Inspector Gareth Williams' mobile danced on his desk, vibrating to signal that a message had come through. Taking a look, he saw it was some information he had requested from the Home Office Large Major Enquiry System (HOLMES), a powerful database used by the UK police for investigations of major incidents. Technically, the HOLMES app was usually restricted for use on computers within police stations or courts. But the technology was sometimes slow and unresponsive, so officers had begun to install the HOLMES app on their phones as it seemed to make it more reliable. In some quarters this practice was frowned upon, but Gareth was a pragmatist.

Sitting back at his desk in the DI's office that was attached to the main CID offices, he looked at the intel that had arrived. After a quick read, he saw that it wasn't relevant to the case he was working. Grabbing the cold toast he'd bought from the canteen about half an hour ago, he munched noisily as he stared at the interminable pile of paperwork on his desk. Gareth ran the CID at Beaumaris nick, which meant that every hour of overtime, every interview and every penny spent on forensics or a phone trace, needed his approval.

Wiping the buttery crumbs from his mouth with the back of his hand, he decided that cold toast was sometimes preferable to hot. Maybe it was something to do with the way the salty butter solidified as it cooled. Through the doorway he could hear snippets of conversations and the odd eruption of laughter as CID officers talked about the various ongoing cases, recent arrests and evidence that had been gathered. He took great pride in his CID team. They were always at their desks early, focused and driven. Often he would have to tell them to go home in the evening, otherwise they'd work into the night.

Reaching over for his coffee, he took a swig and pulled a face. It was now stone cold.

Laura had bought him a coffee mug that plugged in and kept coffee hot but he kept forgetting to bring it to work. *How had the world got so lazy,* he wondered. Pre-grated cheese, voice-activated televisions and heated coffee mugs.

'Boss,' said a voice.

It was Detective Sergeant Declan Flaherty, a stocky Irishman in his late forties who had been part of the Beaumaris CID team for nearly fifteen years. His bearded face was chubby, his mouth full but a little lopsided, and his eyes dark green and thoughtful.

'Everything okay?' Gareth asked.

Declan wore his usual expression of wariness. 'You still okay for tonight, boss?'

Gareth had agreed to come to Declan's son Osian's eighteenth birthday party at the Beaumaris Sports and Social

13

Club later. Osian was sharing the party with a couple of his friends who had also turned eighteen in recent months. Over the years, Gareth had seen Osian grow into a likeable, intelligent and mature young man. The fact that Osian was an outstanding fly half for Beaumaris Rugby Club's U18s had also naturally endeared him to Gareth. He'd been pestering the club secretary to see if he could get Osian a trial for North Wales; Gareth knew that he was that good.

'Of course,' Gareth reassured him.

Gareth was aware that Declan hadn't been himself in recent weeks. Not only had he been preoccupied and quiet, but he had also seemed more fragile and erratic than normal. Gareth hadn't yet broached the subject though, as Declan was a fairly private man.

Ever since Gareth had joined Beaumaris CID as a detective sergeant, he'd liked Declan's pragmatic attitude to policing. It wasn't that Declan broke or even bent the rules. It was that he could apply common sense when it was needed. There were others who would get bogged down in procedure and the policy of modern policing, often losing the actual focus of an investigation. The only thing that let him down once in a while was Declan's very short fuse, but Gareth was willing to overlook it on the rare occasions that he lost his cool.

'Great,' Declan said with a relieved half-smile. 'Thanks. Osian will be made up to see you. And I wouldn't mind someone with me to make sure things don't get out of hand.'

That thought had already crossed Gareth's mind when Declan had first asked him. The thought of thirty eighteen-year-olds letting loose at the Social Club made him shudder.

14

It was a guarantee of excessive drinking, vomit, a possible fight and illicit drug taking. It wasn't what Gareth normally had in mind for a relaxing Friday night after a hard week of police work. But Declan was a mate as well as a work colleague and lending a helping hand was the right thing to do.

'I'm sure it will be fine,' Gareth said and then smiled. 'I'll bring my cuffs just in case Tom Hegerty does his usual trick of causing trouble.'

Gareth knew that Tom had been Osian's friend since primary school but he also knew that Tom was a bit wayward and had been arrested for drunk and disorderly, vandalism and threatening behaviour in recent months.

Declan gave a wry laugh. 'Yeah, I hope he grows out of it or he's going to end up getting into serious trouble.'

'I take it Sue will be there?' Gareth asked.

'Try and stop her,' Declan joked, rolling his eyes with an amused smile. 'New dress, getting her hair done, nails and a spray tan. You'd think *she* was bloody eighteen.'

Sue was Declan's attractive, gregarious wife. From what Gareth could remember, they'd been happily married since their early twenties. The office gossip was that Declan married above himself as Sue's family owned several hotels on the island. That meant they had a nice house, new cars and went on expensive holidays. As far as Gareth was concerned, it was no one else's business and he was pleased for Declan.

'I'll see you later, Dec,' Gareth said as Declan turned to go.

Gareth sat back and for a moment thought of DI Laura Hart. They had been in a relationship for nearly a year,

15

despite a rocky start. He knew he would never replace her late husband, Sam, but in recent months Gareth felt that he'd made progress in his relationship with both Rosie and Jake. He had no children from his previous marriage, so he took delight in his growing connection with Laura's kids. Especially given the fact that he and Laura had agreed in recent weeks to get married, although they were yet to set a date or book a venue.

Looking at his computer screen, Gareth's heart sank as he looked at the time sheets for overtime that he had to print, check and sign off for CID.

Bollocks to that, he thought as he clicked on Google and began to search for wedding venues.

The first image that popped up was the *Viva Las Vegas Elvis Wedding Package* with a couple getting married in a pink Cadillac.

Yeah, I'm not sure that Laura's going to go for that, he thought with a wry smile.

* * *

Laura felt her phone buzz in her pocket as she entered the canteen at Beaumaris nick. The air was thick with the smell of coffee and fried food. It was also bustling with uniformed officers chatting and laughing as they tucked into toast or bacon baps. Now approaching fifty, Laura was trying to be healthy, so she'd started the day with a bowl of porridge sprinkled with berries, nuts and seeds.

If she was honest, she would kill for one of the canteen's legendary bacon baps.

As Laura headed for the coffee machine, she checked to see who had texted her in case it was one of the kids or school.

It was Pete.

Hiya stranger, just checking in to see if you and the kids are all okay? If I was paranoid, I'd think you'd been avoiding me in recent weeks?

Maybe I can drive over this weekend for a catch-up. I need to maintain my ongoing efforts to persuade Jake that City are a far superior football team to that red lot from the other side of Manc.

How's Rosie doing? Been thinking about her.

Pete xx

Laura felt her stomach tense as she read the message.

Detective Chief Inspector Pete Marsons worked for the Manchester Met. He was also a very close family friend and had been Sam's best mate before his death. Laura, Sam and Pete had trained at Hendon Police College together in the nineties and stayed friends ever since. They had even been on family holidays together to Pembrokeshire several times as Pete had kids a similar age to Rosie and Jake.

And Pete had been standing next to Laura when Sam had perished in the warehouse in August 2018.

Neither Laura or Pete were convinced about the results of the Independent Office for Police Conduct's investigation and report on Sam's death that day. In fact, they became increasingly suspicious of the lead officer on the operation, Superintendent Ian Butterfield. The more they investigated

Sam's death, the more they had realised that there had been something much darker going on that day.

It became clear that Butterfield was being paid and blackmailed by the Fallowfield Hill Gang to provide intel as well as tip-offs about arrests and raids. It was also apparent that the corruption stretched into the upper echelons of the MMP.

Just over a month ago, Butterfield had been found murdered at a National Trust property. And to her shock, Laura had been anonymously sent CCTV that showed that it might have been Pete who killed Butterfield that day.

Unable to fathom that Pete might be involved in Butterfield's death, Laura had indeed been avoiding his calls and texts. She now feared that Pete had somehow been mixed up in Sam's death from the very start. She was also afraid that Pete was corrupt and working for the Fallowfield Hill Gang. She suspected that Butterfield was murdered to keep him quiet as he was starting to unravel and was becoming a dangerous liability to the other corrupt officers within the MMP. How was she meant to face one of her oldest friends when she suspected that he might have been responsible for her husband's death? She just prayed that she had got it all wrong and that there was a logical explanation for it all.

'I'll have my usual Americano, please,' said a voice she recognised. It broke her anxious train of thought with a start.

Gareth.

'Bloody hell, you made me jump,' she said.

He smiled at her quizzically and gestured to her phone. 'Why? Up to no good, are you?'

'Oh yeah,' she replied with a withering expression. 'I'm just texting my boyfriend, actually.'

'I'm pretty sure you're too old to use the term *boyfriend*,' he joked.

'Oi. Sod off.' She gave him a playful hit on the arm. 'You're hardly a teenager yourself… Rosie's cooking dinner tonight. I thought we could have a bottle of wine, movie, cuddle. What do you think?'

'Cuddle?' Gareth arched an eyebrow. 'First time I've heard it called that.'

'Pervert.'

'It does sound perfect,' Gareth groaned. 'But I've got that party. Osian's eighteenth.'

'Oh God, rather you than me.' She gave a half-smile. 'By the way, there's something I've been meaning to talk to you about.'

'If it's about your snoring' – Gareth grinned – 'then I've told you that it's a sacrifice I'm willing to make in our relationship.'

'Piss off,' she laughed. 'You snore too.'

'But not like a baby rhinoceros,' Gareth quipped. 'Which I admit is cute, but does keep me awake sometimes. Maybe I'll get you some of those strips that go across your nose.'

Laura rolled her eyes. She knew it was time to tell Gareth her suspicions about Pete, and fill in him on all that had happened since Sam's death. She had tried to keep Gareth out of her quest to uncover the events of that day because Sam was her late husband and it seemed tactless, and, up until recently, she had had Pete to share in her suspicions. Now that she no longer felt she could fully trust Pete, it seemed the right time to divulge all that she knew to Gareth. Even if that was going to be a long and possibly awkward conversation to have.

'I'm serious,' Laura said.

There was an awkward beat between them.

'Oh, right.' Gareth's expression changed. 'Should I be worried?'

Laura put her hand on his shoulder reassuringly. 'God, no. It's nothing to do with us. Just a few things from my past that have cropped up. And I want to talk them through with you.'

Gareth looked as though he was trying to hide the fact that he felt relieved. 'No problem. Maybe we could go out for breakfast tomorrow or something?'

Tomorrow was Saturday, which meant a skeleton staff in CID at Beaumaris and time off for both of them.

'Great,' Laura said, but she felt apprehensive about how Gareth was going to react to discovering some of the stuff she had hidden from him. 'Sounds like a plan.'

'I think I've found somewhere for us to get married,' Gareth said.

'Where's that?' Laura asked with amusement. Gareth was like an excited child. It was cute.

'Well the first option is the *Viva Las Vegas Elvis Wedding Chapel*,' Gareth joked. 'But I thought that might not be completely our thing.'

'No,' Laura said with an amused smile. 'I think we can do better than that. Is there a second option?'

'St Cwyfan's Church,' Gareth replied. 'It's a church in the sea.'

Laura pulled a face. 'Yeah, I'm not sure I want to get married in the sea. Is it one of those things where you have to learn to scuba dive and do the whole ceremony underwater?'

'God no.' Gareth rolled his eyes. 'It's not even technically in the sea. It's on this tiny island called Cribinau, off the coast at Aberffraw. But the church is called *Eglwys Bach y Mor*. You know, Welsh for "the church in the sea".'

Laura arched an eyebrow. 'Yes, thanks, Gareth. Despite what you say, I can speak some Welsh.'

Gareth looked at her with a smirk. '*Byddwch chi'n gwneud priodfferch hyfryd.*'

Laura scowled at him. 'Yeah, I have no idea what that means.'

'You'll make a lovely bride,' Gareth said with a self-satisfied grin.

Laura gave him a playful hit on the arm. 'Show-off.'

CHAPTER 3

Gareth glanced at his watch. It was 9.30 p.m. and the joint eighteenth birthday party was in full flow. Nursing his second pint of lager shandy, Gareth looked around at the centre of the darkened function room of the Beaumaris Sports and Social Club that had been converted into a disco – if that was the right word these days? It sounded old-fashioned. He didn't know and he didn't care. Dancing had never been his thing and never would be. He was far too self-conscious and awkward.

He couldn't help the odd smile at the antics of the young partygoers. The girls were all dressed up – lots of make-up, immaculate hair, impossibly high heels. The boys wore jackets, shirts and smart shoes. Some wore thin pencil ties that wouldn't have looked out of place at the discos Gareth had attended as a teenager in the eighties. He remembered the cover of the album *No Parlez* by pop singer Paul Young, in which he wore a grey jacket and slim tie. And then Gareth remembered that he'd been in a band called The Burned Legion with his brother for about three months in the late eighties. They had three rehearsals – during which he'd tried to learn to play the bass guitar with little success – and tried to play *Life's What You Make It* by Talk Talk. They sounded awful.

God, fashion really does all come full circle, Gareth thought to himself as he sipped his beer. The air was thick with Lynx Africa, perfume and beer fumes. He tried to remember what he used to wear as a teenager. Kuros, Polo and Paco Rabanne. His dad had told him that he smelled *like a tart* when he went out one night. However, this was coming from a man who had to be bullied by his wife to start to wear deodorant at the ripe old age of forty!

A DJ stood behind a long table with digital mixing equipment that looked like it belonged at NASA. *Christ, there isn't any vinyl within a mile of him*, Gareth thought with a wry smile. The music boomed and the bass was making the floor vibrate. Gareth had no idea what most of the records were. Electronic Dance Music, wasn't it? EDM. He thought he remembered reading that somewhere in a Sunday supplement. The whole dance music and rave scene of the late eighties and early nineties had passed him by. His brother, on the other hand, had embraced it. He used to go out with an acid house smiley T-shirt, bandana on his head and baggy jeans, he and his mates heading over to the clubs of Liverpool and Manchester.

Scanning the room, Gareth saw Osian, who was tall and broad-shouldered, with a shock of red hair and freckles. He was deep in conversation with three other teenage boys that Gareth recognised. Tom Hegerty, coal-black hair, thick eyebrows, was grinning and laughing. *At least he's behaving himself,* Gareth thought. There was something about

Tom that always made Gareth feel uneasy on the couple of occasions he'd encountered him, but he made some allowances for him given his homelife. Gareth had nicked Tom's dad Kenny at least half a dozen times over the years for petty theft, receiving stolen goods and other low-level crime. Kenny had made his contempt for the police and any kind of authority very clear so maybe it was inevitable that Tom was going to be a little wayward.

Callum Newell, a young-looking blond boy, was perched on a table with a glowing vape in his mouth. All Gareth knew about Callum was that he was very bright and Declan had told him there had been talk of him going to Oxford when he left school. Although it wasn't unheard of, it was still pretty rare for anyone to go from the state schools of Anglesey to Oxbridge. Those with money on the island often sent their kids over to the mainland to be educated at private boarding schools, such as Ruthin School.

The fourth boy, Ethan Edwards, had mousy hair, a very patchy beard and glasses. Gareth heard that he came from a large farming family just outside Beaumaris, over towards Castellior.

Gareth saw someone approaching and was pleased when he realised it was Sue. She gave him a winning smile as she leaned in to kiss his cheek. 'Hello, stranger.'

'Sue,' Gareth said. If he was honest, Gareth had always found Sue's uber confidence a little intimidating. 'You look well.'

'Thanks. So do you,' Sue said emphatically. She gave him a curious smirk. 'If I was to take a guess, I'd say there was a new woman in your life?'

Gareth felt a little uncomfortable but covered it with a half-smile. 'And I would have to say "no comment".'

Sue laughed. 'Very good, Detective Inspector.' She then looked down at her dark, navy cocktail dress. 'This is vintage. Which is, of course, a posh way of saying "second hand", but I love it.'

'Not my area of expertise,' Gareth admitted. 'But it looks good from where I'm standing.'

Sue hit his arm. 'I hope you're not flirting with me because my husband is coming this way.'

Declan approached, gripping his pint as he weaved in and out of the dancing partygoers. The room was becoming increasingly hot and Gareth could feel beads of sweat appearing on his top lip and brow.

'Everything all right?' Gareth asked, raising his voice over the music.

'Lucy Palmer is being sick outside,' Declan laughed. 'But apart from that, it's all quiet on the Western Front.'

'Glad to hear it,' Sue said. 'I'm going to vape outside so I'll leave you two to it.'

Declan nodded and gestured towards the four friends. 'The boys are off camping for the weekend in the morning. Part of the birthday celebrations. I've bought Osian a few beers to take with him but told him to stay off the spirits.'

'Where are they off to?' Gareth enquired.

'There's a campsite over by Newborough Forest,' Declan explained.

Gareth nodded. 'Oh yeah. I know it. I went there with my *taid* and *nain* when I was about ten.' He pulled a face. 'It was about the time of the Royal Wedding – Charles and

Diana's – and the campsite was decorated with union jacks. My *taid* was fuming. "Bloody English" he kept saying.'

Declan frowned. 'Charles is the Prince of Wales though.'

'Prince of Wales?' Gareth laughed. 'I'm not one of those crazy nationalist "Sons of Glyndwr" types, but the Royal Family should stay in England where they belong.'

The Sons of Glyndwr were a Welsh Nationalist group who had burned down English holiday homes in Wales in the 1980s in reaction to the housing crisis and rise in property prices due to the so-called 'English Invasion'.

'Yeah, well, as an Irishman, I'm with you there,' Declan chortled as he sipped from his pint. 'I visited family up in Belfast when I was a kid. It was a bit scary with all the soldiers, checkpoints and barbed wire. My family hated the English.'

Gareth gestured over to the group of boys. 'They'll have a great time.'

'All part of growing up, isn't it?'

Gareth remembered being taken to Newborough Forest on his camping trip with his grandparents. It had been low tide and they had walked across the beach over to Llanndwyn Island. It had been a stormy day and he recalled that the island had an eerie atmosphere with its derelict religious shrine, Celtic stone cross and two old looming lighthouses at its furthest point. Maybe it had just been his childish imagination.

'Hope the weather holds,' Gareth said and then sipped his pint. The lemonade he'd added to water it down had made the beer too sweet for his taste, but he was driving.

'Forecast is good. As long as they don't get up to no good, eh?' Declan raised an eyebrow with concern.

'Boys will be boys,' Gareth laughed. 'They'll be fine.'

Suddenly, there was pushing, shoving and shouting. A girl screamed.

Gareth put down his pint and moved swiftly towards where the scuffle had broken out. Everyone on the dancefloor had scattered.

Tom was tugging on Callum's jacket as they threw punches at each other. Callum pulled Tom off and put him in a neck lock.

'Oi,' Gareth shouted as he went over. 'Pack it in, the pair of you!'

Declan grabbed Callum roughly by the shoulders. 'Right, get off him.'

Callum shook Declan off angrily and squared up to him.

'Don't be an idiot, Callum,' Declan growled.

Callum stormed off towards the bar.

Gareth put his hand on Tom's shoulder. 'Come on, Tom, outside. You need to cool off.' He frogmarched Tom towards the doors that led outside to the car park.

Some of the partygoers were now videoing the proceedings on their phones with laughs and grins.

Tom pushed Gareth's hands from his shoulders.

'What are you fighting about, Tom?' Gareth asked once they were outside.

'None of your fucking business,' Tom thundered at him before running over to the wall and punching it with his right hand as if he were possessed.

'Woah, woah, Tom,' Gareth said, jogging over and trying to stop him.

'Just leave me the fuck alone,' Tom yelled as he turned and sprinted away across the car park and disappeared.

Osian appeared then, frowning and shaking his head.

'What the bloody hell was that all about?' Declan asked as he joined them.

'I dunno. Tom keeps saying that Callum's sister, Zoe, is fit and other stuff,' Osian explained. 'And I think Callum had had enough.'

Declan gestured to where Tom had run. 'Maybe I should go after him?'

Gareth shook his head. 'Probably best to let him calm down.'

However, Gareth was concerned by Tom's violent outburst.

* * *

As Laura strolled into the kitchen, she spotted Rosie stirring the chicken fajita mix in a pan for dinner.

'That smells amazing,' Laura said.

'Oh God, you made me jump, Mum!' Rosie exclaimed, turning around.

'Sorry, darling,' Laura said. It was clear that Rosie was still jittery after her ordeal. It still haunted her how close she had come to losing her daughter.

'It's fine,' Rosie said, trying to make light of her anxiety.

'*Se ve delicioso*,' Laura said in an exaggerated Spanish accent as she headed for the fridge.

Rosie gave her an amused smile. 'Not sure what that means, but there are Spanish beers in the fridge.'

Laura grabbed a cold bottle of San Miguel. 'I've been using one of those daily language apps on my phone to learn Spanish,' she admitted. '*El niño esta comiendo una manzana.*'

Rosie gave her a blank look as Laura went and opened her beer.

'The boy eats an apple,' Laura said by way of explanation.

'Yeah, that should come in a very handy when travelling in Spain!' Rosie laughed.

'Early days.' Laura shrugged. It was nice to see Rosie smiling and making jokes. There had been days after her abduction when she had spent all her time in her bedroom.

'What's for tea?' Jake asked as he strolled in, engrossed by something he was watching on his phone.

'Chicken fajitas,' Rosie announced proudly.

Jake pulled a face. 'Chicken fa-what, bro?'

'Don't worry, *bro*,' Rosie teased him, 'you'll like it, I promise.'

'Can I have nuggets and waffles?' Jake asked, still staring at his phone screen.

'NO!' Rosie and Laura replied in unison and then laughed.

'Pizza?'

'You're having fajitas, Jake,' Laura said.

'Bit harsh,' Jake mumbled.

Laura watched him wander away. She had navigated the raging hormones of a teenage daughter and was just about to the other side of that. Now Jake was about to hit puberty with a whole new set of delightful problems such as general grumpiness, poor personal hygiene and the discovery of masturbation!

Jesus! I can't wait for all that, she thought sardonically to herself.

The doorbell went and Laura frowned. She wasn't expecting anyone.

'I don't know who that can be,' she muttered.

Jake rolled his eyes. 'Probably that Amazon driver again with more stuff for Rosie,' he replied.

Rosie gave him a sarcastic smile. 'Shut it.'

'You do know that you're killing the planet by ordering all that stuff?' Jake grumbled.

Jake was right. The Amazon driver did seem to be at their door several times a week with various bits of clothing or cosmetics for Rosie. However, if a bit of retail therapy was keeping her daughter's spirits up, Laura wasn't going to say anything.

Wandering down the hallway, she took a swig of her cold beer. The bubbles hit the back of her throat.

God, that's good. Why don't I drink cold beer more often?

She then opened the front door, fully expecting to see the young, curly-haired Amazon driver standing there.

Instead, there was an unexpected figure standing on the doorstep.

Pete.

Oh shit!

She took a sharp intake of breath.

He was holding a bottle of wine and some flowers.

'Hey, if Mohammed won't come to the mountain...' he said with a broad grin.

Oh my God!

Laura's stomach lurched with anxiety. His appearance had completely floored her.

'Pete,' she said as brightly as she could, but her pulse was starting to race. 'What a lovely surprise.'

Jesus! What the hell am I going to do? she panicked.

He stepped forward, kissed her cheek and then gave her a long hug. It felt awkward with all that she suspected about him. But she had to make sure that she didn't display any of the anxiety she was feeling.

'It's been too long, hasn't it?' he said as he took a pace backwards and looked at her with a smile.

She looked at him. Was he really capable of corruption and murder? Pete was one of the good guys. He always had been. And over the years, she had grown to love him like the brother she'd never had.

'It really has.' Laura nodded. Her face flushed a little.

'You look really well,' Pete said enthusiastically. 'You don't mind me dropping in on you like this, do you?'

'Of course not,' Laura replied as she beckoned him inside. 'Don't be silly, you're always welcome here. You know that. And the bed in the spare room is made up.'

'Uncle Pete!' Jake exclaimed as he jogged up the hallway and embraced his godfather.

'Hello, mate,' Pete said, hugging him and lifting him six inches off the floor. 'You're getting too big to pick up these days.'

Laura bristled at their embrace.

'What are you doing here?' Jake asked.

'I haven't seen you guys for ages,' Pete said with a shrug, 'and me and your mum have got some catching up to do.'

'Great,' Jake said with a grin.

Laura felt sick with nerves. 'You're just in time. Rosie's

cooking fajitas.'

'Yeah, they won't let me have chicken nuggets,' Jake said with a groan.

'Won't they, mate?' Pete laughed. 'Your mum's always been a bit of a food nut.'

'Hey!' Laura said, playing along but squirming inside. 'Why don't you both come through.'

They all turned and headed down to the kitchen.

'Rosie!' Laura called. 'Look who's here.'

Laura watched Pete as he walked in front of her, his face lit up with a beaming smile. He looked like the 'old Pete' that she had always known. It would break her heart all over again if he really was involved in Sam's death.

CHAPTER 4

By Saturday lunchtime, Osian and his three friends – Tom, Callum and Ethan – had been dropped off by his dad close to the campsite beside Newborough Beach. Osian was glad that there had been no repercussions from the night before. In fact, Tom had apologised to Callum for his offensive comments about Zoe and they'd hugged it out.

'Where the hell does this pole go?' Callum groaned as they tried to assemble two tents on the far side of the campsite.

'Up your arse,' Tom joked.

Osian remembered putting up tents when he was about ten and in the Sea Scouts, but he was struggling to fathom how it all fitted together now.

The spring sunshine made it hot and hazily bright. Hues of golden light mingled with the azure sky, reflecting off the ripples in the dark sea in the distance. The breeze carried a light scent of freshly cut grass and wildflowers, mixed with a faint trace of the seawater.

Osian closed his eyes for a moment, allowing the sunlight to warm his face. Even though the prospect of his A levels lurked in the back of his mind, he was going to put that to one side and have a brilliant weekend with his best friends. He could feel the buzz of excitement and expectation.

'You should be able to do this, Osh,' Ethan said. 'Weren't you in the cubs or something?'

'Sea Scouts,' Osian corrected him with a frown as he took two steps back to inspect the tent, poles and pegs that were laid out in front of them.

I haven't got a bloody clue, if I'm honest, he thought.

'Assume you were fiddled with in some kind of way,' Callum joked.

'Sod off,' Osian snapped. Osian's time spent in the Sea Scouts seemed to be a source of much amusement to his mates.

'Yeah,' Ethan laughed, 'I'm pretty sure that only paedos run the cubs and scouts.'

'They don't. And it's eight years since I put up a bloody tent,' Osian explained. 'I can't remember a thing. Told you we should have brought one of those pop-up tents.'

'I guess you were too busy letting Akela fumble around in your shorts, trying to find your little tent pole,' Tom snorted.

Osian grinned and quipped, 'Your mum didn't say I had a *little tent pole* the other night.'

They all laughed as Tom shook his head with a withering look.

'I don't know why you're bothering putting up the tents,' Tom snorted with a smirk. As predicted, Tom was now lying back on the grass, wearing sunglasses and smoking a spliff.

Osian had known he wasn't going to help put up the tents. He was far too cool for that.

Tom reached for his phone. The song 'Starlight' by the rap artist Dave started to play very loudly. A couple of middle-aged campers, who were sitting on flimsy folding chairs outside their tent and drinking tea, glanced over and scowled.

'Tom!' Osian hissed. 'Turn it down.'

'Na, bruv,' Tom laughed. 'Fuck 'em.'

Callum shook his head. 'Tom, just turn it down. I don't want to get thrown out of here before we've even got the friggin' tents up.'

Tom grinned and turned the music down. 'Sorry, *Dad*.'

Callum frowned as he continued to inspect the tent pegs. 'If you were a rapper, would you really call yourself Dave?'

'Yeah. Why just Dave?' Ethan agreed. 'Stormzy, AJ Tracy, Skepta. They sound like actual rappers.'

Tom kissed his teeth in an ironic way. ''Cos that's his name, bro. David Omoregie.'

'I suppose he's just lucky his name wasn't Nigel or Gethin,' Osian joked.

Tom jumped up energetically. 'Man, we're going to be so off our faces, we're not going to remember going to sleep tonight. I can't wait, fam.'

Osian didn't know what Tom was talking about. They had only brought a few cans of beer each.

'What do you mean?' Ethan asked. Osian had known Ethan since they joined primary school together. He'd struggled at school and was planning to do an apprenticeship after sixth form rather than go to uni. Sometimes Tom teased Ethan, calling him 'farmer boy' or claiming that he 'bummed' his dad's sheep. Osian didn't like it but couldn't do anything to make Tom stop.

Sitting up, Tom grabbed his rucksack and unzipped it. 'For starters, I nicked these from my dad's garage.' He pulled out two litre bottles of vodka.

'Nice one,' Callum said.

Osian didn't say anything. He had been looking forward to a few beers and listening to music around a campfire or something. He didn't want everyone to get hammered and vomit everywhere. Plus, he was sharing a tent with Callum, who was notorious for being sick when he drank too much.

'Don't give any to that lightweight,' Osian said, pointing to Callum.

Callum grinned and gave him the finger.

'And, I got this from my cousin,' Tom said with a proud grin as he held up a plastic bag with what looked like a large chocolate bar inside.

'Chocolate. Wow,' Osian scoffed sarcastically.

'Yeah, well it's not just chocolate, you losers,' Tom informed them with a triumphant grin.

Taking out the chocolate bar, Osian could see that it had the computer game character Mario on the front surrounded by psychedelic coloured stars and flowers. At the bottom it read: *PSILOCYBIN MUSHROOM CHOCOLATE BAR*.

'Mushrooms?' Ethan asked. 'Who wants to eat chocolate with mushrooms?'

'Jesus, Ethan,' Tom chortled. 'Magic mushrooms, you tit.'

'Oh right,' Ethan replied, but he still looked confused.

'You do know what magic mushrooms are, don't you, Ethan?' Callum asked.

36

'Course I do,' Ethan protested.

'My cousin said this stuff is amazing,' Tom explained excitedly as he opened it up. 'Apparently it makes everything float with colours. And you feel like you're in space.'

'Yeah, well, I'm not taking drugs,' Callum said.

'Pussy,' Tom laughed.

Osian started to feel nervous. He could feel the tension in his stomach. He'd smoked weed a couple of times but didn't really like it. He wasn't sure that tripping on magic mushroom chocolate was going to be his thing but he knew he couldn't say no if the others were doing it.

'I'm up for it,' Ethan said as Tom unwrapped the silver foil, broke off a chunk and handed it to him. Ethan shoved it into his mouth and chewed.

'What does it taste like?' Callum asked hesitantly.

'Chocolate,' Ethan said with a shrug. 'Just eat some, you pussy.'

'Jesus. Give us some then,' Callum said, reluctantly taking a chunk from Tom.

'Come on, Osh,' Tom said.

Osian was still feeling apprehensive. He didn't like the sound of floating around but he wasn't going to be the odd one out.

Fuck it. Let's give this a go.

'Cool,' Osian said, taking a chunk, popping it in his mouth and hoping he didn't lose his mind.

Tom opened the bottle of vodka, glugged from it and then handed it around. 'Lads, we are going to have one mad fucking weekend!'

They all cheered.

CHAPTER 5

Sitting in the afternoon sunshine, Laura closed her eyes for a moment, trying to clear her head. There was a cold glass of white wine in her hand. It was her second. She needed to numb the uncomfortable, uneasy feeling in the pit of her stomach that had been there ever since Pete had arrived the previous evening.

Last night, Pete had joined them all for dinner and then slept in the tiny spare room. He and Jake had taken their dog, Elvis, for a long walk along Beaumaris Beach before they all had lunch.

Laura had thankfully managed to avoid her promise of breakfast with Pete. In fact, she had managed not to be on her own with him for more than five minutes. And that meant they hadn't really talked about Butterfield's murder or the implications it had on their supposed quest to find out what had happened to Sam in Manchester in August 2018.

Rosie could sense that Laura wasn't acting quite herself and had pulled her to one side on a couple of occasions to ask if she was all right. Laura had made a series of flimsy excuses but she knew that Rosie wasn't convinced.

Pete and Jake were now sitting in front of the television watching football, so Laura decided to hide away outside and drink more wine. It wasn't working. The alcohol wasn't turning off the swirling questions that were tumbling around her mind. Had Pete been responsible for the mystery phone call that had lured Sam and his partner Louise to Branning's Warehouse on that fateful day? Did he know when Sam and Louise arrived that they would be taken hostage by the Fallowfield Hill Gang? If Sam had been set up, why? What had Sam discovered? Had Sam uncovered something about Pete's involvement?

Jesus, this is driving me mad!

Letting out an audible sigh of frustration, Laura drank another mouthful of Pinot.

She then saw something out of the corner of her eye.

Through the window to the hallway, she saw a figure coming down the stairs. She could only see him from the waist down but she could see it was Sam. He had baggy navy football shorts on and white socks. She'd recognise those knees anywhere.

It wasn't the first time that she'd caught a fleeting glimpse of Sam in the house. It used to scare her but now she found it a comfort. And sometimes it even amused her.

'Thought I might find you hiding out here,' said a voice, which startled her.

It was Pete.

'Bloody hell!' she yelped.

'Sorry.' Pete pulled an apologetic face.

'It's fine.' Laura forced a smile. 'Just getting a bit of sun,' she said, faking a casual tone.

Laura glanced back through the window but Sam was gone.

'Lovely, isn't it?' Pete said as he sat down on a rattan garden chair close by and stretched out his legs. 'Reminds me of that place we all used to go to in Tenby. What was it called again?'

Pete was referring to a holiday cottage that both families had been to a few summers running when the kids were very small.

'Carew Heights Cottage,' she reminded him.

'That's it,' Pete laughed. 'We played so much table tennis I came back with blisters.'

'Yeah, I think you'll find it was only you and Sam who were actually playing table tennis. For hours and hours.'

'Well, Sam was incredibly competitive,' Pete said quietly.

'And you're not?' Laura snorted and then caught herself. That familiarity now had a dark, uncomfortable sting. It felt agonising to think how long she and Pete had been friends if he really was guilty of betraying her trust.

'The kids were just babies, weren't they?' Pete said, now lost in the memory.

'Jake was a baby. He was still in a pram,' she said as she shifted awkwardly on her chair. 'Not watching the match?' she asked.

'Half time,' Pete said and then glanced at his watch. 'I'm going to have to get going when it finishes and I feel like me and you haven't had a chance to chat and catch up.'

Laura tried to sound relaxed. 'Hey, that's what happens when you have two kids and a dog. There's always something.'

Pete looked over at her and met her eyes. 'I thought you might be trying to avoid me,' he said in a jokey tone, but she knew that he had sensed her unease.

There was an awkward beat.

'What? Don't be daft. Why would I be trying to avoid you?'

Pete sat forward with a serious expression. 'We haven't really talked about what happened to Butterfield. I thought maybe it had all got too much for you?'

'No. I mean, it was a bit of a shock,' Laura said as her pulse quickened. She looked at him. 'But I still need to find out what happened to Sam and why he was murdered. Don't you?'

She scrutinised Pete's expression but he was giving nothing away.

Laura could feel the tension in her body growing. She didn't know how to play this.

'Of course. I'm keeping tabs on the investigation,' Pete reassured her. 'And surprise, surprise, there are no viable suspects yet.'

Laura had to play along as she rolled her eyes. 'Well, there won't be, will there?'

Pete was insinuating that someone else within the MMP had been responsible for killing Butterfield. Maybe he was telling the truth after all?

'Any chance that his murder isn't linked to all this?' Laura asked, but then regretted saying it as it made her sound naive. She was struggling with this conversation given all that she knew.

Why did I say that?

'A corrupt senior police officer who seems to be on the verge of a nervous breakdown goes for a walk and happens to be murdered.' Pete furrowed his brow. 'What do you think?'

'Yeah.' Laura gave a forced smile. 'Now that you've put it like that.' She then thought of Sam's former police partner, Louise McDonald. She and Pete had been surprised to discover that Louise hadn't perished in the explosions and fire in the warehouse along with Sam, and that the Fallowfield Hill Gang had used threats and intimidation to force Louise to work for them. Pete and Laura had finally tracked Louise down to Llandudno, where she was living with a new identity, but before she could reveal the true extent of her corruption and everything she knew about Sam's death, she had been murdered in a hit-and-run. 'Do we think it's the same person that killed Louise?'

Pete shrugged. 'I think it's likely.'

Was that Pete's surreptitious way of confessing to being guilty of Louise's murder as well? It didn't bear thinking about. But he *was* there the night she was murdered. It was now hard to believe it had been just a coincidence.

'If this goes all the way to the top,' Laura said, 'how are we going to get justice for Sam?'

'Leave it with me,' Pete said reassuringly. 'I've got a couple of avenues that I'm going to pursue, so I'll keep you posted.'

'Uncle Pete?' Jake shouted from the door to the kitchen. 'The teams are back on the pitch.'

The sound of Jake's voice calling for Pete made her shiver.

'Okay, mate,' Pete called over. 'Duty calls.' He gave her a meaningful look. 'Don't worry. You and I are going to find out what happened to Sam and bring down those responsible, okay? It's just going to take time.'

Laura felt overwhelmed and confused as she nodded. 'Thanks, Pete.'

CHAPTER 6

It was nearly three p.m. and Osian could feel the anxiety twisting in his stomach – it was making him feel sick. He, Ethan and Tom had been searching for Callum for nearly two hours. They couldn't find him anywhere. It was as if he'd vanished into thin air. The effects of the hallucinogens had started to wear off, which made Callum's disappearance increasingly alarming in the cold light of day.

It had been almost three hours since the boys had ingested the mushroom chocolate. They had then left the campsite and taken a walk through the nearby Newborough Forest, which led down to the beach. As the mushroom chocolate kicked in, Osian had slowly noticed that the sounds of the birds grew louder and clearer but then somehow the birds had begun to sing a song by George Ezra.

The whole concept of time seemed to change. The boys were in a strange, fuzzy, magical otherworld. They had run around the forest, whooping, laughing, shouting and climbing trees.

Osian had also become aware that the beams of sunlight that cut through the tall pine trees were starting to change colour – turning red, turquoise, gold and pink. The light sparkled as though it was full of floating glitter. It was incredible. He could have stood and looked at the shards of light for hours.

By the time the boys arrived at Newborough Beach, Osian had this lovely floaty feeling and a sense of blurred happiness. They had taken off their trainers and paddled in the water, watching the waves foaming and bubbling as they broke on the sand. The sun's reflection in the water made it look metallic – like the sea was coated in aluminium. There were rocks covered in golden brown seaweed that Osian became convinced was a human head covered in dreadlocks. He laughed as he ran his fingers through the long tresses of sea kelp.

There was a family sitting further down the beach. The parents were sitting on a beach towel while their two children paddled in the waves. Osian was paranoid that they could tell that he was 'as high as a kite'. He gave them an awkward wave as he went past, praying they didn't engage him in conversation, and then felt an immense sense of relief that there had been no interaction. It would have been too weird and uncomfortable.

However, it was just after this that Ethan first noticed that Callum wasn't on the beach with them. In their hallucinatory state, his disappearance didn't feel concerning. Osian just assumed that Callum was nearby, lost in a tripped-out space. They called out his name a couple of times before deciding that he would catch them up soon.

But as the mushrooms and vodka wore off, Osian's sense that something was wrong had slowly crept up on him and then the others.

At first they had scoured the beach, retracing their steps. They called Callum's mobile phone but there was no answer. Wandering back through the forest, they yelled out his name, wondering if he was still sitting somewhere in a trance, still feeling the hallucinogenic effects of the chocolate.

By the time they returned to the campsite, there was still no sign of him and they had started to worry. Trekking back through the forest again, they continued to call his phone while shouting his name. They just couldn't find him anywhere. And that felt like a major problem. Newborough Forest was vast, made up of over 2,000 acres of towering Corsican and Monterey pine trees. Callum could have wandered off anywhere.

Soon they were back on Newborough Beach, scouring every dune and pathway.

'Anything?' Osian nervously asked Tom as the other boy tried to call Callum's phone again.

Tom shook his head.

'Maybe he's still off his head and wandering around,' Ethan suggested calmly.

Osian was sometimes jealous that Ethan was able to take everything in his stride, but maybe he had a point this time. Were they getting this all out of proportion?

Tom ended the unanswered call, looking concerned. 'I don't see why. He didn't eat any more than us.'

Osian frowned. 'What if he's fallen down somewhere and hurt himself?'

'Yeah, I hadn't thought of that,' Ethan said, now looking concerned. Then he caught Osian's eye. 'Don't worry, mate. He'll turn up. You know Callum.'

Osian nodded. 'Yeah.' His phone buzzed. He instantly hoped that it was a message from Callum, asking where they'd got to.

However, it was a text message from his dad, Declan.

Everything okay with you boys? Having a good time?

Osian glanced at Ethan and Tom and gestured to his phone. 'It's my dad, asking if we're all okay.'

Tom raised an eyebrow. 'Just tell him we're fine.'

'But we're not fine,' Osian replied, taking a nervous breath. 'We can't find Callum.'

'I'm sure he's okay,' Ethan said, putting on a forced smile. 'He's going to come running down the beach any minute now.'

'Tell you what we do,' Tom said thoughtfully. 'We'll head back through the forest again – that's the last place we saw him – then we go back to the campsite in case he's back there.'

'Good idea,' Osian agreed. 'I'm just worried that his phone is ringing but he's not answering his phone.'

'Come on,' Tom said, giving them a reassuring look. 'He's gonna turn up.'

Osian could see that, despite their different personalities, when it came to the crunch, their friendship that went all the way back to primary school was enduring.

Traipsing through the forest, Osian's body felt heavy and tired. He didn't know if it was the after-effects of the mushroom chocolate, or the worry about his missing friend.

The towering pine trees loomed ominously above them. Their contorted branches twisted to form a dark canopy, making the space below feel enclosed, even treacherous. And then there was a sudden stillness. The wind died and the stir of the trees and the rustle of leaves just stopped, an air of menace hanging heavy in the air until the silence was shattered by the cawing of two crows high up. It sounded like they were calling out an urgent warning. A fox appeared ahead of them. It glared at the boys accusingly and then darted away.

'Callum? Callum?' Tom yelled at the top of his voice.

It was no use.

There was no reply and no sign of him anywhere.

As they approached the campsite, Osian prayed that Callum would be sitting there with all their tent equipment, grinning, and they could all laugh about how he'd got lost.

But Callum wasn't there.

Osian took out his phone. 'I'm calling my dad.'

Tom scowled at him. 'You can't.'

'Why not?'

'Because he's a copper,' Tom explained.

'So, what?' Osian growled. 'He'll know what to do.'

'That mushroom chocolate is illegal, you nob,' Tom said aggressively.

'Okay,' Osian said, trying to think on his feet. 'We won't tell him then. We'll say we got a bit drunk instead. Okay?'

There was a tense silence as they looked at each other.

Tom and Ethan nodded.

Osian took out his phone and dialled his dad's number.

CHAPTER 7

Missing: 2 hours

Twenty minutes later, Gareth and Declan were racing across the island from Beaumaris out to the campsite at Newborough.

'Do you know if they'd been drinking?' Gareth asked as Declan sped around a bend.

Gareth had been pottering at his house when Declan called to say that Osian had rung to tell him that they couldn't find his friend Callum. At first, Gareth dismissed it as teenage boys messing around. But when Declan informed him that Callum had simply vanished nearly two hours earlier, he realised that it might be serious.

'I don't know,' Declan replied. 'I bought Osian a few beers for the trip but I've got no idea what the others brought with them.'

Gareth frowned. 'Drugs?'

'No,' Declan replied immediately. 'I'm pretty sure they're not like that. At least, I know Osian isn't.'

Gareth gave him a questioning look. 'But Tom Hegerty?'

'Good point,' Declan said with a concerned expression.

'If they were drunk, maybe he's fallen somewhere and is now stuck,' Gareth suggested as they turned off the main road and headed down through a wooded area towards the campsite.

'It's still bloody cold at night at the moment,' Declan commented. 'That could be dangerous if he's in only a T-shirt and shorts.'

It was a good point. A night out in the cold could lead to hypothermia and that could be fatal.

'Have you spoken to his parents?'

'I rang Vicky, his mum,' Declan explained. 'I told her we'd call as soon as we know anything.'

'Where's his dad?'

'Mike?' Declan rolled his eyes. 'He's where he always is. Getting pissed with his mates in The Red Lion.'

'You're not a fan?'

Declan snorted, shaking his head. 'No. He's a prick. And when he's drunk, he's a nasty piece of work. I don't know why Vick puts up with him.'

'You've known her for donkey's years, haven't you?' Gareth said.

'We went to bloody primary school together,' Declan said.

'You used to chase her in the playground and pull her pigtails?'

'Yeah, something like that.'

Pulling off the main road, they headed up the bumpy track to the campsite. To the right, the ground sloped down to a line of leafy Spiraea hedges that were beginning to bloom with raspberry-pink blossoms. To the left, there was a gap in the hedgerow and beyond that a sweeping field, which fell down steeply to the dark expanse of Newborough Forest. Over the top, the Irish Sea could be seen stretching away to the glowing horizon.

As they drove around a long bend, Gareth spotted the three boys sitting and waiting nervously on the grass by the campsite. They looked genuinely frightened.

Declan pulled the car into a parking space on the other side of the road and they got out. Now that the sunlight was fading, it was getting decidedly chilly.

'Dad,' Osian said anxiously as he rose to his feet and approached. 'What are we going to do?'

Declan looked at the boys. 'For starters, you need to tell me exactly what you did, where you were going and when you last saw him.'

'We walked down through the forest and onto the beach,' Ethan mumbled in an apologetic tone. 'And he just vanished.'

Gareth's instinct was that Ethan wasn't telling them everything – but he didn't know what exactly it was they were hiding.

'We've looked everywhere,' Osian explained. He looked on the verge of tears.

'Okay, mate. It's fine. He'll turn up,' Declan said. 'Where was the last time you saw Callum?'

Tom looked over and pointed into the forest. 'There's a big fallen tree across the path down there. Callum was standing on top of it. Then he jumped down. The next time I looked back he'd gone.'

51

'And when was that?' Gareth asked.

'A few hours ago.' Osian pulled a face. 'We've been looking for him for an hour and a half, Dad.'

Although it did seem strange that Callum had simply disappeared, there was nothing to indicate anything suspicious – yet.

'Why don't you show us the way you walked,' Gareth said, looking at Declan.

'Have you all been drinking?' Declan asked.

The boys looked at each other sheepishly.

'I'll take that as a "yes" then,' Declan said calmly.

'Not much,' Tom said, shaking his head. 'Just a few cans.'

Gareth spotted Osian and Ethan's expressions. They were definitely hiding something.

'Drugs?' Gareth asked.

There was an awkward silence as the boys looked at each other in a way that confirmed that they had definitely taken drugs.

'Okay, guys,' Gareth said in a friendly tone. 'Believe it or not, we were young once. You're not going to get into trouble. You just need to tell us what kind of state you were all in. What did you take?'

'We had mushroom chocolate, Mr Williams,' Ethan blurted out.

Gareth looked at Declan. It wasn't good that they'd been on hallucinogens. But they were eighteen-year-old boys celebrating so it wasn't exactly shocking news.

'I see,' Declan said, peering at them closely. 'How are you now?'

'We're fine,' Ethan said sheepishly. 'It's worn off.'

'It's okay, Mr Flaherty. We only had a bit,' Tom said nonchalantly. 'We really are fine now.'

Declan glared at him and snapped, 'It's not okay, Tom! It's illegal for starters, and it's bloody dangerous.'

Gareth didn't blame Declan for being angry but now wasn't the time for him to lose his rag. They had to find Callum and it was getting dark – and cold.

'What time did you eat the chocolate?' Gareth said, trying to keep everything calm as he glanced at his watch.

Osian blinked nervously. 'It was just after Dad dropped us off.'

'I left here at about twelve,' Declan said.

Gareth looked at Osian. 'And then what happened?'

'We walked down to the woods. We were running around. You know, messing about,' Osian explained.

'And Callum was with you?'

'Yeah.'

Gareth glanced over at Tom. 'So, what time do you think you saw Callum standing on a fallen tree down there?'

Tom frowned as he thought for a moment. 'One, half one maybe.'

'And none of you have seen him since?' Declan asked to confirm.

They all shook their heads.

Gareth gestured to the woods. 'Right, come on, you'd better show us which way you went and where you last saw him.'

As they turned to go, Osian walked over to Declan and said under his breath, 'Sorry, Dad.'

'Don't worry, mate,' Declan reassured him quietly. 'We just need to find Callum and make sure he's safe.'

For the next few minutes, they tramped across the field that led downhill to the forest. The grass was long, thick and swooshed as they moved through it.

'This is the path we took,' Ethan said as they entered the darkness of the forest.

The temperature seemed to drop significantly as soon as they were under the shelter of the trees, and the canopy of leaves and branches overhead made it difficult to see where they were going.

Now that Gareth knew the boys had taken hallucinogens, he wondered if Callum had imagined he could fly and done something silly. He remembered a case he had attended in Rhosneigr when he was a uniformed officer. A seventeen-year-old boy had taken Ketamine and Acid, jumped from a third-floor window and died. Gareth and his sergeant had been the first on the scene and the sight of the boy's twisted body on the road below had been etched into Gareth's memory forever.

Ten minutes later, Tom pointed to something ahead of them.

'That's it,' he said, gesturing to the trunk of a fallen tree that now blocked the pathway. It was covered in dark green moss. 'He was standing on that tree and dancing around.'

Gareth scanned the area to the right and left for any signs of movement.

Nothing.

'Callum? Callum?' Declan yelled at the top of his voice, which echoed around in the silence.

Reaching the fallen tree trunk, Gareth quickly spotted that there was a small pathway off to the right. To the other side, there were thick brambles. By a process of deduction, he could see that if Callum had left the main pathway, he would have had to have gone right to avoid the brambles.

'My guess is that he went up here,' Gareth said, pointing as he led the way.

'Callum? Callum?' the boys shouted intermittently.

With eyes scanning left and right, Gareth peered into the forest for signs of movement or any clue as to whether Callum had indeed taken this path. The shadows made it difficult to see more than twenty or thirty yards.

Out of the corner of his eye, Gareth spotted something white in the undergrowth to his left.

Crouching down, he moved the undergrowth and wild flowers to one side.

There was a white Nike trainer sitting there.

As the others looked on, Gareth reached into his inside pocket for his blue forensic gloves. He snapped them on and very carefully retrieved the trainer and held it up.

Osian's eyes widened as he whispered, 'Yeah, that's Callum's.'

Gareth's eyes met Declan's – this was not good.

As a couple of leaves fell from the toe and laces, Gareth noticed something else on the smooth white leather toe.

Dark spots and smears.

Blood.

'Shit,' he hissed under his breath as he showed Declan.

Reaching for his phone, he called the Dispatch Centre at Beaumaris Police Station.

'Hi, this is Detective Inspector Gareth Williams,' he said sternly. 'I'm at the forest close to Newborough Campsite. We have a possible major incident here. I'm going to need every available uniform and CID officer here immediately. I also need SOCOs, the canine unit and scramble the helicopter if it's available.'

CHAPTER 8

Missing: 14 hours

It was now three a.m. and Callum Newell had been missing for fourteen hours. The wooded area and the campsite were now a hive of activity. The night sky was lit by the ominous throbbing blue lights of emergency vehicles. The air was filled with the crackle of officers and dispatch talking on Tetra radios. The whole area had been cordoned off with tape and the perimeter was being supervised by uniformed officers.

Pushing through the undergrowth of Newborough Forest with their torches, Gareth and Declan had organised every available police officer in the area, along with some volunteers from the campsite, to form a long line, and they were making their way slowly through the forest, shouting Callum's name as they went.

But they were getting nowhere.

Ever since Gareth had seen the blood on Callum's discarded trainer, he had felt tension in the pit of his stomach. What the hell had happened and where was Callum? Had he been the victim of some random attack while the boys were messing around in the woods on a sunny afternoon? Did Tom have anything to do with it? He had seen them fighting the night before after all.

There was a thundering metallic noise as a black and yellow police EC145 helicopter swooped overhead, its enormous searchlight zipping across the woods. The tops of the pine trees swayed and rocked with the force of its main propeller. The helicopter had thermal imaging equipment on board, so if Callum had fallen somewhere in the woods and was lying injured, it would be able to pick up his bodyheat and then pinpoint his location.

Grabbing his Tetra radio, Gareth clicked the grey button. 'Gold Command to Alpha seven three, are you receiving? Over.'

Alpha seven three was the call sign for the helicopter pilot.

'Gold Command, this is Alpha seven three, we're receiving. Over,' came the reply.

'Any sign of our MisPer yet? Over,' Gareth asked. MisPer was police shorthand for a missing person.

'Negative, Gold Command,' the pilot said. 'I'm going to take us up to one thousand feet and take another look. Over.'

'Okay,' Gareth replied, feeling tense and frustrated. They were in a race against time. Even though it wasn't the depths of winter, if Callum was lying somewhere hurt, he could still end up with hypothermia. 'If that continues to be negative, we're going to need to move the search down to the beach and the sea. Over.'

'Understood, Gold Command,' the pilot replied. 'Stand by. Over.'

Gareth ended the call and gave Declan a dark look. 'As I see it, we're facing two possibilities. First: Callum was off his head, cut himself, wandered off and is now lost or injured. Second: He was attacked or someone has taken him.'

The shouts of 'Callum?' from officers and volunteers continued to echo around the darkness.

Declan pointed to the far end of the forest. 'What if he wandered onto the beach and then into the sea? Maybe he decided to go swimming and got into difficulties. It's not hard to believe, especially given what state he was in.'

'Yeah, that was my thought as well,' Gareth said with a grim expression. 'That would explain why no one can find him. But it doesn't bear thinking about.'

'Over here!' came a shout from an officer about fifty yards to their left.

Gareth's pulse quickened as he and Declan moved as best they could through the trees using torchlight.

He reached out to move branches out of his way, trying to make sure that they didn't just recoil back into his face, all the while praying that Callum had been found alive.

Pushing more branches and undergrowth away, Gareth arrived at where the uniformed officer was standing.

'What is it?' he asked frantically.

A black Under Armour baseball cap was hanging from a branch at about head-height.

Gareth shone his torch on it and then looked at Declan.

'Yeah, that's Callum's cap. He was wearing it when I dropped them off,' Declan confirmed. 'Looks like it snagged on that branch.'

'Why didn't he just take it and put it back on?' Gareth asked, thinking out loud.

Declan looked at him. 'You thinking what I'm thinking?'

Gareth guessed that they had both come to the same conclusion. It was rare that they didn't.

'Given the discarded trainer, the blood and now this cap,' Gareth said, 'my conclusion would be that Callum was being chased by someone through the forest... Or at least, he thought he was.'

* * *

Osian bit at his nails as he sat with the others in a small, deserted café in the main building of the campsite. They had been sitting in silence for a while, trying to take in what had happened. Osian closed his eyes for a second. It felt like he was stuck in a horrible nightmare that he hoped he was going to wake up from soon. He kept looking over towards the glass double doors at the building's entrance and telling himself that any minute now police officers were going to walk in with Callum. He'd tell them how he'd sprained his ankle, got stuck and they'd all laugh about it and go home. And then a more chilling thought came into Osian's head.

What if something terrible has happened?

Tom was leaning forward, staring at the floor. Then he looked up at Osian and scowled. 'What the fuck did you tell them we'd taken mushrooms for?' he hissed.

Osian frowned, angry that Tom was being so self-absorbed when their friend was currently missing. It wasn't a surprise though. 'They need to know everything. If Callum was tripping when he went missing, they need to know that. I'm not going to lie when the truth could help.'

'Just cos your dad's a copper, doesn't mean you have to be a pussy,' Tom said.

'Fuck off, Tom,' Osian said, shaking his head.

'Are we gonna get into trouble then?' Ethan asked nervously.

'No,' Osian replied.

Two uniformed officers walked into the building and for a moment Osian held his breath. Had they found something? Had they found Callum? However, they merely clicked on their radios and then wandered over to a snack dispensing machine and put in some coins.

Osian felt his heart sink again. Then he looked at his mates. 'The only thing that matters is finding Callum. No one cares if we had some bloody mushroom chocolate.'

Tom snorted. 'Easy for you to say. You didn't bring it. I could get done for dealing.'

'Don't be a twat,' Osian snapped. Tom was starting to really irritate him. 'Giving us a couple of chunks of mushroom chocolate hardly makes you Pablo Escobar.'

'Pablo who?' Ethan asked. He suddenly pointed to Tom's knuckles, which were bloody. 'What happened to your hand?'

'It happened when I punched that wall last night,' Tom explained nonchalantly as he licked the fingers on his other hand and tried to wipe the blood away.

'Doesn't look like it happened last night,' Osian noted.

Tom gave him an icy stare.

Osian wondered for a moment if Tom and Callum had argued again while they were in the woods. Did that have something to do with Callum going missing?

Ethan frowned and looked at Tom. 'Why didn't you say

61

anything about Callum disappearing until we got out to the beach?'

Tom glared at him. 'What the fuck are you talking about, Ethan? I was off my tits. I didn't know what the hell was going on.'

'But you were the last person to see him,' Ethan said.

Osian saw a figure approaching out of the corner of his eyes – Tom's dad, Kenny. His thick arms were covered with tattoo sleeves and he wore a black Adidas tracksuit.

'What the fuck's happened?' Kenny asked Tom angrily.

Tom immediately looked scared. 'Callum's missing.'

Kenny didn't look remotely concerned by this. He also didn't make eye contact or acknowledge Osian or Ethan. He never did. Osian suspected it was because his dad was a copper. He'd overheard his dad talking about Kenny having been in prison years ago.

Kenny gestured to the uniformed police officers. 'That lot said you've given your statement so I can take you home.'

Tom looked up and nodded. Osian noticed that Tom always looked on edge, even scared, when his dad was around. It wasn't surprising. By all accounts, Kenny Hegerty was a right nutter.

Kenny clicked his fingers at him. 'Well, come on. I've got fucking work in the morning, lad. Chop, chop.'

As Tom got up and went sheepishly with his dad, Osian noticed the back of Tom's T-shirt for the first time.

Not only was it covered with dirt, it was slightly ripped.

It looked like Tom had been in a fight.

CHAPTER 9

Missing: 17 hours

Laura pulled slowly into Beaumaris nick car park and parked in her regular space. It was 6.20 a.m. and Gareth had called her at ten p.m. the previous evening to tell her that Callum Newell was missing over in the Newborough Forest area. She didn't know much about Callum Newell except that he was a friend of Declan's teenage son, Osian.

All CID officers were to be in by 6.30 a.m. for a briefing, unless there were any significant developments in the interim. She had heard nothing since, but knew that the local BBC Wales radio news was now carrying the story of Callum's possible disappearance, although details were sketchy.

Getting out of the car, Laura took a deep lungful of the early morning air. It was fresh and cold and just what she needed. Pete had left at five p.m. the day before but his stay had thrown Laura's emotional state into turmoil.

The sky above was sauntering from a dark indigo to the shimmering purple and orange of dawn. The noise of an aeroplane high above drew her eyes skyward. The thin white line of its water vapour drew a neat line that dissected the lightening sky in a diagonal shape. It was heading west. She wondered where it was going. Either Ireland, or the next stop after that, which was the east coast of North America.

Taking another deep breath, Laura tried to get her head together as she strolled across the car park, into the station and headed for the CID offices. As she entered, she saw that she was one of the last officers in.

Sitting down, Laura logged on to her computer and sat back for a moment. She glanced at the framed photo of Jake and Rosie sitting on Beaumaris Beach with their dog Elvis, and it brightened her mood immediately.

Looking down at her phone, she saw a BBC news article that had popped up on her feed. A man named Martin Dooley had been found dead in his prison cell in HMP Altcourt with a suspected heart attack. The name rang a bell as she tapped the article to have a read. Then she remembered. Martin Dooley was a disgraced former head of the Merseyside Drugs Squad. In 2013, Dooley had been exposed by *The Sunday Times* as taking bribes from several organised criminal gangs in Liverpool in exchange for giving them intel on future drug raids and operations. He had also used his influence to stop firearms charges being brought against a drug baron's son. When Dooley went to trial, it was revealed that he'd actually approached the major drug dealers in the area, suggesting bribes in exchange for information, tip-offs and evidence tampering. As a detective chief inspector, Dooley became the highest-ranking police officer in UK history to be convicted of corruption when he was sentenced to fifteen years in 2014.

Sitting back in her chair again, Laura reflected on the parallels between the Martin Dooley investigation and trial, and her own suspicions about corruption in the Manchester Metropolitan Police Force. And it struck her that the investigation hadn't been carried out by an internal anti-corruption unit or the Independent Office for Police Complaints. It had been conducted by investigative journalists from *The Sunday Times*. It was definitely food for thought.

Getting up from her desk, she went over to Gareth's office in the corner.

Clearly sensing her presence, he looked up at her. His tie was loosened and his shirt-sleeves rolled up.

He's really very attractive, she thought, looking at his thick forearms.

'Morning,' she said, giving him a quizzical look. 'Have you had any sleep yet?'

'Nope,' he said, shaking his head. To be fair, he didn't look that tired, probably because he was used to late nights. Functioning on little sleep was part of the job.

She went over, touched his arm and then sat down. Officers in CID still didn't know that they were having a relationship, and it was probably for the best as they both wanted to avoid any accusations of favouritism. Plus, if the top brass found out, they would insist that one of them – i.e. Laura – move to another police station. That would all have to change once they got married, but they'd cross that bridge when they got to it.

'Any developments yet?' she asked quietly. She couldn't imagine how Callum Newell's parents were feeling. It didn't bear thinking about, especially given that in the past year she'd had her own experience of both her children being in danger.

'Nothing.' Gareth sighed and shook his head. 'It's like Callum just vanished into thin air.' He looked at her. 'And every hour that goes past, our chances of finding him alive decreases.'

Laura nodded. 'The only saving grace was that it was quite mild overnight. You think he might have been attacked or taken?'

'To be honest, I just don't know.' Getting up from his desk, Gareth pointed to the CID office. 'I'd better get out there. Catch up properly later, okay?'

'Of course,' Laura said as she followed him out. Their little chat about Pete and the MMP might need to be put on hold.

'Right, guys,' Gareth said loudly as he headed over to the scene boards that had been set up overnight. He pointed to the photograph at the top. 'This is Callum Newell. Aged eighteen. A bright, sensible, intelligent young man. Not known to the police, with a stable home life. He went missing at around one p.m. yesterday afternoon,' he said, pointing to another photo showing the four boys at Osian's party the other night. 'He was with three school friends: Tom Hegerty, Ethan Edwards and Osian Flaherty, who most of you know is Declan's son.'

There were a few glances at Declan, who was sitting nearby. Laura could see that he was deep in thought.

Gareth gestured to another photo. 'We have a discarded trainer that has what looks like blood splatters on the toe. We have confirmed that the trainer belonged to Callum, but until we get the tests back from forensics, we won't know if it's Callum's blood. His parents provided us with a couple of things that forensics should be able to use to create a DNA profile.' Gareth walked over to a map and pointed to a red pin. 'About a hundred yards away from the shoe, we found this baseball cap,' he explained, pointing then to another photograph. 'The boys have confirmed that this also belonged to Callum.'

Detective Constable Andrea Jones frowned and pointed over to the image. 'And it was just hanging there on that branch?' Andrea had dark curly hair and olive skin, and had joined Beaumaris CID in September 2021. She and Laura had since grown close, and although she didn't want to admit it, Laura suspected that Andrea – whose parents had both died when she was very young – saw her as a bit of a mother figure.

'Yeah.' Declan nodded. 'The branch is head height, so our theory is that Callum ran under it and the cap caught in the branch, but for some reason he didn't go back to retrieve it.'

Detective Constable Ben Corden sat forward. Blond and handsome, with an athletic build, Ben was a bright young copper whom Gareth had taken under his wing. 'You think he was running from someone?' he suggested.

'That's what we suspect,' Declan replied.

'There is a slight issue here,' Gareth said. 'The boys had taken some magic mushroom chocolate at around 12.30 p.m. So, at one p.m. they were tripping.'

'And so Callum could have been running from some kind of hallucination rather than something or someone real?' Andrea said.

'Possibly,' Gareth replied. 'But we have blood on his trainer. And though we've searched the forest and Newborough Beach thoroughly, there's no sign of him anywhere.'

Ben looked over at Gareth. 'Are we going to extend the search, boss?'

'We have to,' Gareth said. 'But the longer we go on, the more I'm starting to think that Callum was attacked or abducted.'

Declan looked down at a message on his phone. 'Boss, the Canine Unit are in Newborough Forest right now. So far, there's no sign of him.'

'Okay, thanks for the update,' Gareth said.

'What if he went into the sea?' Laura asked. 'If he was off his head on mushrooms and went into the sea, he might have got into difficulties. That would explain why we can't find him.'

'That's another possibility,' Gareth agreed. 'The chopper has done a sweep up and down the coast and hasn't seen anything yet, but we can't rule it out.' He looked at the CID team. 'We'll let uniform, the Canine Unit and the chopper continue the search. But I want to go with my instinct on this. The discarded trainer, the blood and the baseball cap all suggest that someone else is involved in his disappearance. So, we need to track down everyone who was at the campsite, in those woods and on the beach and find out if they saw anything or anyone suspicious.'

'Callum has an account with O2,' Ben said. 'They're running a check on his phone now. If it's on, we might be able to triangulate the signal and find it.'

'Good,' Gareth said. 'And let's get a list of all Callum's phone calls and texts for the past week, to start with. We also need to search through his social media profiles and accounts to see if anything there can shed light on his disappearance. Also, most of you will probably have seen that the media office have put out a press release, but we might need to do a proper press conference later today to ask for tips and further information if we continue to draw a blank.' Gareth took a long swig of coffee. 'Declan, I need you to come with me to the Newells' house. The Family Liaison Officer says that Mrs Newell isn't coping very well and Mr Newell has gone out.'

The FLO was meant to look after the family of any victim of a major crime, acting as a point of contact to explain how the investigation was progressing, but given what they knew about Callum's father, Gareth knew Vicky would appreciate a visit and an update from her old friend Declan.

Ben frowned and then glanced over from his desk. 'Boss,' he said with a dark look, 'the staff at the campsite told us that the assistant park manager, Roy Balmer, went home sick at about 2.30 p.m. yesterday.'

Gareth nodded. 'Okay. That's near the time that Callum went missing. What do we know about him?'

Ben pointed to his screen. 'I ran Roy Balmer through the PNC. He served two years for having sex with a minor in 2011. Plus there's two convictions of possessing indecent images, from 1999 and 2006. He's on the Sex Offender's Register.'

'Christ, I'm surprised he could get a job anywhere,' Declan said.

Andrea frowned. 'But Callum is eighteen.'

Gareth shrugged. 'He's still a teenage boy.'

'And he's skin and bone, so he wouldn't be able to put up much of a fight if someone did try to abduct him,' Declan pointed out.

'Got an address?' Laura asked Ben. If this was an abduction, then there was no time to lose.

Ben nodded.

'Andrea and I will go and talk to him now,' Laura said, getting up from her chair, grabbing her jacket and looking at Andrea, who was doing the same.

CHAPTER 10

Missing: 19 hours

Laura and Andrea were making the forty-minute journey west across the island to the small village of Llangadwaladr where Roy Balmer lived. Leaning over from the passenger seat, Laura clicked on the radio. 'Free' by Ultra Nate, an upbeat dance track from the late nineties, was playing.

'Oh, I love this one!' Laura said with a half-smile. It was nice to hear some familiar, upbeat music and get out of the anxious, dark mood that had pervaded her all day.

Andrea pulled a face. 'Really? It's a bit annoying, isn't it?'

'God, no,' Laura protested. She didn't want to admit to Andrea that the reason she loved the song was that she had heard it years ago in a club in Liverpool when she had taken ecstasy. It was about six months before she'd started to train to be a copper and her sporadic recreational drug taking had stopped.

'Bit of a raver back in the day, were you?' Andrea teased her.

'Hardly,' Laura laughed. 'Okay, maybe a little bit.'

If only she knew!

'Yeah, clubs and dancing passed me by I'm afraid,' Andrea admitted.

Laura raised an eyebrow. 'That's because you're a baby – no offence – or as an old sergeant used to tease me when I was first in uniform, "You're so young, you're barely dry, Constable Hart."'

'Yuck.' Andrea pulled a face. 'Well, there's a phrase I will never be using.'

'What kind of music do you like? Urban?'

'We don't call it "urban" anymore,' Andrea explained in a mock patronising tone.

'No?'

'No.' Andrea shook her head. 'I was reading that it's "reductive", if that's the right word.'

'Reductive?' Laura looked puzzled.

'Basically, labelling various genres of music as "urban" is a politically correct way of saying music made by Black people,' Andrea said.

'That does make sense, now you've said it.' Laura smiled. 'But it also makes me feel very old.'

There was a beat and she could see Andrea was winding up to make a quip about her age.

'Don't even think about mentioning how old I am,' Laura said in a mock cautionary tone.

Looking up, Laura could see that they were now driving through Llangadwaladr, a small village in the south-west of Anglesey that was about two miles east of Aberffraw. It was close to the supposed royal burial ground for the kings of Gwynedd in the fifth century.

Glancing left, Laura saw a small house with a beaten-up old caravan on the driveway. With its rusty metalwork and flaky cream paint, it looked like it might have been parked there since the eighties.

'I think this is it,' Laura said as Andrea pulled the car over onto the grass verge.

They got out and walked along the road. The early morning wind was chilly and Laura buttoned up her jacket.

Looking again at the caravan, she had a thought.

'If Balmer has anything to do with Callum going missing,' Laura said, indicating the caravan, 'we should probably go and have a look in there.'

'Good point.' Andrea nodded as they headed over.

It was a cream colour, with a coffee-coloured stripe along both the bottom and the top.

Laura took out her blue forensic gloves, snapped them on and reached for the handle to the flimsy-looking door that led inside.

It was locked.

'Hello?' Laura called as she knocked hard against the door and then strained her hearing to see if she could hear any movement.

Nothing.

Cupping her hands at the smeared glass of the window, Laura looked inside. The caravan had been stripped of any seats, cupboards or beds. It was an empty shell and there was no sign of anyone or anything.

Laura slowly walked around the caravan and took another final look before assuring herself that there was no one inside – dead or alive.

'Okay, nothing here,' Laura said as she put her gloves back into her pocket.

They headed across the untidy garden to a dark front door. Laura rang the scruffy doorbell, which was more of an old-fashioned buzzer, and it vibrated under her forefinger.

A couple of dogs barked from inside, raising the alarm.

Andrea looked around the garden and then at the house. 'I think this is a property that estate agents describe as being "tired",' she said under her breath.

'Tired? I would have said exhausted to the point of coma,' Laura joked.

Before Andrea could react, the door opened slowly and a man in his sixties peered out at them suspiciously. He had a grey beard, a ruddy, bulbous nose and beady eyes. He was wearing a burgundy cardigan that was covered in dog hair.

'Yeah?' he asked.

Laura and Andrea fished out their warrant cards to show him. 'DI Hart and DC Jones, Beaumaris CID,' she explained. 'Mr Balmer?'

He frowned, looking utterly bewildered. 'Yeah?'

'Is it okay if we come in for a minute?' Laura asked politely. 'There's just a couple of questions we'd like to ask you.'

He looked at his watch. 'Do you know what time it is?' he demanded brusquely.

'I think it's about approaching eight,' Andrea suggested casually.

He glared at her. 'Is that supposed to be funny?'

'No, not at all,' she replied with a polite smile.

He then looked at Laura and grumbled, 'I was about to take the dogs out.'

Laura gave him a forced smile. 'It won't take more than a couple of minutes.'

'I suppose so,' he groaned as he opened the door and ushered them inside.

The house smelled of wet dogs and stale cigarette smoke. There was a rickety table in the hallway with a vase of dried flowers and the frame of the old oval mirror above that was littered with business cards and a couple of post-its.

Balmer ambled slowly down the hallway and turned left through an open door. The living room was cluttered with piles of old books, newspapers and ornaments, and there was a row of empty supermarket-brand whisky bottles on the floor over by the window. Dusty, aluminium Venetian blinds made the room dark and where there were hairline slits, the sun fell in symmetrical lines across the soiled carpet. An old-fashioned television in the corner was showing the BBC news with the volume turned down.

Laura and Andrea went over to a two-seater sofa that was shrouded by a red tartan blanket and covered in dog hair.

Oh God, I hope I don't catch anything, Laura thought as they sat down.

'Just a couple of routine questions. We'd like to check your whereabouts yesterday afternoon,' Laura explained as Andrea pulled out a notebook and pen from her pocket.

'I work at the Newborough campsite,' Balmer explained

with a furrowed brow, giving nothing away. 'I was there in the afternoon.'

Well that's a lie, Laura thought. *Not a good start.*

Andrea looked up at him and asked casually, 'And you were there all afternoon, is that right?'

'Yes,' Balmer said defensively with a surly shrug. 'What's all this about?'

'Can you tell us what time you left the campsite yesterday?' Laura asked, giving him one last chance to be truthful.

'Must have been six,' Balmer said as he scratched his chin nervously. 'It's usually about six, unless it's the winter. Why?'

'That's strange,' Laura said with a frown. She then waited for a few seconds before locking her eyes onto him. 'You see, the staff at the campsite said that you left about 2.30 p.m. yesterday because you weren't feeling well.'

Balmer paused for a second and shifted awkwardly in the armchair, as if something had quite suddenly itched his back.

'Oh yes, that's right.' He nodded. 'Sorry. I forgot that. You know what it's like. One day is much like the next.'

'Not really,' Laura replied caustically. Her instinct told her that he was lying to them.

'My memory isn't very good now that I'm kicking on a bit,' Balmer explained too readily.

Andrea stopped writing and looked over. 'So, you actually left the campsite around 2.30 p.m. yesterday?'

Laura was watching Balmer like a hawk. He was definitely becoming increasingly agitated and his leg was jigging nervously. Why had he lied?

'That's right,' Balmer said, blinking rapidly.

What are you hiding from us?

There were a few awkward seconds as the tension grew.

'Can anyone confirm that you were here at home from mid-afternoon onwards?' Laura asked.

'No.'

'Are you married?'

'No.' Balmer shook his head as though this was a strange question. 'Since my mother died ten years ago, I've lived here on my own.'

'You didn't see a neighbour or talk to anyone on the phone who could confirm where you were once you left the campsite?' Andrea asked.

'No,' he replied. 'Is this about that boy that's gone missing?' He pointed to the dusty old television set. 'I saw it on the news just now.'

'Did you come straight home or did you go somewhere else when you left the campsite?' Laura asked, ignoring his question.

'No, I came straight home,' Balmer said, his voice now uncertain. 'Where else would I have gone?'

'A group of four teenage boys arrived at the campsite at about twelve p.m. yesterday afternoon,' Laura said. 'Do you remember seeing them?'

'Yes,' Balmer replied cautiously. 'I didn't sign them in but I remember seeing them. Was the boy that's missing one of them?'

Andrea glanced over. 'Do you remember anything about these boys when they arrived?

'I remember that none of them could put up a tent properly,' Balmer said, rolling his eyes, clearly desperate to lighten the tense mood in the room. 'They were making a right meal of it. I offered to help them actually.'

'What did they say?' Andrea asked.

'They said they were fine and then fell about laughing,' Balmer explained. 'I'm not sure why.'

Laura looked at him for a second. 'Did you see any of them after you left the campsite?'

'No, of course not.'

'And you left the campsite and went straight home?' she asked again, hoping to trip him up.

'Yeah. As I said, I wasn't feeling well.'

Laura didn't bother to point out that wasn't what he'd said initially and that he had already lied once about his whereabouts the day before.

She gave him a quizzical look. 'But you're all right now though?'

'Yes.'

She looked around the room. There were doors on the far side that led out to the back but they were covered by long, dark curtains. There was an atmosphere in the house that was making her feel uneasy but she couldn't pinpoint what it was.

'Mind if we have a look around?' she asked.

Balmer didn't answer for a beat and then shrugged. 'Yeah. I haven't got anything to hide.'

We'll see about that.

Laura studied him for a moment. Despite what he had said, his nervousness seemed to have gone up a notch. Was Callum Newell being held somewhere in the property against his will?

Getting up from the squeaky sofa, Laura and Andrea went out into the hallway, before sticking their heads into the small kitchen. It smelled of sour milk.

Laura gestured to Andrea that they should search upstairs.

'We're going to have a look upstairs,' she said to Balmer.

'Help yourself,' he said, clearly trying to sound unflustered.

They climbed the bare wooden steps that creaked loudly, passing various old photos of Anglesey that hung on the wall. If Laura was to guess, she'd say that they had been taken in the sixties or seventies. Several featured a much younger Balmer sitting on the beach with an older woman, whom she assumed was his late mother.

Christ, Dr Freud would have a field day in here.

They got to the top and moved along the landing, which had threadbare dark red patterned carpet. A wooden shelving unit halfway along had some old-fashioned toys arranged on it: a spinning top and two dinky blue and yellow Meccano cars with silver nuts and bolts. A large china doll with a brightly coloured face sat on the top.

'This place is giving me the creeps,' Andrea whispered.

'Yeah,' Laura agreed. Even though it was warm outside, there was a strange chill inside the house. 'I keep expecting to see a jar with a head inside.'

Glancing into a bedroom to the left, Laura could see that it had belonged at some time to a woman. There was an old dressing table, with a mirror, hairbrush and dusty bottles of perfume displayed on top. The double bed was made and a vintage-looking dress and overcoat had been laid neatly on the mustard-coloured, candlewick bed cover.

Laura gave Andrea a look. Balmer had mentioned his mother had died ten years earlier, so it was all a bit Norman Bates to see her room and clothes laid out as if she was actually still alive.

They went inside and Laura crouched and looked under the bed while Andrea opened the old pine wardrobe, which was crammed full of women's clothes on hangers.

'Okay, I am now officially freaked out,' Andrea whispered with a shudder.

'You won't find anything in there,' growled an angry voice.

Shit!

Laura nearly jumped out of her skin.

Balmer had managed to get up the stairs and along the landing in silence.

'That's okay, Mr Balmer,' Andrea said. 'We're just having a quick look around and then we'll let you get on with your day.'

'Well, I think you've seen enough,' Balmer said, sounding flustered. 'I'd like you to leave now, please.'

Laura looked at Andrea.

Something in here is all wrong.

She ignored him as she took a look in the second bedroom, which was sparse but neat and tidy. She guessed it was where Balmer slept.

They went in and checked under the bed and in the wall cupboard.

Nothing.

Laura stopped outside the bathroom, which had a stained avocado suite that looked like it was from the seventies.

'Thank you, Mr Balmer,' she said with her best professional smile.

Walking along the landing back towards the stairs, Laura could feel his eyes burning into their backs. Even though everything seemed a little sinister here, there was no sign of Callum anywhere.

They went down the stairs and back into the hallway.

Laura reached into her pocket, pulled out her card and handed it to Balmer. 'If you think of anything that might help us, please give me a call.'

He didn't say anything, simply walked towards the front door to let them out. It was clear that he was desperate for them to leave.

Out of the corner of her eye, Laura spotted something. Behind the table in the hallway was the wooden panel on the wall. However, there seemed to be an opening of about an inch around the edge, as if there was a door – it just didn't have a handle. It was well disguised by the vase of flowers and the mirror.

Who has a hidden door with no handle?

Laura raised an eyebrow. 'Just one more thing, Mr Balmer. Have you got a cellar in this house?'

Balmer shook his head. 'No.'

Liar.

Laura looked at Andrea, who had now spotted what she was looking at. 'So, if I move that table, I'm not going to find a door just there?' she asked, pointing to the gap in the wooden panelling.

'Oh, that,' Balmer said, clearly trying to hide his escalating anxiety. 'It's just a coal cellar.'

Laura frowned. 'But I just asked you if you had a cellar and you said no.'

'I just keep coal down there,' Balmer babbled. He was starting to unravel.

Andrea went over to the table and moved it. 'You won't mind if we go and have a look then?'

'Don't you need a search warrant?' Balmer snapped as he moved the table back. His eyes roamed nervously, like a rabbit caught in headlights.

Andrea exchanged a concerned look with Laura. Something was definitely wrong.

'No, we don't,' Laura said, keeping her voice calm. 'Not if we think that a serious crime has been committed or someone's life is in danger.'

'Why don't you show us the cellar, Mr Balmer?' Andrea suggested, quietly moving the table away from the wall.

Balmer was now fidgeting. 'I can't.'

'Why not?' Laura asked.

'You can't go down there!' he mumbled.

Andrea pushed at the wooden panel where the oval mirror was located, but met with resistance.

'Open this door, now,' Andrea barked.

Fumbling in his pocket, Balmer took out a set of keys, went over and reached up to a lock that was about six feet above the ground and had previously been hidden behind the mirror. Everything about the clandestine door was highly suspicious.

Balmer pushed the door open and stepped back, revealing wooden steps leading down into the darkness.

Laura could feel her pulse quicken as she pulled a small Maglite torch from her pocket.

'Mr Balmer,' Laura said sternly, 'I'd like you to take us down to the cellar.'

Balmer nodded and blinked nervously as he went to the doorway and flicked a light switch inside. His whole body seemed to squirm.

Laura followed him to the top of the flimsy-looking staircase, which descended into the cellar. The air was thick with damp but also something else that she recognised. It smelled like baby oil, or white musk.

Laura gestured him forward.

They followed Balmer down the stairs into a large, shadowy cellar. To their left, there was a workbench with tools attached to the wall. Next to that was a set of shelves with some old blankets, a petrol can and a small step ladder.

As she glanced right, Laura immediately spotted a desk, office chair and a computer with a large, expensive-looking monitor. It looked totally out of place. Above the computer were twenty or thirty photographs neatly arranged on the wall.

Taking a few steps towards the desk, Laura could now see that the photos were of naked boys in their early teens. Some of them were posing but other images were of them having sex.

Oh God...

Laura took a nervous breath as her stomach lurched.

'Jesus,' Andrea said under her breath as her eyes widened in disgust.

'It's not what you think,' Balmer babbled anxiously.

'I'm pretty sure it is,' Laura said dryly. 'Roy Balmer, I'm arresting you on suspicion of…'

Suddenly, Balmer gave her an almighty shove. She clattered into Andrea, lost her balance and fell to the cold stone floor, grazing the palms of her hand.

Glancing up, she could see Balmer striding up the staircase. He slammed the door behind him and disappeared.

'Bloody hell,' Laura said, jumping to her feet and dusting herself down. 'You okay?' she asked Andrea, who was rubbing her head.

'Yeah, fine,' Andrea replied, wincing.

Sprinting over to the staircase, Laura bounded to the top and pushed at the door, only to find that Balmer had locked it from the other side.

'Fuck!' She groaned in frustration.

Andrea looked at her. 'Want me to give it a try?'

'Go for it,' Laura said, moving over to allow Andrea to come past her to the top step.

Bracing herself, Andrea smashed her shoulder against the door.

CRASH!

Nothing.

Please don't tell me we're stuck in here.

'Hang on,' Andrea said as she crouched and then hit the door with her whole weight again.

It flew open.

'Nice one,' Laura said as they ran out into the hallway.

'Where the bloody hell is he?' Andrea growled.

Dashing into the kitchen, Laura glanced out of the window. She could see Balmer doing his best to run across the field at the back and escape.

'Call for back-up and stay here,' Laura said. 'And see if there's anything down there that relates to Callum Newell.'

'Why? Where are you going?' Andrea asked.

Laura pointed at Balmer. 'I'm taking that fucker down.'

Sprinting out through the back door, she raced across the narrow, untidy back garden and jumped over the fence. She dropped down into the field and looked up. Balmer was about 150 yards away but he was hobbling and struggling to run very fast. There was no way she was going to let him get away.

With her arms pumping, Laura broke into a steady run, confident that she would be able to catch him. Her head was whirring. Balmer was looking like a viable suspect in Callum's disappearance. Would Balmer reveal where Callum was or what had happened to him? Was Callum still alive and being held somewhere?

Balmer darted left, heading for a steep hill.

Bad move. You're never getting up that, you tosser, Laura thought.

To the right, barbed-wire and an aluminium fence marked out a field where cows were grazing. A couple of them looked at Laura with disinterest as she sprinted past.

Balmer was less than a hundred yards away.

She was running flat out and her shoes were beginning to rub against her heels. With the back of her hand, Laura wiped the sweat from her forehead.

Seventy yards and closing.

Balmer glanced back at her anxiously. His escape had slowed to a lumbering jog.

'Stay there!' Laura yelled.

Surely he could see he wasn't going to get away.

Fifty yards.

Her early morning walks and swimming meant that she was in relatively decent shape, but her lungs were still starting to burn with effort as she sucked in air.

Twenty-five yards.

Balmer turned and looked shocked to see that she had virtually caught him up.

'Roy, just stop there!' She gasped. 'You're not going anywhere.'

Balmer turned, stumbled and fell to the ground.

A moment later, Laura was on him. She grabbed her cuffs, pulled his hands behind his back and cuffed him.

'Where is Callum Newell?' she thundered.

'I don't know,' Balmer snivelled. 'I don't know who that is.'

Laura grabbed his cuffs so that they tightened around his wrists, causing him pain.

'Ow,' he yelped, 'that hurts!'

'Where is he, Roy?'

'I swear…' He whimpered. 'I've got nothing to do with that boy going missing.'

'Then why did you run?' she snapped.

'Why do you think?'

'Roy Balmer…' She puffed out a laboured breath. 'I'm arresting you for the possession of indecent images of children. You do not have to say anything, but anything you do say can be used in a court of law.'

CHAPTER 11

Missing: 23 hours

Gareth and Declan were sitting opposite Vicky Newell. With nervous fingers, she smoothed her blonde ponytail and pulled a few fine strands of hair so that they came over her forehead. She was sitting hunched and gripped by anxiety on the sofa in her tidy living room. Zoe, her twenty-one-year-old daughter, sat beside her, holding her mother's hand.

Zoe was attractive, with auburn hair knotted on the top of her head. She had strong features that were both delicate and defined. Unlike her mother, she sat up straight, the picture of poise, calmly assessing the situation before reacting.

On the other side of the room, PC Layla Whittle, the FLO – Family Liaison Officer – sat quietly on a dining room chair. She had blue-green eyes and a choppy mess of brunette hair that surrounded her elf-like face.

'Why aren't you out there looking for him?' Vicky asked

Declan with a distraught frown. Her face was red and puffy from crying.

'We've got trained officers, tracker dogs and a helicopter out there, Vick,' Declan said, leaning forward as he tried to reassure her. 'We're doing everything we can, I promise you.'

The tone of his voice immediately revealed the close relationship going back years that Declan and Vicky had.

Vicky nodded but it was clear that she wasn't convinced. Her eyes roamed nervously around the room.

Gareth looked at her and said gently, 'We do need to find out as much as we can about Callum and what he's been doing in recent weeks to see if there are any clues as to what's happened to him.'

Zoe gave them a suspicious, almost hostile look. 'What does that mean?' she demanded.

'Is there anything out of the ordinary that's happened to him or anyone in the family recently?' Declan asked.

Vicky shook her head. 'No, nothing. I don't understand it.' Her eyes filled with tears once more. 'What if he's just lying there and he can't shout out?'

Zoe passed a tissue to her mum, who wiped her face.

'I can't imagine how difficult this is for you, Mrs Newell,' Gareth said.

'It's Vicky...' she said with a sniff.

'The longer Callum is missing, the more that we're convinced that someone else is involved in his disappearance,' Gareth explained.

There was a beat as Vicky and Zoe registered the suggestion and twin looks of horror came over their faces.

'What? You think he was attacked?' Zoe asked, her

expression returning to neutral. Gareth thought her eerie calm might just be her way of dealing with her brother's disappearance. Some people bottled up their emotions for fear of losing complete control.

'Something like that.' Declan nodded and then said quietly, 'There were traces of blood on his trainer that we found.'

'Oh God!' Vicky gasped as she visibly shook.

'It's okay, Mum,' Zoe said, putting a reassuring hand on her shoulder.

Gareth took a moment before broaching their darker theories about what might have happened to Callum. He took a breath before saying as gently as he could, 'Actually, with his discarded trainer and baseball cap, we think Callum might have been chased.'

'Chased? Vicky sobbed at the news, looking over to Gareth in utter disbelief. 'Who would do that?'

'That's what we wanted to ask you, Vick,' Declan said gently. 'Is there anyone you can think of that Callum has had contact with? Or anyone that might want to harm him?'

'Of course not,' Vicky snapped as she rubbed her tears from her face. 'Callum's not like that. You know him, Dec. He wouldn't hurt a fly.'

'No, of course not,' Declan agreed, trying to placate her. 'We're just looking for anything out of the ordinary, that's all.'

Vicky shook her head and wiped the tears from her eyes. 'What if some horrible paedophile took him?'

'We are exploring every avenue in this investigation,' Gareth said quietly.

There was a tense silence.

Declan pointed out to the hallway and the stairs. 'Mind if we go and have a look at Callum's bedroom?'

'Yeah, of course,' Vicky murmured as she continued to huddle into herself, arms folding tightly.

'Do you want me to come with you?' Zoe asked, making to get up.

'It's all right. You stay here with your mum, Zoe,' Declan suggested with a kind expression.

Gareth and Declan got up slowly, made their way into the hallway and began to go up the thick carpeted stairs. The house smelled of freshly brewed coffee and toast, and even though it was mild out, the central heating was on, making the house uncomfortably warm.

Mounted on the wall alongside the stairs were a series of professional studio photos of the family that Gareth guessed had been taken about ten years ago. The images had been printed on canvas and even though they featured Mike Newell, it was clear that he wasn't comfortable in the images and seemed to be keeping his distance from the others. In fact, it looked almost as if he wanted to be anywhere but in the studio having photos taken with his family. It wasn't that surprising though. From what Gareth knew, Mike was a nasty drunk who was rarely at the family home – and when he was, he was verbally and emotionally abusive.

'What about the dad?' Gareth asked under his breath, pointing to one of the images.

'Mike?' Declan asked as they got to the top of the stairs. 'Do we need to be looking at him?'

Declan then thought for a second. 'He's a horrible

91

little prick. But I can't see why he would go all the way to Newborough to either abduct or attack Callum. That doesn't make sense.'

'Fair point,' Gareth conceded as he rubbed his hand over his scalp. However, there was no denying the fact that the data showed that 90 per cent of all murders were committed by people known to the victim – mainly family members. 'But I do think we need to interview him as soon as possible,' he insisted.

They made their way slowly down the narrow landing.

'Here we go,' Declan said, pointing to a door on their right as they both pulled on their blue forensic gloves. 'This is Callum's room.'

The bedroom was just large enough for a double bed, and the walls had a variety of posters stuck up very precisely, showcasing things like Japanese Anime, *Star Wars* and *Call of Duty*.

Gareth looked at them. He was vaguely aware of the Japanese animation graphic novels and television series. It seemed to be what lots of teenagers were into these days, which was a far cry from Enid Blyton or *Smash Hits* and *Shoot* magazines – the staples of his own teen years.

There was an open laptop on a desk with some books and scribblings on a notepad. Gareth moved the books to take a look at the covers, finding *Catechism of the Catholic Church*, *The Puzzle of God* and *God, Freedom and Evil*.

Gareth furrowed his brow. 'Is Callum very religious?' he asked.

'Not that I know of,' Declan replied as he looked up from

where he was searching the bottom of the pine wardrobe. 'Bit of a boffin. Very bright.'

Looking down at the notepad, Gareth noticed there was some writing saying: *DNA Cells PT.* Gareth picked up the notepad and showed Declan. 'This mean anything to you?'

'I'm not sure,' Declan replied. 'I think he was doing some kind of Science A level. Chemistry, maybe. Osian did tell me ages ago.'

'And maybe he was doing some kind of religious studies,' Gareth suggested, pointing to the books.

Either way, there was nothing so far that gave them any clue as to what had happened to Callum and Gareth knew that the clock was ticking. They were nearing twenty-four hours since Callum's disappearance, and though 80 per cent of all missing children and teens were usually found within that period, after that, there was a declining correlation between time missing and young people being found unharmed or alive.

'There's something under here,' Declan said from where he was kneeling and looking under the bed. He fumbled around and then pulled out a thick roll of banknotes.

Gareth frowned. It looked like a lot of money.

'Fifties and twenties,' Declan said as he thumbed through the bundle. He looked over at Gareth. 'We're talking thousands, not hundreds.'

CHAPTER 12

Missing: 23 hours

'Interview conducted with Roy Balmer, Sunday, 12.30 p.m., Interview Room 2, Beaumaris Police Station. Present are Roy Balmer, Detective Constable Andrea Jones, Duty Solicitor Patrick Clifford and myself, Detective Inspector Laura Hart.'

Balmer was now dressed in a grey sweatshirt and matching bottoms, the clothes he'd been wearing when Laura arrested him, having been taken for extensive DNA analysis. His mouth had also been swabbed for a DNA sample and his nails clipped.

There was an ongoing search of Balmer's property by SOCOs and uniformed officers. However, so far, there was no sign of Callum Newell and nothing at the property to suggest that Callum had ever been there or that they knew each other in any way.

Balmer gave Laura a blank stare and then leaned in to talk to Clifford, whispering something in his ear.

Laura raised her eyebrow. 'Roy, do you understand that you are still under caution?'

Balmer peered over at Laura and said very quietly, 'No comment.'

Are you kidding me? Laura thought with frustration.

Andrea shifted forward in her seat as she clicked her pen. 'Roy, I'd like to advise you that opting for a "no comment" interview isn't in your best interests here. The evidence against you is overwhelming and so some explanation is going to be needed.'

Laura sighed. 'If you offer no explanation or defence, that will be taken into account in court.'

Balmer didn't respond as he picked at the nails on his right hand and ignored her.

'Roy, can you tell us where you were yesterday afternoon?' Laura said.

Balmer looked down at the ground. 'No comment,' he said, now sounding like a bored child.

'When we initially asked you that question, you told us that you were at the Newborough campsite until about six p.m.,' Laura said. 'Do you remember telling us that?'

'No comment.'

'However, it wasn't until we told you that your co-workers informed us that you'd gone home sick at 2.30 p.m. that you suddenly remembered when you actually left work yesterday. Don't you think it's strange that you couldn't remember what you were doing barely twenty-four hours ago?'

Balmer gave a fake yawn and replied, 'No comment.'

Laura bristled at Balmer's attitude. This was a sex

offender who had disgusting images of young boys having sex plastered on the walls of his home. Boys no older than her son, Jake. It made her so angry to think of what those children had been through for the thrill of Balmer's twisted perversion, but she knew she needed to keep calm and not let her seething loathing of him show.

'Roy,' Andrea said, looking up from the pad that she was writing notes on. 'You admitted to us that you spoke to Callum Newell and his friends yesterday when they were trying to put up their tents. Did you see or speak to Callum after then?'

Balmer didn't reply for a second but then let out an audible huff of impatience. 'No comment.'

Laura pulled a folder towards her and took out a piece of paper. 'Could you take a look at this document for me? For the purposes of the tape, I'm showing the suspect Item Reference 393T.' She then looked at Balmer with disdain and gestured at the sheet. 'Can you tell me what this document is, Roy?'

Balmer glanced at it, bristled and then sniffed nervously. 'No comment.'

'Fine. For the record, this document is a list of previous criminal offences that you've been charged and convicted of,' Laura said. 'You served two years of a four year sentence for having sex with a minor in 2011. Plus you have two convictions of possessing indecent images – one in 1999 and the other in 2006 – both for which you served time in prison. Is there anything you can tell us about that?'

Balmer continued to look down at the floor. His foot was now jigging nervously. 'No comment,' he said very quietly.

'As a convicted paedophile, can you see why we might think you have something to do with Callum Newell's disappearance, Roy?' Andrea asked.

Balmer didn't respond. Bringing up his past convictions had rattled him, as intended.

Balmer was now hunched over.

'Did you tell your work colleagues that you weren't feeling well and then wait for Callum and his friends to head off to the woods from the campsite?'

'No comment,' he said in a whisper. The line of questioning was clearly getting to him.

'Come on, Roy,' Andrea said. 'You approached Callum in those woods, didn't you?'

'No comment.'

'And then something happened,' Laura said. 'Callum ran and you chased him, didn't you?'

'No comment.'

'Roy,' Laura said loudly. 'I need you to tell me what happened between you and Callum yesterday afternoon.'

Balmer scratched his face and then looked up very slowly. There was now something cold and unnerving about his expression.

'You're right,' he said with a sneer.

Laura frowned. 'What precisely am I right about, Roy?'

There was an uneasy silence.

Balmer gritted his teeth and shuddered with rage. 'Please stop using my name. I hate my name.'

'Okay,' Laura said. 'Just tell us what I'm right about.'

He fixed her with a stare. 'I am a paedophile.'

Laura nodded. 'Yes. And I need you to tell me what

happened between you and Callum yesterday afternoon.'

'Don't you understand what I'm telling you?' Balmer said, shaking his head in obvious frustration.

'Of course I do,' Laura reassured him. 'Where's Callum? Can you tell me that?'

Balmer let out an aggravated groan. 'I'm a paedophile. So yes, I am sexually attracted to pre-pubescent children, in particular boys. *But* I have no interest in that boy. He was in his late teens. That's not my thing. It never has been. I had nothing to do with that boy going missing.'

CHAPTER 13

Missing: 23 hours

'It's about three thousand pounds,' Declan said, holding up the evidence bag that contained the roll of money they'd found under Callum's bed. He and Gareth were back in the Newells' living room.

Vicky looked baffled. 'I don't understand where he'd get that from.' She looked at Zoe.

'No, I don't know either,' Zoe admitted. 'I don't see how this is going to help find my brother. Have you heard anything?' she asked anxiously. Gareth observed Zoe for a second, noticing how keen she seemed to move the conversation away from the money. What was that about? Was she hiding something from them?

Declan leaned forward with his hands clasped. 'Look, I know this is difficult for you, but I promise we will tell you as soon as we hear anything.'

'You don't know how difficult this is, Dec,' Vicky snapped, her eyes still watery and bloodshot. 'It's not Osian out there missing, is it?'

'No, it's not,' Declan admitted very quietly.

Even though he understood how emotive this all was, Gareth was keen to move the conversation back to the matter in hand. 'As we mentioned, we're looking for anything out of the ordinary in Callum's life in recent weeks. If you really don't know where this money came from then—'

'Are you calling us liars?' Zoe asked angrily. 'Maybe he saved it up.'

'Come on, Zoe,' Declan said with a pleading tone. 'How is Callum going to save up three thousand pounds?'

'I don't know, do I?' Zoe snapped.

There was clearly something about the money that was making Zoe very jittery.

'Are you sure that you don't know anything about this money, Zoe?' Gareth asked politely.

'No,' Zoe said, looking offended. 'How would I know anything about money under Callum's bed?'

There were a few seconds of tense silence.

Gareth couldn't be sure but his instinct was that there was something Zoe wasn't telling them. Her reaction to the discovery was definitely off but it wasn't something he felt comfortable pursuing again just now.

'We noticed some religious books in Callum's bedroom,' Gareth said instead, looking at Vicky. 'Is Callum very religious?'

'No, not really,' Vicky said, sounding a little defensive. 'He's doing a Religious Studies A level, that's all.'

'Mum,' Zoe said under her breath, as if to prompt her to say more.

'What?' Vicky huffed.

They were clearly hiding something else.

'Please,' Declan said gently. 'Anything, however insignificant it may seem, could be the key to us finding Callum.'

'We need to tell them about that bloke David,' Zoe whispered.

Gareth shot Declan a look.

'What bloke David?' Declan asked.

Vicky looked at them with a reluctant expression. 'Callum had been going to see some bloke recently. David Coren. He told us it was research for his RS A level.'

'Okay,' Gareth said. 'And why is that an issue?'

'Because David Coren runs some weird pagan cult thing,' Zoe blurted out.

'It's not like that, Zoe,' Vicky said tetchily. 'I think they're just druids, that's all. Not everyone's cup of tea, I know, but your grandad was into all that stuff too.'

Gareth knew that Anglesey was one of the UK's hotbeds for modern druidism. Beaumaris had a standing stone circle that locals referred to as their 'mini Stonehenge', which dated back to the Bronze Age and 'The Age of the Druids' – around 100 BC.

'When you say that Callum had "been going to", what exactly do you mean?' Gareth asked.

'Callum had become interested in druids and paganism while doing his A level,' Vicky explained. 'He went to see this bloke called David Coren who lives near here. He's married. I don't think there was anything weird about it. Honestly. I've met him a couple of times and he seems really nice.'

'Yeah, well, most paedophiles do, Mum,' Zoe near

growled. 'They don't wear a big paedophile badge around their necks, do they?'

'Zoe!' Vicky said disapprovingly.

Gareth looked at Zoe. 'You had your doubts about David Coren?'

'I don't know.' Zoe shrugged. 'It's just that Callum talked about David a lot. I thought it was weird. And Mum did too, if she's honest.'

Vicky narrowed her eyes and looked at Declan. 'I think Callum was just looking for a decent male role model. He wasn't going to find one here, was he?'

'I look out for him,' Zoe insisted. 'Callum's my little brother. I just want him back home with us.'

Gareth could see that Zoe and Callum clearly had a close relationship.

Declan had been quietly mulling over this new information and had started to frown. 'You're not talking about the people that live over in Lon Capel, are you?'

'Yeah,' Vicky replied. 'Why? You know them?'

Declan's face fell as he nodded. 'It's a religious cult called The Fair Men.'

* * *

It was early afternoon by the time Osian stirred in his bed. He had slept very fitfully, waking constantly to check his phone for news about Callum on Twitter and the BBC site.

What the hell had happened to Callum? Why hadn't anyone found him? Where was he? There had been posts on Twitter claiming that he'd been abducted, which made Osian feel sick with worry. Why had he run off and left his trainer and baseball cap? The fact that they'd all been tripping on mushroom chocolate meant that none of them had been thinking straight. Did that explain it?

A knock at the door interrupted his dark train of thought.

'Hello?' he said, his voice still croaky from sleep.

The door opened and his dad appeared holding a cup of tea.

'Hello, mate,' Declan said with a concerned expression. 'I just popped back from work to check how you're doing.'

Osian blinked and looked at him with a faint flicker of hope. 'What's going on? Have you found him?'

'No, I'm sorry,' Declan replied, shaking his head sadly as he approached and put the cup of tea down on his bedside table. 'Here you go, mate.' He sat down on Osian's bed. 'We are doing everything we can though.'

The scene was familiar as his dad often brought him tea and sat on his bed while they chatted about rugby on Sunday mornings. Their team was Leinster. Based in Dublin, they'd been incredibly successful in recent years and Osian and his dad had been to the Aviva Stadium in Dublin a few times to watch Leinster play.

'I don't understand where he can be,' Osian said quietly as he sat up and pulled up his pillow. He felt numb, as though none of this was really happening.

'Don't worry,' Declan reassured him quietly. 'We'll find him. He's out there somewhere.'

However, there was something about the tone of his dad's voice that sounded hollow, as if he didn't really believe what he was saying. Did he know something that he hadn't told Osian?

Osian took a nervous breath as he looked at his dad. 'Do you really think someone could have taken him or… attacked him?'

Declan took a few seconds to respond. 'We just don't know, mate. I wish there was more I could tell you.' He reached over and gave Osian a reassuring pat on the shoulder. 'I know this is really difficult for you but your mum and me are here if you need anything, all right?'

'Yeah.' Osian nodded but he didn't really know what that meant.

Glancing down at his watch, Declan got up. 'I'd better get going. I'll see you later, okay?'

'Thanks, Dad,' Osian said as he sipped his piping hot tea and watched his dad go.

Osian was suddenly grateful he had such a good relationship with his father. Some of the kids at school teased him for having a copper for a dad, but Osian was secretly proud that his father was out there doing something meaningful, even if it wasn't very 'cool'.

Osian's phone buzzed. It was a message from Ethan.

heard anything?

Osian started to type.

No, nothing. My dad says they're still looking.

Ethan: *heard from tom?*

Osian: *no*

Ethan: *hes not answering my texts or calls*

Osian: *has he seen them?*

Ethan: *yeh, just not replying*

Osian: *maybe he's upset?*

Ethan: *yeah*

Osian: *I might pop round and see if he's ok*

Ethan: *I went round earlier to check*

Osian: *What did he say?*

Ethan: *his mum said he gone out somewhere. Meeting someone?*

Osian: *where? Who?*

Ethan: *dunno*

Osian was confused. Why wasn't Tom responding to the texts or calls? And who was he going to meet?

CHAPTER 14

Missing: 26 hours

Laura and Andrea arrived at Newborough Beach after learning that the search was now focusing on the eastern end. They had eventually called a halt to the interview with Balmer when it became clear he wasn't going to give them anything beyond 'no comment'. However, due to the images and computer found in his cellar, he was still being held on the charges he'd been arrested on until he could be brought before a magistrate the following morning. Laura and Andrea had discussed it afterwards and admitted they just didn't know for sure if Balmer had attacked or taken Callum or not. There was nothing in the house, cellar or in his car to suggest a connection with Callum, but Laura had interviewed sociopathic fantasists in the past whose ability to lie convincingly was frightening, and it was always possible that could prove to be true with Balmer.

A gull squawked overhead, breaking her train of thought. The beach was as Laura remembered it as a child. At the far end was Llanddwyn, a seventy-four-acre island, which she thought looked like it had been plucked from a dark Welsh fairy-tale. At its centre stood the eerie ruins of Saint Dwynwen's church, built in the sixteenth century on the religious site that had been there since AD 465. As children, she and her sister, Emma, had loved hearing the ill-fated story of Saint Dwynwen, who was the daughter of King Brychan Brycheiniog in the fifth century. The folktale told of Dwynwen's love for a young man, Maelon, whom she was unable to marry as her father had promised her hand in marriage to someone else. Devastated by this, she prayed that she would fall out of love with Maelon to ease her pain. In response to her prayer, an angel granted Dwynen three wishes: Maelon was made to forget all about her; Dwynwen remained unmarried for the rest of her life; and God promised to look after and protect any couple that was truly in love, so they wouldn't face the same cruel separation that Dwynwen and Maelon suffered. Dwynen then moved to the island of Llanddwyn, where she lived out the rest of her life as a hermit. Saint Dwynen became the Welsh patron saint of lovers and Dydd Santes Dwynwen – St Dwynwen's Day, on 25 January – was still the Welsh equivalent to Valentine's Day. Laura and Emma had always thought it was such a beautiful but tragic story.

Taking a long deep breath of the sea air, Laura then realised that she hadn't been down this part of Newborough Beach since she was nine or ten. She recalled Emma, with trousers unevenly rolled up over her knees, holding a net and jar as they both waded among the rockpools. Her *nain* and *taid* – Welsh for 'grandmother' and 'grandfather' – had brought green striped foldable chairs, a huge red tartan blanket and a picnic that day. Even though it had been blazing hot, her *nain* and *taid* had remained almost fully clothed, with hats and an old orange umbrella to shield them from the sun.

Laura and Emma had played in the rockpools and paddled in the sea, squealing with delight as the waves whooshed over their feet and shins, splashing droplets of cold sea up onto their faces. It was only with the hindsight of age that she realised what a carefree, glorious time that had been in her life.

'It's getting warm,' Andrea said, blowing out her cheeks as she took off her jacket and slung it casually over her shoulder.

As they strode down the vast beach, Laura looked down at the shells that were in a multitude of shapes and sizes, all smooth white, and flecked with green algae. The sea breeze blew noisily about her face with a fresh, salty bite.

Laura glanced at her watch, which glinted in the sunlight. Callum was still missing and the clock was ticking with an ominous steadiness. And that meant two things. Firstly, they were less likely to find Callum alive. And secondly, it was highly probable that someone else had been involved in Callum's disappearance.

Up ahead, the beach was crowded with uniformed police officers, detectives, dog handlers, search dogs and SOCOs who were scouring the beach and the ground behind for anything that might give them a clue as to what had happened to Callum.

'That's the problem with a MisPer like this,' Laura said

sadly. 'We don't know if Callum is missing due to accident, misadventure or if he's been taken. It's hard to get the investigation focused.'

'I think if he was injured and lying somewhere, we would have found him by now,' Andrea said.

Laura looked to her left at the warren of towering sand dunes and pathways, and then the thick, dark lines of conifer trees. 'You know what, I'm not convinced we would. This place is huge,' she remarked.

Gareth and Declan walked towards them, Gareth giving a half-wave.

Laura nodded towards the dark expanse of the Irish Sea to their right. 'Of course, he could have ended up in there.'

Gareth took his Ray-Ban sunglasses from his pocket and put them on. Laura couldn't help but notice how attractive and rugged he looked as he approached.

'Have we found anything, boss?' Andrea asked.

'Nothing.' Gareth shook his head in frustration. 'One of the dogs picked up on a scent from one of Callum's T-shirts in the dunes earlier on. But so far, we can't seem to find anything down here.'

Laura looked at him. 'But that does mean that Callum was down on this part of the beach at some point, doesn't it?'

'Yes. Callum was down here.' Gareth gestured to the dunes and forest behind them. 'But this place is so big, I'm not sure if it helps us very much.'

Declan's Tetra radio buzzed and he answered it.

Suddenly, there was a thudding noise from overhead as the police helicopter arrived and hovered over the sea, the force from its rotor blades creating concentric circles on the water's surface.

Declan gestured to his radio as he looked at them and said over the noise, 'The chopper's scoured the whole of this area. There's nowhere else to look, boss.'

Gareth pulled a face and pointed in the opposite direction, towards the sea. 'Unless he went in there. And then he could be anywhere, God help us.'

'He would have been taken out by the tidal currents,' Declan explained. 'And if he was taken out into the Irish Sea, we'll never find him.'

'Which takes us back to the theory that he was abducted,' Laura said.

'Yeah,' Gareth agreed. 'Any trace on Callum's mobile phone yet?'

Andrea shook her head. 'Still waiting, boss.'

'Social media?' Gareth asked.

'I've looked at his Facebook, Twitter and Instagram and there's nothing of interest,' Laura said. 'I need to check to see if he had TikTok or Snapchat. Given his age, it's likely that he did.'

'Okay,' Gareth said. 'Callum's mother and sister said that he'd become interested in some religious group in recent months. Declan says they're based in Lon Capel.'

Andrea's eyes widened. 'The Fair Men?'

'That's right,' Declan replied. 'You know them?'

'Yeah,' Andrea said. 'They've been around for donkey's years. Some sort of offshoot of druid worshippers and pagans. But they've definitely got a community down in Lon

Capel. My aunt used to tell me to keep clear of them when I was kid.'

The others frowned.

'But my aunt was pretty bonkers. She made up mad stories all the time,' Andrea offered.

Gareth looked at Laura and Andrea. 'Bloke's name is David Coren. Bit of a long shot, but you two should go over there now. Then I want a full briefing of all CID at five p.m.' He gave them a dark look. 'And move quickly. Every second counts more than ever now we're past the twenty-four hour mark since Callum went missing.'

CHAPTER 15

Missing: 27 hours

Half an hour later, Laura and Andrea were heading south-west from Beaumaris towards Lon Capel. Andrea was driving and Laura was researching *The Sunday Times* investigative reporter who had exposed DCI Martin Dooley back in 2013 – a woman named Claudia Wright. As far as Laura could see, Claudia still worked at *The Sunday Times* and she'd managed to track down her email address. Maybe she should reach out anonymously and see whether Wright would be interested in all that she knew about Sam's death, Butterfield, the Fallowfield Hill Gang and the MMP? Laura felt safer talking to a journalist than another police officer, which was disheartening. The only other option would be to talk to an anti-corruption unit in another police force, but her instinct was to talk to someone like Claudia Wright first.

'Everything okay, boss?' Andrea asked, breaking her train of thought.

Laura knew that between looking at her phone and

thinking about contacting Claudia Wright, she hadn't actually uttered a word for nearly twenty minutes. And usually her and Andrea's time in the car was spent chatting.

'Yes, all fine,' Laura said with a kind smile. It wasn't a topic that she felt she could share with Andrea, for all sorts of reasons. 'Just some stuff that I needed to sort out.'

Clicking onto her Gmail account, Laura bit the bullet and began to compose an email to Claudia Wright with as much detail as she dared to share with her. Even though Laura was working a major incident, she feared that Pete was potentially dangerous to her and even her family and so she needed to disclose what she knew to someone outside of the police force as soon as possible.

Ten minutes later, they arrived in the tiny village of Lon Capel, which was just over four miles north-east of Newborough Beach. It was no more than a hamlet, with a garage, an old Methodist church and some holiday cottages.

At the far end, there was a collection of old-fashioned-looking bungalows, which were decorated with strange ribbons and circular wooden decorations that were carved with solstice symbols and hung around the front doors.

As Andrea pulled the car over to park, Laura looked down at her phone where she had been doing some very hasty research after finishing her email to Claudia Wright.

'Okay, The Fair Men are an order overseen by the High Priest, David Coren,' she said, reading from their website.

'Right,' Andrea replied as she unclipped her seatbelt. 'It was Andrew Coren who was running The Fair Men when I was a kid.'

'Maybe it's his son?' Laura suggested as she got out

and then peered at the slightly eerie sight of the decorated bungalows. 'No cars?' she observed.

'Yeah, I don't think they believe in modern stuff like that,' Andrea said, raising an eyebrow. 'Although, to be fair, I don't know very much about them except that we were scared of them when we were kids and made up horrible stories.'

Laura spotted the largest bungalow at the end of the row and thought it was as good a place as any to look for David Coren. 'Let's start there.'

Walking up the road, Laura got the distinct feeling they were being watched even though she couldn't actually see anyone.

This feels distinctly weird.

They got to the last bungalow, walked up the garden path and arrived at the front door, which was decorated by various wooden symbols, ribbons, a crown made from dried flowers and other strange-looking artefacts.

Laura pulled a face at Andrea and then knocked on the door.

A few seconds later, a man in his forties with long, straw blond hair in a ponytail, glasses and smiley blue eyes answered the door.

He was wearing a dark brown hooded robe that had embroidered edges. Around both wrists were a plethora of silver, wooden and leather bracelets.

'Hello?' the man said with a cheery but curious expression.

'DI Hart and DC Jones, Beaumaris CID,' Laura explained, showing her warrant card. 'We're looking for a David Coren.'

'That's me,' Coren said as he opened the door a bit wider. Not only did he appear to have been expecting them, he seemed downright pleased to see them.

'Is it okay if we come in for a minute?' Andrea asked. 'We've got a few questions that we'd like to ask.'

'Of course, of course,' Coren said, beckoning them in with a serious look on his face. 'I'm assuming that you've come because of what's happened to Callum Newell?'

Laura nodded as they came into the neat hallway. On the walls were a couple of dark oil paintings depicting Pagan celebrations on a beach. Next to them was a black canvas with an intricate circular pattern and lettering that read: *Wiccan Wheel of the Year.*

As they followed Coren into a living room, he gave them a concerned look. 'Is there any news about Callum?'

'Not at the moment,' Laura said as she and Andrea went over to the sofa, which was covered by an olive green throw.

The room itself felt old-fashioned and it would be hard to date as there seemed to be no technology, just dark furniture and bookshelves that were crammed with books and ornaments. It also smelled of joss sticks and lavender.

Andrea pulled out her notebook and pen. 'Can you tell us the last time you saw Callum?'

'Gosh,' Coren said with a frown. 'Erm, I think it was about a week ago, although I would have to check.'

Laura looked at Coren, trying to get a handle on him. His manner seemed to be superficially friendly, even charming. But she wasn't buying it. It felt like an act.

'And where did you see Callum?' Andrea enquired.

'He came here last week,' Coren explained casually, as

115

though he had nothing to hide. 'He had tea with me and my wife.'

Laura waited for a second and then asked, 'Is your wife here?'

'No,' Coren said, shaking his head. 'I'm afraid she's tending to a lost soul from our flock. Metaphorically, that is.'

'How did Callum seem when he was here?' Laura said.

'He seemed fine.' Coren sniffed and scratched his nose. 'We talked about his interest in religion as he's doing a Religious Studies A level.'

Laura sat forward. 'There didn't seem to be anything troubling him?'

'Nothing apart from the usual,' Coren said with a knowing expression. It was clear he wanted them to ask him what he meant.

Andrea looked over at Laura and at her nod, gave Coren what he wanted. 'The usual?'

'I don't think Callum's home life is that stable,' Coren said. 'I get the feeling that his relationship with his father, Mike, is very difficult.'

Laura wondered if there was anything in this. As far as she knew, CID hadn't managed to speak to Mike Newell yet.

'And he told you about that, did he?' Laura enquired.

'A little,' Coren said with a serious expression. 'Reading between the lines, I think his father is very hard on – even unkind to – Callum. As you're probably aware, Callum is a very intelligent young man, and for some reason, Mike Newell seemed to dislike or mistrust Callum for it.'

Laura and Andrea shared a look.

Andrea gestured to her notepad. 'Just to confirm, you haven't seen Callum since he came here last Sunday?'

'No,' Coren stated.

'And you've had no communication with Callum since then? No phone calls, texts?' Laura confirmed.

'No, I'm afraid not.'

Looking around at the books and the wall hanging covered with symbols, Laura asked, 'And you and your wife – and this community – are members of The Fair Men Order? Is that correct?'

'Yes,' Coren replied. 'We are an essentially pagan community, although we have those who believe in a more druid-type of worship. We explore and celebrate the rich spiritual history and connections of this magical island. But we're fully transparent about what we do and what we believe. And despite some silly rumours around here, there is no more ritual to our worship than your average Catholic mass.'

Laura nodded. Coren seemed very self-assured.

'And Callum had joined The Fair Men?' Andrea said.

'No, nothing like that,' Coren replied. 'But he was definitely interested in talking about what we do, our beliefs and rituals. Of course, we hoped that one day he might join us—' Coren stopped abruptly, as though he had been about to say something but had stopped himself.

Laura looked directly at him. 'Please, if there's anything, however small, it might provide a clue to help us find Callum.'

Coren looked a little awkward. 'It's just that I know that Callum and his father got into a physical fight about ten days ago. Callum had told him that he'd had enough of his drinking and tantrums and that he was going to move out of the house and come and live with us here. His father told him that no son of his was running away to join some "weird religious cult". In fact, he said he'd prefer Callum to be dead than come and live here… Sorry, I should have told you that when you first arrived.'

Laura and Andrea exchanged a look. They needed to find and interview Mike Newell as soon as possible.

CHAPTER 16

Missing: 28 hours

Gareth was now running on caffeine and adrenaline alone. He had managed about half an hour of sleep since the investigation began, but had noticed that he was nodding off into unintentional micro naps at his desk. Taking a deep breath, he rubbed his face, trying to summon the energy to go out and brief CID on the investigation.

Come on, Gareth, you got this.

'Hey,' said a friendly voice.

It was Laura.

Even though they had been in a relationship for nearly a year, he still got a little fizz when he saw her. It was something about her deep chestnut eyes and the faint smile that lit him up.

'Hey,' he said as he smiled and then pushed himself up out of his office chair with a groan.

'No offence, but you look like shit,' she joked.

'No offence taken. I feel like shit,' he admitted.

Laura pointed to the sofa on the far side of his office. 'Why don't you grab an hour of sleep after the briefing, before you collapse.'

'Yeah, maybe,' he said to placate her. He couldn't rest while there was a missing teenage boy out there, especially when it was all so close to home. He got a flash of memory of Callum and his friends laughing and drinking on Friday night. He owed it to all of them to find out what had happened.

'Do you want my coffee?' she asked as they headed for the door. 'It's hot and I can pop and get another one in a bit.'

'Yes,' he said with a grateful smile. 'Thanks.' He took the coffee as he headed across to the scene boards, then took a long swig. He looked out at the CID team and then pointed to the clock on the wall as it hit five p.m. 'Right, guys, Callum Newell has now been missing for approximately twenty-eight hours. According to our search team, if he was lying somewhere in Newborough Forest, they would have almost certainly found him by now. As most of you know, one of the search dogs caught Callum's scent at the far end of Newborough Beach this morning. However, we didn't find anything in that area.' Gareth pointed at the photo of Callum's trainer. 'Anything from forensics on this blood?'

Andrea shook her head. 'I'm chasing it, boss.'

'Can we chase it harder, please?' Gareth said sternly as he ran his hand over his cropped head. He knew that he sounded annoyed but it was vital to know if it was Callum or someone else's blood. 'We are also going to need elimination DNA samples from Osian, Ethan and Tom. And the Newell family.'

Ben looked over with an urgent expression. 'Boss, Digital Forensics have found the signal from Callum's mobile phone.'

Gareth's attention was immediately pricked. 'Where is it?'

Ben moved swiftly over to the map of Anglesey on the wall. 'They've narrowed it down to this area here,' he explained, pointing.

As Gareth moved closer, he could see Ben was pointing to an area about two miles north of Newborough Beach, the forest and the campsite. It was a big breakthrough and although they couldn't be certain that the phone was on Callum's person, it was a possibility, which gave them reason to hope.

'Are they certain?' Declan asked.

'Yeah, they're certain,' Ben said. 'The signals around there aren't very good so it's proving difficult to triangulate its location exactly. But they think they might be able to pinpoint more exactly later today, once they've had a chance to work on it further.'

'When they say exactly, what do they mean?' Andrea asked.

'They mean they're going to try to narrow it down to fifty to a hundred yards,' Ben replied.

Gareth looked at the map again. This was all very significant.

'Right, so if Callum's mobile phone is a couple of miles north of our search area…' Gareth said, thinking out loud.

'…It means our theory of Callum being chased, attacked and taken is even more likely,' Declan chipped in.

'Exactly. Anything else?' Gareth asked.

Ben shifted in his seat. 'Forensics have been all over Balmer's car and home. Nothing to suggest that Callum Newell has ever been in either.'

'Right.' Gareth nodded. 'But Balmer is being held on the other charges?'

'Yes, boss,' Laura replied. 'He's up in front of a magistrate tomorrow.'

Gareth pointed to the map. 'Okay, we need a thorough search of this new area please.' He looked at Laura and Andrea. 'What happened over on Lon Capel?'

Laura frowned for a moment. 'Andrea and I spoke to David Coren, who is the High Priest of The Fair Men. He's a little bit odd but, to be fair, articulate and pretty open about why Callum had been visiting them.'

Gareth raised an eyebrow. 'Did you think there was anything sinister there?'

'Not really,' Laura replied. 'I didn't think he was hiding anything from us and I can't see any motive. Andrea?'

Andrea nodded. 'Nothing he told us made me think he was involved in Callum's disappearance.'

Laura's phone rang and she answered it.

'But Coren did tell us that Mike Newell and Callum have a very strained relationship. Sounds like Mike is verbally, if not physically, abusive to the family when he's been drinking. Mike and Callum had a physical fight about ten days ago.'

Andrea turned a page of her notebook. 'In fact, Mike told Callum that he would prefer him to be dead than to go and join some "weird religious cult", as Coren said he put it.'

Gareth nodded. That was definitely something that needed looking at.

'If Mike thought that Callum was going to run off and join these Fair Men, that might give him motive to abduct him on Saturday afternoon,' Declan stated.

'I've had a call from the FLO,' Laura said, gesturing to her phone as she got up from her desk and grabbed her jacket. 'Mike Newell is at the family home so Andrea and I can go and have a word.'

'Good. In the meantime, I have to get this press conference done,' Gareth said with a grimace. 'After that, Declan and I will pay a visit to Digital Forensics to put the pressure on. We need to pinpoint that mobile phone's location as soon as possible.'

CHAPTER 17

Missing: 28 hours

Osian turned the corner on his bike, pedalling hard and enjoying picking up speed. Feeling the fresh air against his face, he took a deep breath. It was just good to be out of his bedroom and the house.

After the texts from Ethan, Osian had decided to go and check on Tom. It wasn't like him to go off radar and not return messages or calls – especially when they could see that he had read them.

Cutting down New Street, close to the centre of Beaumaris, he then turned right into Rose Hill. Osian had always had a soft spot for Rose Hill, ever since he was a child. It was narrow and lined by cute, terraced houses. In recent years, they had all been painted – mostly white, but others in sky blue, pink and mustard. Osian thought the road looked continental. It was how he imagined the roads in the south of France to look.

A few seconds later, he whizzed past Beaumaris gaol and courts. He remembered that in Year Eight at school he had done an extensive history project on Beaumaris' Victorian gaol. He had learned about the penal treadmill where prisoners were forced to walk on steps cut into cast-iron wheels to pump water for hours on end. Osian thought it was barbaric. The gaol had also seen the infamous execution of a prisoner called Richard Rowlands in 1862 for murdering his father-in-law. Rowlands protested his innocence even in his last seconds, and it was said that he cursed the church clock from the gallows, claiming that if he were innocent, the four faces of the church clock would never show the same time again. The clocks were still out of sync over 150 years later.

A moment later, Osian turned right by the Liverpool Arms Hotel and began to cycle along the seafront. The tide was out and a steep-slanted corridor of sunlight fell along the wet sand, which glistened with a blue-white colour. Above, a huge seabird swooped and banked silently on the invisible currents and undulations of wind coming in from the Menai Strait.

It was the Easter Holidays, so the front was busy with holidaymakers.

Slowing his bike, Osian turned into Mill Lane, where Tom lived with his parents in a small bungalow. Osian hoped that when he knocked to see if Tom was home and if he was okay, it would be Kathleen Hegerty, Tom's mum, who answered. Kathleen was a quiet woman who looked like she had the weight of the world on her shoulders but she was friendly enough.

Stopping his bike, Osian hopped off so he could wheel it along the pavement.

His attention was drawn to a small, blue car that at that moment pulled up outside Tom's bungalow. Osian knew instantly who the car belonged to – Zoe Newell, Callum's older sister. If he was honest, he'd had a crush on Zoe for years, but he suspected lots of boys did. Unfortunately, she normally looked at Osian with a mixture of indifference and disdain.

What's Zoe doing outside Tom's house? Osian wondered.

He slowed a little and then peered over at the car.

Tom was sitting in the passenger seat, smoking a spliff.

What the fuck!

Osian stopped in his tracks then edged closer to the hedgerow and behind a tree, where he was fairly confident that they couldn't see him.

Tom wound down the passenger window and blew smoke out in a huge plume.

Zoe looked upset and appeared to be wiping tears from her face.

Tom leaned over to console her.

Osian couldn't say he was entirely shocked. In recent months, he'd seen Tom and Zoe having little chats on their own when they'd all been at Callum's house. Plus he'd seen Tom flirting with Zoe at the beach a few weeks ago and had seen her reaction. It had made Osian more than suspicious at the time.

As Tom put his arms around Zoe inside the car, Osian couldn't help but feel a pang of jealousy. They began to kiss passionately.

Jesus!

Tom got out of the car, and gave Zoe a little wave before she drove away.

Taking the handlebars of his bike, Osian wondered if he should just turn around, cycle home and forget what he'd seen.

Tom was loitering around outside the house, clearly avoiding going inside as he looked down at his phone.

Just go and talk to him.

Taking a breath, Osian began to wheel his bike up the steep pavement towards his friend.

'You okay, bro?' Osian called as he approached.

'Hi, fam,' Tom said and then put his phone away hurriedly, instantly looking shifty. 'Have you heard any news about Callum?'

Osian shook his head. 'No, nothing.'

'What about your dad?' Tom asked.

'He says the police are doing everything they can,' Osian replied.

Tom frowned and said quietly, 'I just don't understand what happened.'

'No,' Osian agreed. 'Me and Ethan have been trying to get hold of you.'

Tom hesitated and then shrugged. 'I haven't felt like talking to anyone really after what happened. I've just shut myself away, you know? Sorry.'

'Yeah.' Osian nodded. 'You haven't seen anyone then?'

Tom frowned at him. 'No.'

Yeah, well, I know that's a lie.

'Must be horrible for Callum's mum and dad. And for Zoe,' Osian said.

'I suppose so, yeah.' Tom nodded.

Osian looked at him.

What the fuck are you lying for? What's going on?

CHAPTER 18

Missing: 29 hours

Laura and Andrea were sitting in the living room at the Newells' home. They had been talking to Mike for about five minutes but he had already made it clear that he wasn't happy answering their questions.

'Can you tell us where you were between twelve p.m. and five p.m. yesterday afternoon?' Andrea asked.

In his forties, he had a scraggy beard and unkempt hair. His eyes were baggy and his face was slightly puffy, probably from drinking.

'Why do you need to know that?' he asked in an annoyed tone.

'It's just routine,' Laura reassured him.

'Why aren't you out there looking for my son?' he snapped.

'We have every available officer looking for Callum. But we also need to get a clear picture of where everyone in Callum's life was when he went missing.'

'I was in The Red Lion,' Mike replied gruffly. He looked like he wanted to be anywhere else rather than talking to them.

'Can anyone verify that?' Laura asked.

Mike scowled at her and said loudly, 'Why do they need to bloody *verify* it? My son is out there missing, so what the fuck are you two doing here asking me where I was?'

'If you can calm down please, Mike, I've just explained. These are just routine questions in an investigation like this,' Laura said calmly, but his attitude was starting to grate on her.

'Sounds like a bloody waste of time to me,' he mumbled as he ran his hand through his hair. He looked worried. 'I just don't understand where he can be.'

Laura looked at him. 'How would you describe your relationship with Callum?'

Mike took a few seconds to reply but then seemed to take offence. 'Eh? He's my son.'

'Do you get on?' Andrea said.

'Yeah… I suppose so,' Mike replied with a shrug.

Laura frowned. 'You don't sound very sure about that.'

'We don't always see eye to eye on stuff but he's a teenager. That's what they're like, isn't it? So, sometimes I have to put him straight, that's all.'

'*Put him straight*?' Laura said with a quizzical expression. 'Can you tell us what you mean by that?'

'Jesus.' Mike furrowed his brow. 'You know, when he's out of order or got something wrong. I let him know.'

'Have you ever been violent towards Callum?' Andrea asked.

'No,' Mike growled but then thought about it for a moment. 'I've given him the odd clip around the ear when it's been needed. But that's what my old man did to me and it never did me any bloody harm.'

Laura shot Andrea a surreptitious look – she didn't like the sound of that.

'We understand that Callum had been spending some time with a man called David Coren and his wife,' Laura said.

'Oh yeah,' Mike snorted with a caustic expression. 'Right shitshow that is.'

Andrea looked up from her notepad. 'I take it you don't have much time for David Coren or his religious beliefs then?'

'Fucking joking aren't you?' Mike sneered. 'Like all those religious weirdos, he's just a paedophile using some cult to get with teenagers. Like that bloke over in America when they all died in that fire.'

Laura assumed that he meant the Waco Massacre in 1993 in Texas, when members of a religious cult – called the Branch Davidians, under the guidance of David Koresh – died in a fire during a siege.

'Do you believe that Callum was in a sexual relationship with David Coren then?' Laura asked bluntly.

'No!' Mike looked horrified. 'When the fuck did I say that! That's not what I meant. Jesus! I just meant that that Coren bloke's a freak.'

'I'm confused. You said you thought David Coren was a paedophile who was using his status in The Fair Men to attract teenagers.'

131

'I didn't mean Callum,' Mike spluttered, floundering for the right words to explain what he was trying to say. 'I meant that Callum spending time with them was just bloody weird. Why does a man his age want to spend time with an eighteen-year-old boy? It's not right, is it? It's just not bloody normal.'

'Were you concerned that Callum might run away and join their religious order?' Andrea enquired.

'No,' Mike said defensively. 'Why would you say that?'

Laura looked over. Her last question had obviously rattled him and his eyes roamed nervously around the room.

She waited for a few seconds for the tension to rise. Was that it? Was Mike's fear that Callum was going to run away so great that he had followed them down to Newborough and confronted his son there?

Vicky Newell opened the door and looked in sheepishly.

'I'm sorry but I couldn't help overhearing,' she said to Laura before turning to Mike and adding, 'I don't think we should lie. Our son is out there somewhere and these detectives are just trying to do their job.'

'What the fuck are you on about?' Mike asked angrily.

Vicky turned to look at Laura and Andrea. 'Sorry, Mike, but you *were* worried that Callum would end up running away and going to those people in Lon Capel,' she said, getting very emotional.

'You need to rein yourself in, Vicks!' Mike thundered as he suddenly stood up and clenched a fist.

Laura could instantly see Vicky flinch – she was scared about what Mike was going to do next.

'Please sit down, Mike,' Laura said calmly but firmly. 'We need you to calm down because this isn't helping.'

'I'm not having her question me like that in my own home,' Mike said through gritted teeth.

'That's a joke. You're never here,' Vicky muttered as she retreated towards the door with tears in her eyes. 'You didn't even bother to go down there to look for your own son. Why is that, Mike, eh?'

The question seemed to hang in the air for a few awkward seconds.

It was a good point. Why hadn't Mike gone down to Newborough to help search for Callum? Did he know something they didn't?

'You told me you wanted me here,' Mike said, shaking his head. 'Bloody hell, I can't win, can I?'

'You weren't here, Mike,' Vicky said, sounding distraught. 'You went to the pub.'

'I was worried about Callum,' Mike protested.

Vicky pursed her lips in anguish. 'We're all worried.' She pointed upstairs. 'Zoe's scared out of her wits up there. You know how close they are.'

There was a tense silence.

Laura made eye contact with Vicky and gave her a look to imply it might be better if she left them now.

Vicky obliged, turning and walking out of the room.

Mike was hunched with clenched fists, his face red.

'Please, Mike,' Andrea said. 'Sit down.'

Laura waited until Mike eventually sat down and puffed out his cheeks. 'Sorry. It's all been very stressful.'

'Your wife does have a point,' Laura said. 'Why didn't you race down to Newborough to look for Callum?'

Mike blinked as though he couldn't remember. 'I dunno. Thought it would be better if I stayed here for any news.'

'But you didn't stay here, did you?' Andrea reminded him.

'No,' he muttered.

Laura fixed him with a stare. 'Is it right that you told Callum you would prefer him to be dead than go off and join a religious cult?'

'No,' Mike sneered. 'Who the hell told you that?'

'You didn't say that?' Andrea asked to clarify.

'No.' Mike shook his head and got up out of the chair. 'Look, I'm not answering any more of your bloody questions. Just get my son back.'

Mike stormed out of the room.

Laura shot a look at Andrea. He was definitely lying.

CHAPTER 19

Missing: 31 hours

Gareth looked out at the crowd assembled for the press conference. There were journalists from local papers and a radio station but none of the nationals or television crews that had descended upon the room back during the Henry Marsh case. The story of Callum's disappearance was still low down on the news agenda, and Gareth hoped it stayed that way.

Sitting next to Gareth was Kerry Mahoney, the Chief Corporate Communications Officer for North Wales Police, who had come over from the main press office in St Asaph. Gareth had met her before and found her to be a rather pompous woman on first impression.

'I'm surprised they've asked me to travel all this way to cover this,' Mahoney said under her breath in a supercilious tone. 'No offence, but don't teenagers go missing every five minutes and then turn up with their tails between their legs?'

Gareth looked at her. 'We've got enough evidence to suggest that we should be concerned for his safety. Plus we need the general public's help as witnesses.'

'Okay,' Mahoney said with a shrug. 'I guess it's your reputation that's on the line when he waltzes into his home after a day-long bender.'

Jesus, she really is a little treat, isn't she?

Gareth gave her a forced smile but didn't reply. Instead he cleared his throat and started. 'Good afternoon, everyone. I'm Detective Inspector Gareth Williams of the Anglesey Police and I'm the senior investigating officer on this case,' he said. 'We are concerned for the safety of this young man, Callum Newell.' Gareth turned and gestured to a large photograph of Callum. 'Callum is eighteen years old. He went missing yesterday afternoon at around one p.m. while walking with his friends in Newborough Forest. For the past twenty-four hours, Anglesey Police have carried out an extensive search of both Newborough Forest and Newborough Beach using trained officers, helicopters and our canine unit, but at the moment, we have found no sign of Callum. I'd like to appeal to any members of the general public who were in the vicinity of Newborough Forest, Newborough Beach or Llanddwyn Island yesterday afternoon to contact us if they saw Callum. I'd also appeal to anyone who thinks they saw anything suspicious or out of the ordinary in that area to ring our helpline.' Gareth leaned forward in his chair. 'I've got time to take a couple of questions.'

A young female journalist at the front of the room indicated that she wanted to ask a question and Gareth nodded in her direction. 'Cerys Jones, *Daily Record*.

Obviously that area is coastal. Do you think that Callum might have entered the water and got into difficulties?'

Gareth nodded. 'That is one line of enquiry that we're pursuing and we have so far conducted an aerial search of that whole coastline.' Gareth pointed to a middle-aged journalist who was standing towards the back of the room. 'Yes?'

'Do you believe that Callum's disappearance is a matter of misadventure, or are you looking for anyone else in connection with his disappearance?' the journalist asked.

'As I said, we are looking at several lines of enquiry. And yes, one of them is the possibility that someone else was involved in Callum's disappearance, which is why we have appealed to the public to contact us if they saw anything suspicious in the area,' Gareth explained.

The journalist frowned. 'Newborough Forest and Beach are very popular tourist destinations on this island and we're in the middle of the Easter holidays. Do you think the public should be worried that Callum's disappearance isn't an isolated event?'

Oh great. I wasn't prepared for that can of worms to be opened.

'No, I don't think the public should be concerned for their safety in the area,' Gareth replied, feeling slightly on the back foot. 'My advice is for them to take the normal type of precautions. That's all I've got time for today, so thank you.'

As Gareth got up, Mahoney raised her eyebrow and gave him a smug look. 'The Anglesey Tourist Board are going to love you, Gareth.'

* * *

Twenty minutes later, Gareth and Declan were sitting with a Digital Forensics officer on the ground floor of Beaumaris nick. The room comprised two rows of state-of-the-art computers facing each other. Above this were black shelves that contained audio and digital tracking machinery, which glowed and made low humming noises.

The officer – thirties, beard, glasses – pointed to the digital map of Anglesey on a large monitor mounted on the wall. 'Do you want the good news or bad news?' he asked them as he pushed his thick glasses up the bridge of his nose.

'Bad news, I guess,' Gareth said with a shrug. He wasn't in the mood to enter into anything light-hearted.

'Okay, this is the bad news here,' the officer said, pointing to a red circle highlighting an area of about six square miles north of Newborough.

'What are we looking at?' Declan asked.

'Because the mobile phone signal is so weak in this area, we can only find one cell tower that has received a signal from the mobile phone we're looking for. To get an accurate reading, we need two cell towers to get that signal and we then triangulate those coordinates to narrow down the location. It's not unusual in somewhere as remote as this.'

Gareth let out a frustrated sigh. He knew that finding Callum's mobile phone was key to discovering where he was and what had happened to him.

'But you can guarantee that this mobile phone is not in Newborough Forest, the campsite or on the beach down there?' Gareth asked, pointing to the areas on the map.

138

'No, it's definitely not in any of those places,' the officer confirmed.

'Which fits in with our theory that he was chased and possibly abducted,' Declan said.

Gareth then turned to look at the forensic officer. 'When you say it's hard to locate, what exactly do you mean?' he asked.

The officer pointed to the red circle again. 'This is about as good as we can get.'

Gareth looked at him. 'You said there was good news?'

'Possibly,' the officer said hesitantly. It wasn't a good sign. 'There is a slim chance that the mobile phone has automatically logged onto a broadband provider at its location.'

'A slim chance?' Gareth asked with a quizzical expression. 'How do you mean?'

'If, for example, the phone had a pre-programmed wireless code set up already, it would automatically log into that broadband address when it was within range.'

'So, in layman's terms, if Callum Newell is somewhere where he's previously logged on to the wi-fi on his phone, then the phone would automatically log in again?' Gareth asked, making sure that he fully understood.

'Yes. Exactly, sir.'

Gareth arched his eyebrow. 'And how does that help us?'

'If the phone has logged into a wi-fi network, we can track the IP address. And then we can identify the location and address of that wi-fi,' the officer explained.

'Sounds like a long shot,' Declan said.

'It is, I'm afraid,' the officer admitted as he pointed over to two more Digital Forensics officers who were at another computer. 'We're trying it now though. Let me see how we're getting on.'

The officer left and went over to talk to his colleagues.

For a moment, Gareth felt overwhelmed by the fact that Callum had now been missing for so long and they still hadn't found a concrete lead. He knew questions about why Anglesey Police hadn't managed to find him were starting to trend on Twitter. Gareth was also starting to get pressure from the top brass on the island to make some kind of breakthrough. And his comments at the press conference about someone else potentially being involved in Callum's disappearance hadn't gone down very well either.

Declan moved closer to the screen. 'My guess is that Callum is being held by someone in this area,' he said, pointing to the map.

Gareth gave him a dark look. 'Or he's somewhere in here but he's dead.'

As the officer came back over, Gareth saw that he was holding a print-out. He also saw that the man had a trace of a smile on his face, as if he had good news.

'Well, it was a long shot,' the officer said as he looked at them both, 'but we've managed to trace the IP address.'

'To where?' Gareth asked as his pulse quickened.

'A property in Lon Capel called Dynion Mwyn,' the officer said as he went over to the screen and pointed. 'Just here.'

Gareth exchanged a look with Declan.

'David Coren,' Gareth murmured.

CHAPTER 20

Missing: 32 hours

Laura looked down the deserted road in Lon Capel. There were two unmarked police cars and three patrol units parked in the road close to David Coren's house, Dynion Mwyn. CID and uniformed officers were waiting silently for the signal to approach the property and execute the Section 18 Search Warrant that Gareth had obtained an hour ago from a local magistrate. If Callum Newell's mobile phone was in David Coren's home, there was a strong possibility that Callum was also somewhere in the vicinity too. They had checked with Vicky Newell and got details of the make, model, colour and distinctive stickers on Callum's phone.

Was Callum being held against his will somewhere inside? Or had he sought refuge among the Dynion Mwyn community? Were they just hiding him or had something altogether darker taken place in the last two days?

Laura peered back down the road. She could see the large gardens spread out at the back of the houses of Lon Capel.

A woman in a nondescript summery dress was hanging out washing on a line, oblivious to their presence. Two small children ran around the garden, playing with a ball. It struck Laura how timeless they all looked. But that's how the whole road felt.

She hadn't noticed it before, but the houses were all identical. They had been painted the same sandy colour. Front doors and windows all a dark olive green.

The more she looked, the more creepy and unsettling the whole scene felt.

As the wind picked up, the sounds of various wind chimes rang out in unison. There was something decidedly eerie about the sound of the wind chimes, the identical houses and the police officers waiting in silence.

Laura could feel the growing tension in the air.

This place is giving me the willies.

Gareth gave a nod as three uniformed officers moved purposefully down the side of the house to the rear. They didn't want Coren trying to do a runner out the back.

'Okay, everyone,' Gareth said quietly. 'Let's do this.'

He turned and walked to the front door, pulled out the search warrant from his pocket and gave an authoritative knock.

Laura couldn't help but find Gareth attractive as she watched him take charge.

The door opened slowly and David Coren looked out. When he saw the group of officers his eyes widened in shock.

'David Coren?' Gareth asked.

Coren's furrowed his brow. 'Yes?'

'DI Williams, Beaumaris CID,' Gareth said firmly, showing both his warrant card and the search warrant. 'I'm here to execute a Section 18 Search Warrant on this property. Any attempt to interfere in my officers search will result in you being arrested for obstruction. Do you understand what I've said to you?'

'Yes, b-but I don't understand,' Coren stammered. He stood back in disbelief as Gareth entered the property and then directed the officers inside.

Laura looked at Andrea as they walked up the garden path and followed the uniformed officers inside.

'DI Hart?' Coren said as he stared at Laura, aghast, as though she might help him in some way. 'What is all this about? I really don't understand.'

'We have reason to believe that a mobile phone belonging to Callum Newell is located at this premises,' Laura explained calmly.

'What?' Coren snorted and pulled a face. 'That's not possible.'

Laura watched as officers fanned out, entering rooms on the ground floor and going up the staircase.

A woman in her forties – slim, red hair pulled into a ponytail, no make-up, with intense blue eyes – strode out from the kitchen.

'David,' she asked with a strident tone. 'What on earth is going on?'

Laura assumed it was Coren's wife, Moira.

Before David could explain to her why the police officers were there, Ben appeared from a door which led to a study.

'Nothing obvious in there, boss,' Ben said, gesturing back to the room.

Gareth nodded. 'Thanks, Ben.'

Ben headed away to the kitchen.

Andrea then came out of a door to a small dining room. She had a female uniformed officer in tow.

'Anything?' Gareth asked.

'No.' Andrea shook her head. 'Clear in there, boss.'

'Great,' Gareth said in a frustrated tone. He looked at Declan and gestured. 'Come on, Dec. I want to have a look in that garage.'

As the house continued to buzz with activity, Gareth and Declan marched out through the front door.

Coren looked at Laura and stammered fretfully, 'If you'd just l-let me—'

'Why are you here?' Moira asked angrily, interrupting her husband.

'We have a search warrant,' Laura explained.

'That's not what I asked you!' Moira snapped.

Four uniformed officers appeared at the top of the stairs and began to come down the steps.

'Anything?' Laura gave them an expectant look.

'Sorry, ma'am,' the burly uniformed sergeant said as he got to the bottom step. 'We've done a initial search under beds, drawers and in wardrobes, but we can't find it.'

Laura shared a look with Andrea. It seemed that they might have made a mistake and would now have some explaining to do.

Then Ben appeared from the kitchen with a meaningful expression on his face. 'Boss?' He wore blue forensic gloves and was holding a transparent plastic evidence bag.

Inside was a white iPhone 11.

As Ben turned it, Laura immediately spotted a yellow sticker reading '*CAUTION – NO BAD VIBES!*' plus a black and white sticker saying '*EXPLICIT CONTENT*'.

Bingo!

It was Callum's phone.

'I found it inside the bread bin in there,' Ben explained, pointing to the kitchen.

Taking the bag containing the phone, Laura looked at Coren. 'Is this your phone?'

'N-No,' Coren stammered, 'but I—'

'David Coren, I'm arresting you on suspicion of the abduction of Callum Newell,' Laura said sternly. 'You do not have to say anything, but it may harm your defence if you do not mention when questioned something that you later rely on in court. Anything you do say may be given in evidence—'

'This is ridiculous!' Moira exclaimed.

Ben took out his cuffs, pulled Coren's arms behind his back and cuffed him.

'I can explain this…' Coren protested.

'Leave him alone,' Moira cried.

Laura looked at Coren for a moment. 'David, I need you to tell us where Callum is right now,' she growled.

'I don't know. I promise you, I-I…' Coren stammered.

'Last chance,' Laura snapped angrily. 'Where is Callum?'

Coren shook his head. 'I wish I knew…'

Laura gave Ben a frustrated look.

Two uniformed officers marched Coren out of his house.

Moira glared at them. 'Where are you taking him?'

'Beaumaris Police Station,' Laura explained and then fixed Moira with a stare. 'I need you to tell us where Callum is.'

'David's just told you,' she replied, sounding frustrated. 'We haven't seen him. We don't know where he is. And we're just as worried about Callum as you are.'

Laura raised an eyebrow and said, 'Mrs Coren, I would like you to attend as well for voluntary questioning.'

'Are you joking?' she said, shaking her head.

'No, I'm not.' Laura then looked for Gareth. 'DI Williams?' she called loudly.

Gareth and Declan were talking outside. She pointed to the evidence bag.

'We've got the phone,' she explained with a serious expression.

'Good,' Gareth said as he spotted David being taken towards the car and took a moment to process the discovery. 'Right, I want every inch of all these properties searched,' Gareth thundered to the officers. 'Every attic, cellar, garden shed. Everything. And interview everyone. Someone in this community knows something or has seen something.'

* * *

Missing: 32 hours

Laura pressed the button on the recording equipment and said, 'Interview conducted with David Coren, Sunday, 9.30 p.m., Interview Room 1, Beaumaris Police Station. Present are David Coren, Detective Inspector Gareth Williams, Duty

Solicitor Patrick Clifford and myself, Detective Inspector Laura Hart.'

Laura raised her eyebrow as she looked at Coren. 'David, do you understand that you are still under caution?'

'Yes, I do,' he replied nervously.

Gareth reached for the evidence bag that contained Callum's iPhone. 'For the purposes of the tape, I'm showing the suspect Item Reference 283D. Can you tell me what you can see in this bag, David?'

'It's a mobile phone,' he replied. His voice was shaky.

Unlike many of the people they interviewed, Laura assumed this might be the first time Coren had ever been in a situation like this. He was clearly rattled.

'Would it surprise you to know that this iPhone belongs to Callum Newell?' Gareth said.

'We've been through this in the car,' Coren sighed in despair. 'A member of our congregation found this phone when a group of us were on Newborough Beach on Saturday afternoon. They handed it to me and I brought it home. I had no idea that it was Callum's phone.'

Laura looked over at Gareth. She wondered if Callum had decided to run away and was hiding out somewhere in Lon Capel?

Gareth arched an eyebrow. 'Come on, David. That seems to be an extraordinary coincidence, don't you think?'

'It's the truth.' Coren shrugged but he looked scared. 'Why would I lie about it?'

'You would lie about it if you knew where Callum was, what had happened to him or if you had something to do with his disappearance,' Gareth said.

'But I don't.' Coren shook his head. 'I keep telling you that.'

Laura sat forward on her chair. 'What were you doing on Newborough Beach on Saturday afternoon?'

Coren took a few seconds to compose himself. 'We were preparing for the festival of Ostara. It's the Spring Equinox. We were casting a circle and building an altar on Llanddwyn.'

'How many of you were there?' Laura asked.

Coren frowned and thought for a moment. 'About twelve of us, I think.'

Gareth waited for several seconds and then said in a tone that verged on affable, 'Come on, David. Callum Newell is a vulnerable teenage boy whose home life is verging on abusive. For whatever reason, he's been coming here for some kind of guidance and support. He went missing on Saturday afternoon somewhere in Newborough at the exact time that you and your disciples—'

'They're not my disciples,' Coren said.

'Followers. Whatever you want to call them. The fact is, you were on Newborough Beach preparing for a pagan festival when Callum went missing, and we found Callum's phone in your house. Just tell us what happened and where he is,' Gareth said.

'Seriously, I wish I could,' Coren said, shaking his head. 'We didn't see Callum. I promise you.'

Laura leaned forward and softened her expression. 'Look, David, maybe you bumped into Callum by sheer coincidence on Saturday afternoon. We think that he was running away from something in the forest…'

'I've told you,' Coren said, now sounding like he was unravelling. 'Jonathan found the phone on that stretch of beach that leads down from the coastal path.' Coren looked up at them with a pleading expression. 'I'm not lying to you. You can talk to Jonathan. You can talk to anyone who was there with me.'

Gareth snorted. 'We'll be talking to everyone who was with you, don't you worry about that.'

'You do understand that if, for whatever reason, Callum came to you and asked you to help him run away or hide,' Laura said quietly, 'and you are concealing his whereabouts from us, that is a criminal offence and you, and whoever might have helped you, will be in serious trouble?'

'But I don't know where he is!' Coren whimpered. 'I don't understand why you don't believe me!'

There was a knock at the door and Andrea opened it and looked over at Laura with an expression that suggested it was something significant.

'Can I have a quick word, boss?' Andrea said.

Laura nodded, got up from the interview table and said, 'For the purposes of the tape, DI Hart is leaving the interview room.'

Laura stepped out into the corridor to talk to Andrea.

'What's going on?' Laura asked.

'There's something you need to see.' Andrea took out her phone and showed her a photograph. It was hard to see but it looked like the burned remains of something inside a large steel drum. 'SOCOs found this on the land at the back of the Coren's property.'

Laura's heart sank. 'What is it?'

'Looks like someone has been burning clothes,' Andrea replied.

Looking again at the image made Laura feel very uneasy.

'Can you send that over to me so I can confront Coren with it?' Laura asked.

'Of course.' Andrea nodded as she tapped at her phone. 'That should be in your inbox now.'

'Great, thanks.' Laura said. 'Can you also ask the SOCOs if they can give us some idea of what was being burned? Colours, patterns, that sort of thing?'

'Will do.'

Laura went back into the interview room and sat down. They knew that Callum had some kind of relationship or friendship with Coren. They had found Callum's mobile phone in his house. And now they had found evidence of clothes that had been burned. Coren had a lot to answer for.

'For the purposes of the tape, DI Hart has now re-entered the room,' Gareth said.

Laura took out her phone and waited, allowing the tension in the interview room to intensify before she opened the photograph that Andrea had sent over and turned it to show Coren. 'For the purposes of the tape, I am showing the suspect an image from my mobile phone.' She then looked at Coren. 'David, can you tell me what you can see in this photograph?'

Taking reading glasses from his grey joggers, he put them on and peered at her phone screen. He looked confused. 'I'm not really sure. There appears to be something burned in a barrel…' His voice trailed off.

Gareth looked at the photo with a quizzical expression.

'Our forensic team have just found this on the land at the back of your home, David,' Laura said quietly. 'Can you tell me what it is?'

Taking off his glasses, he looked at her, perplexed. 'No. I've never seen it before.'

'For the record, the image shows the remnants of clothes that have very recently been burned within a large steel drum,' Laura said.

'I told you... I... I don't know,' Coren murmured, looking very shaky. 'I mean, I'm not the only person who has access to the land at the back.'

Gareth slammed the flat of his hand down on the desk, making Coren jump. 'Come on, David! You need to tell us what happened to Callum. And you need to tell us right now!'

Coren dissolved into a shaky mess as he covered his face with his hands. 'I think I'm going to be sick,' he whispered.

The duty solicitor, Clifford, looked over at the detectives and said, 'I think my client could do with a break, don't you?'

'He can have an hour,' Gareth said, unable to hide his annoyance.

'I'd like ninety minutes,' Clifford said.

Gareth glared at him. 'Fine. We will resume in an hour and a half then.'

CHAPTER 21

Missing: 33 hours

Ten minutes later, Laura and Gareth walked purposefully across the car park towards one of the unmarked police cars.

Laura let out a frustrated sigh. 'Coren is up to this in his neck, isn't he? Or is there something that I'm missing here?'

'No. He's definitely hiding something,' Gareth agreed.

Laura got to the passenger door, opened it and got in. 'Maybe Coren and Callum really were having some kind of relationship? If Callum threatened to tell his parents, it would have been a scandal.'

'True. I'm wondering if he might have lied to us about not seeing Callum. Maybe he spoke to him down at the beach by Llanddwyn Island,' Gareth said, thinking out loud as he pulled the car out of the car park. 'The conversation could have gone wrong, leading Coren to chase Callum through the woods and attack him.'

Laura gave Gareth a dark look. 'It's an interesting theory. The question is, if he's not at Coren's, where is Callum now?'

'I don't know.' Gareth ran his hand over his scalp. 'But if the clothes in that drum really are Callum's, it's not likely that he's alive, is it?'

'No,' Laura said quietly, shaking her head. 'Probably not.'

* * *

It was dark by the time Laura and Gareth arrived at Lon Capel. The place was swarming with officers – SOCOs in full forensic suits, uniformed officers and CID going door to door and the Canine Unit using dogs across the land at the rear of the houses in The Fair Men's community. Above them, the large round moon was turning from silver to a mottled gold against the night sky.

As they parked, she could see that many of the residents were out on the street, looking concerned as they talked and watched the events develop. She also noticed that their clothes were formal and old-fashioned. Everyone was dressed in shades of brown, green and dark grey, and there wasn't a tracksuit, hoodie or a pair of trainers to be seen.

On the other side of the road was an Armed Response Unit. They were dressed all in black, in Kevlar protective vests and helmets. Carrying the usual Heckler & Koch MP5 machine guns, they also had Glock 17 handguns strapped to their hips. Laura had started the training to be an Authorised Firearms Officer before joining CID, but she'd realised that it wasn't for her after they'd spent a training day taking part in various hostage scenarios in an old, abandoned warehouse. With her heart pounding and covered in sweat, Laura had to admit that being an AFO wasn't what she wanted. The training had confirmed something else for her though – that she wanted to train to be a hostage negotiator.

Looking up now, she saw Declan and Ben approaching.

'Have we found anything?' Gareth asked, unable to disguise his frustration.

'Not yet, boss,' Declan replied.

'What about the burned clothing?' Laura enquired.

'Forensics have taken it back to the lab for testing,' Ben replied. 'Impossible to tell what it was before it was burned though.'

Declan pointed to an area behind the houses. 'There's a couple of sheds over there. One of them has got a couple of padlocks on, but no one seems to have a key.'

'Have we got bolt-cutters?' Laura said.

'No,' Ben said, shaking his head.

'Then we kick the door down,' Gareth said. 'Come on.'

Getting out their torches, they marched across the road and through a gap between two houses, emerging onto a stretch of uneven grass that banked up at the back. Two huge wooden sheds sat side by side in the darkness and several officers stood beside the padlocked double doors of one.

'Go ahead and knock that door down,' Gareth called as they approached.

Uniformed officers took the heavy steel battering ram – known ironically as 'The Big Red Key' – and swung it back before slamming it into the padlock. The thick lock held its own against the 16kg battering ram and Gareth was visibly annoyed.

Laura shared a concerned look with Declan. She wondered what they would find on the other side. The thought made her feel uneasy.

The officers swung The Big Red Key again and this time it did its job and the thick wooden doors flew open with a bang.

Moving swiftly inside, the officers disappeared into the dark.

Laura used her torch as she followed behind and was instantly hit by an overwhelming putrid smell.

Jesus!

The officers inside were quickly putting hands over mouths and noses as they moved around the interior of the shed.

Andrea gave her a quizzical look but Laura already knew what the smell was.

It was the unmistakable stink of death – of rotting flesh.

The inside of the shed was cavernous and shadowy. There were shelving units stacked against the walls, along with workbenches, ladders, piles of chairs and large objects covered with dark green tarpaulins.

Gareth glanced back at her with a dark look as he used his torch to see where he was going and stepped over some old pots of paint.

Laura prayed that the stench wasn't anything to do with Callum. She wasn't a forensics expert, but she assumed that if Callum's body had been hidden in the shed since his disappearance, and given the heat, it might well smell just like this.

Moving her torch slowly over the area in front of her, she saw a large shape under a grey tarpaulin. Looking down she saw a tyre and realised there must be a small car underneath.

Andrea appeared next to her. The colour had drained from her face.

'You okay?' Laura asked under her breath. She was breathing through her mouth, given the terrible odour.

Andrea winced. 'I've been better.'

Laura gestured to the tarpaulin. 'Can you give me a hand to move this so we can have a look underneath?'

Andrea nodded as she popped her torch in the breast pocket of her jacket and they moved the tarpaulin and revealed an old two-seater Fiat sports car. It was covered in dirt and rust but they could see it had once been orange.

Worryingly, the smell had intensified significantly now that the tarpaulin had been moved.

As Laura took her torch and moved its beam, she saw the tell-tale sign of blowflies buzzing in the air. They seemed to be circling around the smashed window and rear seat of the car.

Whatever – or whoever – was inside the car, they were dead and had been there for a while.

Laura felt her stomach turn at the thought of it.

She remembered being a young PC on the beat in Salford. She and her sarge had been called by a neighbour to the flat of an old man who hadn't been seen for a few days. When they eventually got inside, they discovered that he had died and fallen onto an old-fashioned two-bar electric fire. His dead body had been effectively cooking where it had fallen for over three days. Laura had been sick on the spot when she saw what had happened. Her sarge hadn't blamed her, saying it was one of the worst things he had seen in twenty years of policing.

'Found something, Laura?' Gareth called over.

Laura gave him a significant nod. 'There's something in this car.' She put her hand over her face and cautiously moved forward as she used her torch to look inside.

The light disturbed the flies, which began to fly and swirl noisily, adding to the eerie scene.

Laura saw a shape on the back seat and her pulse quickened as she took an unsteady breath.

She squinted.

The shape was small – too small to be a person.

Gareth came over from the left, using his torch to illuminate the back seat.

Laura saw ginger fur and then legs.

'It's a fox,' she said quietly, feeling relief. 'It's okay. It's just a bloody fox.'

CHAPTER 22

Missing: 33 hours

It had been ten minutes since they'd discovered the dead fox and searched the rest of the two sheds. There was nothing there that aroused any suspicions. In fact, since the SOCOs had found the remnants of burned clothing, nothing else had been discovered. Gareth was becoming increasingly frustrated.

'We haven't done anything wrong!' snapped a voice.

Moira Coren was marching towards them, holding a lantern, with a red face and glaring eyes. She had been briefly questioned under caution at the station but then released.

'You going to pay for that?' Moira asked Gareth through gritted teeth as she pointed to the broken padlocks and splintered wood of the shed doors.

Gareth fixed her with a withering stare. He wasn't in the mood for niceties. 'Mrs Coren, as I assume you're aware, we're looking for Callum Newell, a vulnerable teenager that you and your husband have "befriended" in recent months for whatever reason—'

'Hold on a second,' Moira interrupted. She looked like she was going to explode. 'You made that sound like there was something inappropriate about myself and David offering Callum support and friendship.'

Gareth arched his eyebrow. 'Was there?'

'Was there what?' Moira virtually spat out her words.

'Was there anything inappropriate between you or your husband and Callum Newell?' Gareth asked sternly.

'I'm pretty sure that's defamation,' Moira huffed. 'I should talk to my solicitor.'

Gareth gave her a nonchalant nod. 'Actually, talking to a solicitor isn't a bad idea, Mrs Coren. Because if your husband has harmed Callum in any way, *you* will be charged with perverting the course of justice. And if Callum has been murdered, that will carry a life sentence for you.'

'Don't be ridiculous!' Moira spluttered. 'Callum isn't dead. He's probably run away and he's hiding from that scumbag of a father of his.'

Laura gave her a quizzical look. 'Why do you say that?' They'd already heard Coren's suspicions about Mike Newell but this was the first time Moira had mentioned the man.

'Callum has lived in a dysfunctional home all his life,' Moira said with a withering frown. 'And his father is abusive to him, his sister and mother. That's why he came here. He knew that David and I would listen to him. And, if you ask me, he's out there somewhere hiding away.'

Gareth wasn't convinced. The mobile phone and the burned clothing were leading him to believe that the answer to where Callum was, lay in this community in Lon Capel.

* * *

Laura and Andrea were sitting on a threadbare sofa covered with a thin, flower-printed throw, which had been tucked down the back. Laura could actually feel the springs beneath her.

Opposite them sat Jonathan Leary, the man identified by David Coren as having found Callum's mobile phone on the beach close to Llanddwyn Island. He was a huge man with a shaggy beard and hair that needed a trim, a fat neck and a yellow smock that strained over his chest. His forehead glistened with sweat.

'And you found the mobile phone when you all left the island?' Andrea asked to clarify as she scribbled in her notebook.

'Yes,' Jonathan replied in a Yorkshire accent. 'It was still low tide then so we were able to walk straight across the beach.'

'Was the phone just lying there?' Laura asked. 'Or did it look like it had been hidden?'

'Oh no,' Jonathan said, shaking his head. 'It was just lying there. You know, like it had fallen out of someone's pocket on the sand.'

'What did you do then?'

'I picked it up and looked around to see if anyone was looking for it. But they weren't. Then I told David,' Jonathan replied. 'He said he'd take it and ask around to see if anyone had reported a phone missing.'

'And did he?' Andrea asked, looking over.

'How do you mean?'

'Did he ask around to see if anyone had reported it missing?'

Jonathan shrugged. 'I dunno. I didn't ask him.'

'Did you notice if the phone was turned off?' Laura asked.

'It was out of power,' he explained. 'I tried to turn it on but nothing.'

'Did you see anyone around when you were there?' Andrea said.

'There were some people heading over to Llanddwyn. And a few further down on Newborough Beach,' Jonathan said.

'Could you describe them?'

'Not really,' Jonathan said in a matter-of-fact tone. 'They were a long way down. A couple of kids paddling and their parents sitting on the sand. I wasn't really paying close attention.'

'Yes, we're aware of this family. We're trying to trace them,' Laura said and then looked over at him. 'And at no point did you see Callum Newell?' Laura asked.

'No,' he said adamantly.

'Can you explain what you were doing on Llanddwyn Island?' Laura asked. David Coren had explained it to them already but they needed to compare accounts to see where – if any – the holes were.

Before Jonathan could elaborate, Gareth and Declan appeared out of the darkness at the back door with urgent expressions.

Laura looked over as if to say 'What's going on?'

Gareth indicated with his hand that Laura and Andrea should join them. 'Can I have a quick word outside?' he asked quietly.

Whatever it was, it seemed serious.

'Excuse us for a second,' Laura said politely to Jonathan as they got up from the kitchen table.

They went outside and Gareth took them a suitable distance away.

'What's going on?' Laura asked.

'A dog walker has found a body on the far side of Llanddwyn Island,' Gareth explained.

CHAPTER 23

Missing: 34 hours

By the time Laura and Andrea parked up in the car park close to Newborough Beach, a major incident had been called for the discovery on Llanddwyn. They had both been lost in thought on the short journey, especially when uniformed officers reported that the victim was a young man, perhaps even a teenager. There was little doubt in Laura's mind that it was Callum.

Getting out of the car, Laura and Andrea retrieved their torches and made their way down a sandy footpath towards the beach. They heard the deep thundering sound of the black and yellow police EC145 helicopter as it swooped overhead and then hovered over the island to their right, its huge searchlight cutting through the darkness to the ground below. There were already uniformed and CID officers on the beach and island and the SOCO van had parked on the sand.

Thinking of Vicky and Zoe Newell, Laura felt her stomach tighten. She couldn't imagine the anguish they would feel if it really was Callum's body that had been discovered.

'It still doesn't make sense, does it?' Andrea said as they walked across the beach towards Llanddwyn.

'No, it doesn't,' Laura muttered. 'There's been no suggestion that the victim had been buried or there had been any attempt to hide the body, and there's no way our search team and helicopter would have missed someone over there.'

The moon was bright over the black water. Laura looked down as her boots made tiny splashes in the shallow rivulets of water that criss-crossed the illuminated beach.

'You think he drowned?' Andrea said.

'The postmortem should tell us that,' Laura said, trying not to run away with theories quite yet. As Laura's first detective sergeant used to say to her in Manchester, 'Slow and steady wins the bloody race, DC Hart.'

Taking the footpath that bisected the island, they passed the shadowy ruins of St Dwynwen's Church.

Further along, up on a small mound, was a stone Celtic cross that had been erected to commemorate the death of St Dwynwen. For a moment, Laura glanced at its base, using her torch to read the inscription that she remembered from childhood visits:

They lie around did living tread, this sacred ground now silent – dead.

Andrea paused to see what she was reading and then looked at her. 'A cheery thought,' she noted darkly.

For a moment, Laura wondered if there was any connection between the religious past of the island, the

164

inscription and the fact that a body had been found there. She took a deep breath, conscious of the eerie stillness, the only sounds that of their feet crunching on the footpath and the helicopter hovering in the distance over the small beach at the far end of the island.

As they came to the beach itself, they saw the grisly sight of a forensics tent, which had been erected over the body. The scene was lit by huge halogen arc lights, which turned the area into virtual daylight. The dim rumble of a diesel-powered generator filled the air, competing with the noise of the helicopter, and white figures of the SOCOs in their forensic suits moved to and fro as the lines of blue police tape fluttered in the breeze.

Laura's heart sank with sadness. She had held on to the hope that Callum had simply run away and was in hiding somewhere. But that was now quickly diminishing. It was always so distressing when she worked on a case where a young person had lost their life. She would never get used to it, and she never wanted to.

Two uniformed officers in hi-vis jackets were stationed at the rocky outcrop down to the beach itself. Up to the right loomed the iconic Twr Mawr Lighthouse, with its white, conical tower that resembled a great windmill.

Laura took out her warrant card as they approached the uniformed officer who was holding a clipboard on which she was recording a scene log. 'DI Hart and DC Jones, Beaumaris CID,' she explained as the officer scribbled down their names by torchlight.

'Thank you, ma'am,' the female officer said. In her twenties, she had dark hair pulled back from a round face.

'Were you first on scene?' Andrea asked, raising her voice against the battering wind that was coming in from the sea.

The officer nodded. 'We got here just after the victim was discovered.'

'Okay, thank you, Constable,' Laura said as she and Andrea began to tread carefully over the rocks that led down onto the beach, which were covered in Chorda Filum seaweed, known as bootlace weed or dead man's rope.

Looking up, Laura spotted Gareth and Declan coming out of the forensic tent dressed in a white nitrile forensic suits and white rubber boots. She could also see that the SOCOs had laid down a series of aluminium stepping plates to preserve the sand around the crime scene for footprints and forensic evidence.

Gareth glanced over and saw them approaching, but before anyone could say anything, Laura saw Declan surreptitiously wipe a tear from his face. He looked shell-shocked and pale. It had to be Callum lying under the tent.

'It's him, isn't it?' Laura asked quietly.

Gareth nodded with a dour expression. 'Yes,' he said under his breath.

Laura looked at Andrea and indicated they needed to have a look. They made their way across the sand just as the tent was lit up with a sudden burst of light as a SOCO leaned in to take a photograph.

Laura and Andrea were handed suits, masks and boots to put on. Once everything was on, Laura drew in a deep breath before stepping inside. A SOCO was taking another photograph – the flash further illuminating the material of the tent for a millisecond – and as he moved out of Laura's way, she allowed her eyes to rest on Callum's body.

He was fully clothed, in a Nike T-shirt, trackies and one trainer on his right foot. For a beat, she thought about her son, Jake, and found her breath catching in her throat.

Callum's skin had a grey-blue tinge and his hair was matted, dishevelled and sprinkled with sand. Thankfully, his eyes were closed.

Laura crouched on her haunches and gazed at Callum's innocent, young face.

What happened to you, Callum? she wondered.

For a moment, Laura was taken back to the terrible night when she had rescued Rosie. It could have so easily been her daughter lying dead like Callum if she hadn't found her in time.

Laura knew that Callum's family would have spent the day clinging to the fading hope that their son had simply decided to run away. Or that he'd fallen, injured himself and had become trapped somewhere. That the search team would find him alive and bring him home. Vicky and Zoey would have been thinking that they'd hug him and tell him off for worrying them all so much. And in years to come, they could laugh at family get-togethers about the time Callum went missing for two days.

But the dark reality was that none of that would ever happen now.

Callum was dead.

Getting back up, Laura and Andrea wandered outside to where Gareth was deep in conversation with the chief pathologist.

Declan was sitting down on a rock, looking into space. Laura knew that he was likely thinking about the fact that he would now have to go home to Osian and tell him that one of his best friends was dead.

Gareth nodded a thanks to the chief pathologist and turned their way.

'Does she think that he drowned?' Laura asked.

'That's her initial thought,' Gareth explained, 'but she can't be specific until she does a preliminary postmortem.'

'Anything suspicious?' Andrea said.

'There's a cut on the top of his head and some marks on his neck,' Gareth replied, 'but that could have been caused by rocks if he was washed ashore.'

'*If* he was washed ashore?' Andrea said.

'Given the scale of the search, there is no way that Callum has been lying here for the past thirty-three hours and no one saw him. So the other option is…'

Laura arched an eyebrow as she finished Gareth's thought. 'That someone put him here more recently.'

CHAPTER 24

Gareth and Declan had been driving for about ten minutes in a sombre silence, edged only by the hum of the car's engine. They were heading for the Newells' home to break the devastating news about Callum's death.

As Gareth glanced to their right, he could see that the moon had been covered by a blanket of clouds and it appeared to be raining over the inky sea in the distance. Buzzing down the window, he let the cold air blow in against his face. Even from here, he could smell the salty bite of the sea. He took a deep breath, knowing that the next few days were going to be extremely intense for him and the whole CID team.

As he closed the window, he glanced over at Declan, who was driving but clearly deep in thought.

'You okay?' Gareth asked, even though it felt a slightly absurd question to ask.

'I remember when Callum was born,' Declan said quietly.

There were a few seconds of silence.

'I was made up for Vicky and Mike,' Declan continued.

Gareth nodded. 'You've known them a long time.'

'Vicky was the first girl I ever kissed. We had just moved over from Ireland. I was about fourteen and at some party at Becky Green's house. We had been drinking cider and I was trying to show off by climbing a tree in the garden. I fell off and onto my back like a right eejit. It winded me but I was laughing my head off lying there on the grass. Vicky came over to see if I was okay and the next thing I knew, she was on top of me and we were kissing.'

Gareth gave him a kind smile. 'The first girl I kissed was Suzie Townsend. She was a year older than me, which is a big thing when you're fifteen.'

There was a beat as Declan slowed at some traffic lights.

Gareth glanced over again. 'So, was Vicky your first girlfriend?'

'For about three weeks,' Declan said with a snort. 'Then she snogged Jason Andrews. He was a big tosser who played rugby. I told all my mates I was gonna beat him up but he would have killed me… Me and Vicky became friends after that though.'

'What do you think of Mike Newell?' Gareth asked.

Declan thought for a few seconds and then said, 'He and Vicky got together when she worked at her dad's timber yard. They were only young but he seemed like a decent bloke. A bit laddy but he soon calmed down when Callum was born. But in recent years he's gone off the rails. Mike's little more than a functioning alcoholic now.'

Gareth frowned. 'Was there any specific reason why things changed?'

'Nah. Mike's old man Terry Newell was a nasty, violent drunk,' Declan explained, 'and as we say in Ireland, Mike just "got the gene" passed down to him.'

'Alcoholism?' Gareth asked to clarify.

'Yeah,' Declan said with a nod as they pulled up outside the Newells' house. He gave Gareth a dark look once he'd switched off the engine. 'I know that Callum hated Mike. And I think the feeling was mutual.'

For a few minutes they sat in silence in the car.

Gareth could see how much Declan thought of Vicky. In fact, he wondered if, despite how young they were, Declan ever thought of Vicky as 'the one that got away'.

He looked over at his friend. 'Are you sure you're okay to do this?'

Declan nodded. 'Yes. If Vick is going to hear this news, she needs to hear it from me.'

As Gareth got out of the car, he felt the tension tighten in the pit of his stomach. However many times he had to break the news of a death to a family, he would never get used to it. Their reactions also varied wildly. Sometimes there was stunned silence. Other times anger and complete denial. And sometimes an explosion of terrible grief and pain.

They walked along the verge and up the garden to the front door, which was lit by a light over the porch. The news about Callum was made all the more difficult as they couldn't yet tell the family what exactly had happened to Callum or how or why he had died.

Declan took a deep breath and rang the bell.

A few seconds later, Vicky came to the door. She looked terrified when she saw them standing on the doorstep.

'No!' Vicky gasped as she put her hand to her face. 'Dec? Please God, no.'

'I'm so sorry, Vick,' Declan whispered.

Vicky began to shake all over and then staggered. Declan quickly moved forward and took her in his arms.

'No, no, no…' Vicky sobbed, trying to get breath.

'Mum?' came a voice. 'What is it?'

Zoe appeared at the door and put her hand to her face.

'Is it okay if we come in?' Gareth asked very quietly.

'What's going on?' Zoe asked in a panic. 'Have you found Callum?'

They moved inside the house and Gareth closed the front door behind them.

As Declan comforted Vicky, whose sobbing was intensifying, Zoe's eyes roamed wildly around the hallway. 'What is it?' she asked, her face stricken with terror.

Gareth looked at her. 'I'm so sorry but we have some very bad news about Callum… He's dead. He was found on the beach on Llanddwyn Island.'

'No,' Zoe said, shaking her head as though he was lying to her. 'Why are you saying that?'

'I'm really sorry,' Gareth said gently as he gestured to the door to the living room. 'Shall we go in here?'

They moved slowly into the room and Vicky and Zoe sat on the sofa together, holding hands and staring silently into space.

CHAPTER 25

Osian was sitting on his bed, looking at his phone with his headphones on. He was trying his best not to dwell on the ongoing search for Callum but the overwhelming uncertainty was driving him mad. What had happened just didn't feel real. It was something you might see on a TV drama, the news or crime documentary. It wasn't something that happened on an island like Anglesey.

Then his mind turned to what he'd seen earlier when he went over to Tom's. He was still trying to make sense of it. If Tom was with Zoe, did Callum know? Is that what they had been fighting about at his party at the Sports and Social Club? But why? It might have been a bit weird Tom going out with Callum's older sister, but it wasn't something they'd need to get into a fight over, was it? Or maybe Callum didn't know and Tom had made another one of his unpleasant, inappropriate comments about Zoe. Osian realised now that Tom had likely made those jokes as a way of covering up what was really going on.

Out of the corner of his eye, Osian spotted his bedroom door opening slowly. Then his dad stuck his head around and looked at him. There was something in his dad's expression and eyes that immediately concerned him – an ominous look of dark solemnity.

With his stomach twisting with anxiety, Osian took off his headphones and gave his dad a quizzical look.

'All right, mate?' Declan said quietly. His voice sounded shaky.

Osian sensed his dad's uneasiness. He took a breath and sat upright.

Sitting down on the edge of his bed, Declan glanced at him apprehensively. 'I've got some very bad news, son,' he whispered.

Osian's whole body froze with his father's words.

Please God, no.

A devastating wave of fear, pain and confusion rushed through his very being.

'We've found Callum,' Declan said as he reached out and took Osian's hand. 'I'm so sorry but he's dead.'

Osian shook his head. It was too much. He didn't understand.

Did he really say that Callum is dead? That can't be right.

Feeling his lip tremble, Osian's eyes filled with tears as he stared at his dad.

'He's dead?' Osian whispered. He felt himself detaching from everything around him.

'I'm so sorry, son,' Declan said with a pained expression.

Osian moved forward, putting his arms around his father and burying his head into his chest as he sobbed.

His dad just held him.

Moving back, Osian rubbed the tears from his face and sniffed.

'Where?' Osian asked as he took a deep breath to try and compose himself.

'On the far end of Llanddwyn Island,' Declan said gently, putting a hand tenderly to his son's face.

'He drowned?'

'We don't know yet,' Declan replied.

Osian thought for a few seconds. 'I thought the island was searched?'

'It was,' Declan said and then hesitated before explaining, 'We think he might have been in the sea and then washed ashore.'

Sitting back on his pillows, Osian was hit by another wave of grief and pain. He'd known Callum since they were in Year 1 at Primary School. They'd had sleepovers at each other's houses, played rugby together, been on school trips…

Pursing his lips, Osian blew out his cheeks but the tears came again. How could it be possible that he would never see his friend again?

A figure appeared at the door. It was his mum, Sue.

'I'm so sorry, Osian,' she whispered as she came over to him. She sat on the side of the bed and wrapped her arms around him as he sobbed once more.

CHAPTER 26

It was nearly nine a.m. when Laura pulled into the dark, empty car park that looked over Beaumaris Beach. Glancing at her watch, she saw that she was five minutes early for her meeting with Claudia Wright from *The Sunday Times*. Claudia had replied almost immediately to Laura's email yesterday afternoon and had suggested they meet as soon as possible. Despite the events of the last two days, Laura had agreed as she was keen to get the ball rolling.

As Laura turned off the ignition, she felt a pang of anxiety. Meeting Claudia and telling her everything that she knew felt risky – even dangerous. Laura knew she would have to tread very carefully to make sure that every step of the way she made sure that she and her family were protected and kept out of danger.

Staring out of the windscreen, she heard the soft moan of the wind coming in from the Menai Strait. She buzzed down the window to get some fresh air and try to clear her head. The sound of the waves collapsing onto the nearby shore had a soothing, regular rhythm that jarred with Laura's growing tension, making her think about the unremitting nature of the tides and the moon – and the fact that they would still be here centuries after she was gone.

The realisation brought with it perspective. Her lifespan was a tiny, imperceptible fragment of the planet's timeline. What if she didn't need to spend it trying to find out what had happened to Sam on the day he died? What would he say to her about her efforts if he was actually sitting next to her at this precise moment?

Looking at the passenger seat, she imagined Sam sitting there in the morning light. She looked into his dark, hooded eyes, taking in his serious expression.

'Seriously,' Sam said very quietly. 'You don't need to do this, Laura.'

'I do,' she replied. 'I need to find out what happened to you and who is responsible.'

'Why?' Sam frowned, his dark thick eyebrows arching. 'It won't bring me back. I'm gone. And if you think that I deserve some kind of justice, I really don't. Not if it puts you and the kids in any kind of danger.' He locked eyes with her and she felt the emotional intensity of his presence, believing in that moment that he was really there. 'It can't be worth it. I don't need it.'

'What if I do?' Laura asked. 'What if I can't rest until I know why you were killed?'

Before Sam had time to answer, Laura's attention was drawn to another car pulling into the car park.

It had to be Claudia Wright.

Glancing back at the passenger seat, she saw that it was now empty. Sam was gone.

177

Opening the door, Laura got out and the salty air stung her nostrils.

The sleek black Audi A5 was parked across from where she had stopped. Walking over cautiously, Laura went to the passenger side and looked inside.

The window buzzed down.

A woman in her forties – brunette, sharp features, quick, intelligent eyes and expensive-looking hair and clothes – looked back at her.

'Claudia?' Laura asked.

Claudia nodded and Laura opened the passenger door, got in and sat down.

She took out her warrant card to show Claudia. 'Just so you know I am who I say I am.'

'Detective Inspector Laura Hart,' Claudia read out loud and then looked at her with a meaningful expression. 'Thank you for meeting me, Laura. As you said, it's definitely safer for us to meet face to face.'

'If I'm honest, I'm not sure that I'm doing the right thing,' she said quietly. 'But I didn't know where else to go.'

'Everything you tell me today is off the record until you tell me otherwise, okay?' Claudia reassured her. She had a tone that calmed Laura immediately.

'Okay. Thanks,' Laura said.

'You said that you had something about the Manchester Metropolitan Police that you thought I might find interesting,' Claudia said, taking out a notepad and pen. 'And given that you've managed to track me down, you must know that I've written several articles for *The Sunday Times* exposing police corruption over the past fifteen years.'

178

'Yes, that's why I contacted you,' Laura said.

'You have concerns that there is police corruption in the MMP?' Claudia asked to clarify.

'Yes,' Laura said with a nod. 'Serious concerns.'

Claudia arched an eyebrow. 'How serious are we talking?'

'Murder, tip-offs and bribery,' Laura said.

Claudia stopped writing and frowned. 'Sorry, did you say murder?'

'Yes.'

'The reason I've acted on this so quickly,' Claudia explained, 'is that colleagues of mine from *The Sunday Times* investigated the MMP back in 2018. I don't have the full details of that yet, but from what I remember, their investigation covered very similar ground to what you mentioned you wanted to discuss with me. Why don't you try and run me through everything from the beginning.'

Laura took a breath and then looked at Claudia. 'In August 2018, my husband, a serving uniformed officer with the MMP, was killed in an explosion during a police operation against a well-known organised crime group in Manchester.'

Claudia's eyes widened. 'Yes, of course. I remember it. He was killed along with his partner, if I remember correctly?'

Laura pulled a face. 'Yeah, that's where it starts to get complicated. I believe that my husband was lured to his death that day because he had uncovered some form of corruption in the MMP.'

Claudia nodded as she wrote. 'You think he was deliberately targeted?'

'I know he was,' Laura replied. 'And I have very strong

suspicions that Detective Chief Inspector Pete Marsons is corrupt and taking bribes from the Fallowfield Hill Gang. I also suspect he might be responsible for the murders of two officers who had become a liability in this corruption.'

Claudia's expression revealed her surprise. 'Can you tell me how you know all this?'

Laura gave her a dark look. 'Because DCI Pete Marsons was, until recently, one of my closest friends and godfather to my son.'

CHAPTER 27

As Laura pottered around the kitchen, her mind was whirring. The meeting with Claudia Wright had gone as well as she could have hoped, but there was part of her that worried that by going to a newspaper she was opening a can of worms that might have terrible ramifications for her and her family.

Claudia wanted Laura to go on the record with all that she knew but she had explained that she needed time to think about the ramifications of that. However, she also knew that as a proud police officer, she couldn't rest knowing that Sam's death had been a result of corruption in the MMP. She owed it to Rosie and Jake to find out why their father had been taken from them, and to ensure the people responsible were held accountable for their actions.

'Is there anything you want on this food order?' Rosie asked as she wandered in looking at her phone.

Rosie's relationship with food had always been tricky and uncomfortable – though thankfully it had never developed into any kind of serious eating disorder – but ever since her

181

abduction, she had been increasingly particular in what she ate... to the point of obsessiveness. Laura knew that Rosie's need to feel in control was a reaction to what had happened to her, and unless it became detrimental to her health, she'd decided she wouldn't mention or challenge her daughter's demands.

'Let me have a quick look,' Laura said, reaching out to take Rosie's phone to look at the family's online shopping order, which Rosie had now taken control of.

Rosie smiled. 'Don't you trust me?'

'No,' Laura joked and then reached out a comforting hand and put it on her shoulder. 'I'm kidding. I just need a few toiletries, that's all.'

'Jake wanted some hair gel so I added that,' Rosie explained.

'Hair gel?' Laura raised an eyebrow in amusement. 'Who's he trying to impress?'

'I don't know,' Rosie replied with a shrug. 'But he does keep mentioning a girl called Hannah in his class.'

'Does he now?' Laura said, feeling her heart warm that Jake might be getting his first crush but also the pang that came with it, knowing that he was growing up. She scanned the list and frowned. 'What's Matcha?'

'It's powdered Japanese green tea,' Rosie explained.

'It's what?' Laura laughed.

'Good for memory, brain function and energy. And loads of other things,' Rosie replied.

'Well I could definitely do with some of that then.'

Hearing the front door close, Laura knew that Gareth had arrived. She felt a twinge of anxiety. Having met with

Claudia, it was more important than ever that she come clean to Gareth about everything to do with Sam's death, Butterfield and what she suspected about Pete. She still wasn't sure how he was going to react, but she would take it in her stride.

Laura handed the phone back to Rosie. 'Looks great to me, darling.'

Rosie frowned. 'What about your toiletries?'

'Oh, next time,' Laura said as she went to talk to Gareth. He looked exhausted.

'Jesus, I need a beer,' he said.

'It's not even noon!' she said, though not altogether surprised by his vehemence.

'I haven't gone to sleep yet so time means nothing at this point,' he replied.

'Fair enough.'

They kissed and she wrapped her arms around him for a few seconds.

'Stupid question,' Laura said, looking at him, 'but how did it go at the Newells' last night?'

He gave her a dark look. 'They're devastated, as you can imagine.'

'What about Declan?' she asked. She knew that Callum's death was incredibly personal to him.

'He's trying to keep it together,' Gareth explained, 'but I can see how upset he is. And he had to go home and break the news to Osian and Sue afterwards, which would have been heartbreaking.'

'Oh God,' Laura said, pulling an anguished face.

There were a few seconds as they both took in the

magnitude of the previous day's events.

Laura gave Gareth a meaningful look. 'There is something else I need to talk to you about. And I know this might not be great timing, but if I don't get it off my chest, I'm going to explode.'

'Okay,' Gareth said and then frowned. 'Can I get that beer first?'

'Yes, of course,' she replied, giving him a kind smile.

'Good,' Gareth said as they went into the kitchen.

He grabbed a beer and Laura poured herself a cup of tea.

'Let's go to the study,' Laura suggested.

'This is all very clandestine,' Gareth joked.

She felt guilty about making a song and dance about it all. And she was becoming increasingly anxious about how he was going to react to her having kept it all secret from him.

The study was cluttered and untidy. Laura made a mental note at least once a week to go in and tidy it, organise her paperwork, books etc., but because it was tucked away on the far side of the ground floor, the old adage 'out of sight, out of mind' rang true.

Laura closed the door behind them and pulled a face to show that she was feeling apprehensive.

Gareth had perched himself on a chair over by the cluttered desk. He looked at her and raised an eyebrow. 'Christ, is it that bad?'

Laura didn't answer for a few seconds.

'Okay, you're scaring me a bit here,' he admitted, sitting forward.

'It's not about us. Well, not really,' Laura sighed as she

sat on the thick arm of the sofa. The seats were occupied by cardboard boxes. 'I just don't know where to start with it all.'

Gareth gave her an understanding nod. 'At the risk of stating the obvious, maybe at the beginning?'

'Okay,' she said and then took a sip of tea. 'It started off with me and Pete believing that there was more to Sam's death than was ever discovered.'

'Okay,' Gareth said. He seemed relieved – obviously he'd imagined that what Laura was about to tell him was going to focus on something more tricky or unpleasant than her late husband. 'There was an IPOC investigation, wasn't there?'

Laura nodded. 'We didn't think it was thorough enough. I don't want to go into every minor detail, but we concluded that Sam and his partner had been lured to Brannings Warehouse deliberately. We think Sam had somehow come across evidence of police corruption involving the Fallowfield Hill Gang.'

'He was set up by someone inside the MMP?' Gareth's eyes widened. 'That's terrible, Laura.'

Laura nodded. 'It gets worse. Do you remember that when we first met a few years ago, I told you that Sam and his partner, PC Louise McDonald, had both died in the explosion and fire at the warehouse?'

'Yes, of course,' Gareth replied. 'I remember seeing her funeral on the news. They had the bagpipes as they took her coffin into the church.'

'Except she didn't die in that fire,' Louise explained. 'And she wasn't in that coffin.'

Gareth looked utterly bewildered. 'Now I'm completely lost.'

'Corrupt officers from the MMP and members of the Fallowfield Hill Gang faked Louise McDonald's death – she was on their payroll. Pete and I tracked her down to Llandudno.'

There were a few seconds as Gareth tried to process this.

'Before we could speak to her,' Laura continued, 'she was killed by a hit-and-run driver. I'm convinced that she was murdered to stop her revealing the identities of the corrupt officers within the MMP.'

She briefly explained about Superintendent Ian Butterfield, the officer in charge of the police operation at Brannings Warehouse the day Sam had died – how he had visited her home, drunk and dishevelled, revealing that he was trapped by the corruption he was involved in.

The blood had drained from Gareth's face as he looked at her aghast. 'Butterfield was found murdered in the Peak District, wasn't he? Why didn't you tell me any of this?'

'I wanted to but...' Laura said, searching for the right words to explain. 'We had just started to see each other and it seemed crass and tactless to tell you that Pete and I were looking into the death of my late husband. I thought if you knew that I was investigating Sam's murder, you'd run for the hills. In fact, that would have been a completely normal reaction.'

'So, you just hid all of this from me?' Gareth mumbled, clearly struggling to make sense of it all.

'I'm so sorry,' she said with a pained expression. 'At first, I didn't want to jeopardise things between us. And then Pete and I got too far down the road for me to start to explain. And it's just kind of snowballed in the past few months.'

Gareth furrowed his brow. 'So why tell me now?'

Laura winced, knowing this last revelation would be the most difficult. As far as Gareth knew, Pete was one of Laura's oldest and closest friends. They had met on several occasions in Beaumaris and they had got on really well.

There was a tense silence.

Gareth locked eyes with her. 'What?'

'I think Pete's involved,' she whispered.

'What?'

'I really hope I'm wrong but I think he set up Sam. And I suspect he killed Louise and Ian Butterfield,' Laura said.

CHAPTER 28

Gareth had left Laura's home after a fitful and all too brief nap and was now ensconced in his office, wading through paperwork but finding it hard to concentrate. The revelations about Pete Marsons, Sam's death and corruption within the MMP had rattled him. He wasn't naive enough to believe there weren't bent coppers in the UK police force. There always had been, and sadly that was never going to change. There were 150,000 police officers in the country and it only took a tiny percentage to abuse their position of power and trust to tarnish the force as a whole.

Ben knocked on Gareth's open door. 'Boss, we're ready for you.'

Christ, is that the time already?

Glancing out of his office, he saw that the CID team had assembled towards the front of the room in preparation for a briefing.

Getting up from his chair, Gareth nodded. 'Thanks, Ben.'

He needed to get his head back into their investigation, rather than focusing on the internal debate about what

Laura should or shouldn't have told him in the past year.

'Okay, everyone,' Gareth said loudly in an attempt to energise himself as he marched towards the scene board. He stopped, took a moment and then looked out at the assembled detectives. 'As I'm sure you're all aware by now, Callum Newell's body was discovered on the beach at the south end of Llanddwyn Island just before midnight last night. Although we are waiting for the preliminary postmortem, we are going to treat his death as suspicious until we get those results.'

'Can I just check, boss,' Ben said, 'Callum's body had been in the water and washed up onto the beach. Is that correct?'

'According to the SOCOs, forensics and the chief pathologist, Callum's body had signs that he had been in the water for some time,' Gareth explained. 'So, yes, we believe that at some point on Saturday afternoon, Callum entered the water somewhere on Newborough Beach. We have no idea if he was alive when that happened, if it was an accident, a misadventure or if there was someone else involved. However, given the trainer and baseball cap we found, I'm sticking to our original hypothesis that someone else was involved in Callum's death. And that means we are going to continue our lines of enquiry into who that might be.' Gareth turned and pointed to a photograph. 'What is the latest on Roy Balmer?'

Andrea straightened. 'He went in front of a magistrate in Mold this morning. He was charged with possession of indecent images and released on bail to appear at Crown Court.'

'And we still have nothing forensically to link him to Callum, do we?' Gareth asked to clarify.

'No, boss,' Andrea replied.

'Okay, as far as I can see there's no point investigating Balmer any further,' Gareth said. He then turned to the board again. 'David Coren. We have Callum's mobile phone in his possession. Laura?'

As he looked over at her, he realised that his feelings towards her were somehow different. The enormity of what she had told him earlier that morning weighed heavily on him.

'Andrea and I interviewed Jonathan Leary, one of The Fair Men, who claims to have found the phone on the sand at Newborough Beach,' Laura explained.

'What did you think?' Gareth asked.

'He seemed pretty genuine to me,' Laura explained. 'Andrea?'

Andrea nodded. 'Yeah. There was nothing about him that suggested that he was lying to us or hiding anything.'

Ben frowned. 'Weren't The Fair Men preparing for some kind of ceremony on Llanddwyn on Saturday afternoon?'

'That's right,' Laura said.

'Doesn't that strike anyone as a big coincidence? Especially given Callum's connection with David Coren?' Ben questioned.

'Possibly,' Gareth admitted. 'So, we know that Llanddwyn was searched extensively on Saturday and Sunday and the search team have confirmed that there was nothing on that beach at the south end when they searched there.'

Ben nodded. 'That's my point though, boss. Doesn't it

feel a little spooky that Callum was found there, given the religious significance of the island to druids and pagans? And that a religious cult were performing a ceremony on that island when he disappeared.'

Gareth frowned. 'Are you saying you think Callum's body was placed on the beach rather than being washed up there?'

'I don't know, boss,' Ben admitted. 'I just know that I've heard you say multiple times that as detectives we should never believe in coincidences.'

Gareth gave Ben an encouraging nod for airing his instincts. He had a lot of time for Ben, whom he had mentored since his arrival in Beaumaris CID. Their mutual love of rugby gave them a special bond. 'Let's see what the postmortem tells us and go from there. But we should bear it in mind…' Gareth took a breath. 'Have we managed to get a call log yet for Callum's phone?'

'Just got it, boss,' Ben replied. 'I've got several unanswered calls from a mobile phone the day Callum was murdered. The number doesn't match those of any of his friends or relatives.'

'Okay,' Gareth said, 'let's see if we can run a trace on it. What about the money that we found hidden under Callum's bed?'

Andrea signalled with her pen. 'Forensics are still checking for prints and DNA, but I'll give that a chase, boss.'

'Thanks, Andrea,' Gareth replied and then went to review the board again.

Declan looked over. 'Are we still looking at Tom Hegerty, boss?'

'I think we have to,' Gareth replied. 'We know that Tom and Callum got into a physical fight on Friday night, apparently over some remarks that Tom made about Callum's sister, Zoe. And as far as we know, Tom was the last person to see Callum alive. Unfortunately, the statements from the three boys about Saturday afternoon are incredibly vague because of the drugs that they had taken. But at the moment we do know that there was some kind of issue between Tom and Callum. And under the influence of drink and drugs, that might have escalated.'

Declan nodded in agreement and added, 'And if Tom attacked Callum, he might have ended up in the sea unconscious or dead.'

'It might have been nothing more than teenage boys dicking around and taking the piss, but we'll get a clearer idea of that when Tom's questioned, which I want done asap,' Gareth said. 'Any forensics back on the boys that were with Callum?'

Ben signalled for Gareth's attention and explained, 'Nothing that flagged up anything suspicious. Obviously they have Callum's DNA on their clothes, hair etc., but nothing came up that might indicate anything untoward.'

'Okay.' Gareth then turned and pointed to a photo. 'Of everyone that was in Callum's life, Mike Newell raises the most concerns for me at the moment. He's a functioning alcoholic with a violent temper, and he and Callum were clearly at each other's throats a lot of the time.'

Andrea nodded. 'Mike was angry that Callum had found some kind of father figure in David Coren.'

'And Mike said he'd prefer Callum to be dead than go off and join a religious cult,' Declan pointed out.

Ben frowned. 'He has an alibi.'

'The local pub where he virtually lives,' Declan said dubiously.

Gareth looked over at Laura. 'Laura, can you go with Andrea to the preliminary postmortem right now?' He then glanced at Declan. 'Dec, we'll go and check Mike's alibi.' Gareth then looked out at the assembled CID team who had plenty of leads to follow up on or chase. 'Okay, guys, let's give this our best work today.'

As Gareth went back into his office, he realised that he'd all but blanked Laura as he turned to go.

He didn't care. He was feeling hurt and so he shut the door behind him, even though he was aware that he was being childish.

CHAPTER 29

Laura pushed through the double doors into the hospital mortuary, followed by Andrea. The acrid stench of preserving chemicals and detergents filled the air, clinging to the back of her throat and making it difficult to breathe for a few seconds.

The temperature had dropped to a ghostly chill and she glanced around at the mortuary examination tables, gurneys, aluminium trays, workbenches and an assortment of luminous chemicals. The walls were a sterile white that glowed under the fluorescent lighting overhead, casting harsh shadows on every surface. In the corner, a single window let in a sliver of light that only served to make the darkness surrounding her feel even more oppressive.

Looking around, she spotted Chief Forensic Pathologist Professor Peter Lovell. In his fifties, Lovell was dapper and charming. He was on the far side of the mortuary, taking photographs and using a small white plastic ruler to give an indication of scale. Attached to his scrubs was a small microphone, as postmortems were all now digitally recorded.

As Lovell moved away from the metallic gurney, Laura saw the pale, naked corpse of Callum Newell laid out. Now that all the forensic evidence had been taken from him, Lovell was establishing cause of death, plus anything else that might help the investigation.

Laura approached and her gaze fixed on Callum's lifeless body. She couldn't help but feel saddened.

As usual, Lovell was dressed in pastel blue scrubs.

'It's hard when they're this young,' Lovell commented sadly as he gestured to Callum. The front of his torso had a large scar where he'd been cut open for examination. It had been stitched up with blue thread.

'What can you tell us?' Laura asked as they approached. She found herself compelled to look at Callum's face. Such tragic innocence. There was something about Callum's murder that had struck an emotional chord with her.

'Can you tell us the cause of death?' Laura asked. It was vital they knew as soon as possible if this was misadventure or something more sinister.

'Yes.' Lovell nodded with a grim expression and pointed to the dark marks around Callum's neck and throat. 'He died from manual asphyxiation.'

'He was strangled?' Laura asked, surprised.

'Yes,' Lovell replied quietly. 'Your victim was murdered.' He pointed again. 'You can see the pattern of finger-marks around the windpipe here, which have caused a very particular pattern of bruising. Plus there was no water in his lungs, which confirms he was dead before he went into the sea.'

'Can you tell us how long he's been dead?' Andrea asked.

'Being in the water does make getting an accurate time more complicated,' Lovell admitted, 'but I would say that he died early on Saturday afternoon, which fits your timeline. My guess is that he was strangled close to the shoreline and then his body was put into the water, where it was taken out and then brought back in by the tides.'

Laura took a few seconds to process this. Lovell had confirmed they had a murder case on their hands, but so far, they had very little to go on. 'Is there anything else that might help us, Professor?'

'Actually there is something,' Lovell said as he moved towards Callum's mouth and used a small metal instrument to move Callum's top lip back. 'Can you see here that these two front teeth are cracked?'

Laura leaned forward and peered closer. 'Yes.'

'Well, we found fragments of those teeth inside his stomach,' Lovell explained.

Andrea raised a quizzical eyebrow. 'At the risk of being rude, how does that help us?'

'No, no. That's a good question,' Lovell conceded with a reassuring expression. 'It means that when Callum stopped breathing, his mouth closed. Nothing has entered or left it since he died.'

'Okay.' Laura nodded but she still had no idea where Lovell was going with this.

'Sorry, I'm not being very clear here. If you look at this broken tooth, you'll see there's a couple of tiny specks of blood where it's broken. At first, we assumed that it was Callum's blood, but we checked his mouth and gums and found no cuts or signs of bleeding.'

'So… you don't think it's Callum's blood on his tooth?' Laura asked to clarify.

'Exactly. It can't be. I'm sure that a DNA test would confirm that for you.'

'So whose blood is it?'

'My theory is that Callum bit his attacker very hard during the struggle,' Lovell explained. 'In fact, so hard that he cracked his teeth and drew blood. So, your killer would have a very nasty bite mark and bruise on their body somewhere.'

Laura and Andrea exchanged a look – that was very helpful.

'However, the blood on the tooth was in his mouth for a long time, which means it could have been diluted and we might not be able to get a full DNA profile from it.'

'But it's possible?' Laura asked hopefully.

Lovell shrugged. 'It's possible, but a bit of a long shot, if I'm honest.'

CHAPTER 30

Gareth and Declan pulled into the car park of The Red Lion pub, which was on the road out of Beaumaris. With its large sign proclaiming 'Sky Sports' and 'Burger and a pint for £5', it was clearly aiming for a different type of customer than some of the fancier gastropubs in the town.

Getting out of the car, Gareth felt his mobile phone buzz in his pocket. He took it out and saw that it was Laura.

'Hi, Laura,' he said, not knowing if this was a social or professional call. Declan was within earshot, standing by the car, so he had to choose his tone and words carefully.

'According to Lovell, Callum Newell was definitely murdered,' Laura explained. 'Cause of death is asphyxiation by strangulation – manual – and as there's no water in his lungs, he was dead before he went into the water.'

Gareth took a moment to process this. Even though he wasn't surprised, he needed a second to get his head around the fact that this was now a murder investigation, with all that that entailed. 'Any idea how long he'd been in the water?'

'Lovell's best guess was some time on Saturday afternoon,' Laura said. 'And he also thinks that Callum bit his attacker.'

'Bit them?' Gareth asked, making sure he'd heard her correctly.

'Callum had cracked teeth with the attacker's blood on,' Laura explained. 'Lovell seems to think it was result of a violent bite…. If they can get some DNA off the blood sample, it might help identify our murderer.'

'Okay, thanks, Laura,' Gareth said. 'See you later.' He then turned to look at Declan, who apparently already knew what he was going to say.

'Callum was murdered, wasn't he?' Declan asked with a dark expression.

'Strangled and then put into the water. Saturday afternoon.'

Declan gestured sadly to The Red Lion. He didn't seem surprised at the news but it was still horrible. 'We'd better go in here then, boss,' he said quietly.

As Gareth looked up, he noticed that the weather had changed quite suddenly. The bright sunshine had been replaced by dark, granite-coloured clouds, and the air had become heavy and portentous, filled with the smell of wet earth and dark anticipation. It felt like the darkness was swallowing the sky above them as the wind began to whip around them.

They marched quickly across the car park, aware that the heavens were about to open.

Opening the door to the public bar, the first thing that grabbed Gareth's attention was a fruit machine, flashing and beeping beside the door. The lighting was stark and fluorescent, giving the pub around it a drab and soulless atmosphere.

Heading for the bar, a bartender in his late teens approached, looking self-conscious. His pale face still bore signs of acne and his clothes hung on his skinny frame as if he was trying to hide himself from the world.

At the far end of the bar, another man stood chatting to some men who looked like regulars, perched as they were on stools, nursing their precious pints. In his forties, the man was thick-set, with a shaved head and tattoo sleeves. He was so engrossed in conversation that he didn't initially notice Gareth and Declan's appearance at the bar.

'What can I get you?' the young bartender asked in a polite tone that lacked confidence.

Gareth flashed his warrant card. 'DI Williams and DS Flaherty, Beaumaris CID. I wonder if you could answer a couple of questions for us?'

The blood drained from the young bartender's face. 'Erm, yes. O-Okay,' he stammered hesitantly.

Gareth unlocked his phone and showed him the screen. 'Do you recognise this man?'

The young bartender peered at the image for a second and then replied. 'Oh yeah, that's Mike.'

'Mike Newell?' Declan asked to clarify.

'That's right,' the young bartender said with a frown. 'Is Mike okay?'

Gareth gave him a reassuring look. 'We're just asking a few routine questions, that's all.'

'Is it about his son?' the young bartender asked with a serious expression. 'I can't believe what's happened. Terrible.'

Declan looked at him. 'Did you know Callum Newell?'

'No,' the young bartender replied. 'I never met him.'

'Is Mike a regular in here?' Gareth asked, knowing the answer.

'Oh yeah,' he replied with a nod. The bartender seemed relieved that the focus of their questions was Mike, rather than anything closer to home. 'He's in here all the time.'

'Were you working here on Saturday afternoon?' Declan asked.

He thought for a couple of seconds and then replied, 'Yeah. I was here all afternoon and evening.'

'Can you tell us if you saw Mike in here on Saturday at any point?' Gareth enquired.

'Everything all right, Jack?' asked a gruff voice.

The shaven-headed bartender had wandered down to see what was going on.

Jack froze and looked hesitant. 'Erm, hi, Stu... I...' He gestured to Gareth and Declan. 'Just talking to these police officers about Mike.'

Pushing back his shoulder and puffing out his enormous barrel chest, Stu looked at them. 'Mike?'

'That's right,' Gareth said, annoyed that Stu had prevented Jack from answering their question about Mike and his whereabouts on Saturday afternoon at the time of Callum's disappearance.

Stu nodded to Jack. 'It's all right, I can take it from here. Go and see if Suzie needs any help in the kitchen, eh?'

Stu maintained steady eye contact with Gareth, as if to indicate that he wasn't someone to be messed with.

Jack scurried away and disappeared.

Gareth could predict just how this was going to go. If Mike was a popular regular in The Red Lion, Stu was going to cover for him, whether or not Mike had been there at the time of Callum's disappearance.

Declan put his hand casually on the bar, but Gareth could see out of the corner of his eye that he was irritated by Stu's aggressive manner. 'We're just checking that Mike Newell was in this pub on Saturday afternoon.'

'Yeah, he was,' Stu said immediately, without thought. 'All afternoon and evening.'

'And you're sure about that?'

'You calling me a liar?' Stu sneered.

Gareth saw Declan bristle with anger. He'd seen Declan lose his cool with men like Stu before. They seemed to wind him up more than anyone else.

Declan ignored Stu's question and gestured to the regulars who were sitting at the other end of the bar. 'And if I have a chat with your customers down there, they're going to tell me the same, are they?'

Stu gestured with a pompous laugh. 'Be my guest, *mate*.'

Gareth decided to call his bluff. He was constantly amazed by the audacity and bare-faced lies that people had told him over the years.

Walking along the bar, Gareth took out his warrant card again as the three men, all in their sixties and seventies, turned to look at him.

To his and Declan's frustration, the men confirmed what Stu had told them. However, there had been enough shifty glances in Stu's direction to suggest that they might be colluding to give Mike an alibi.

Gareth and Declan left the pub and headed for their car.

'What are you thinking, Dec?' Gareth asked.

Declan took a moment and then said, 'I'm thinking that if Mike Newell was in there all afternoon and evening, why are they making such a song and dance about telling us?'

'My thoughts exactly,' Gareth agreed. 'What's that line? "He doth protest too much"?'

'"My lady doth protest too much, methinks",' Declan corrected him. 'It's from *Hamlet*, boss.'

'Didn't realise you were such a fan of the Bard,' Gareth said with an amused arch of his eyebrow.

However, Declan was no longer listening. Instead he was looking at something across the road.

'What's wrong?' Gareth said, following his gaze to an off-licence with a large window and a big red sign reading 'Bargain Booze'.

'Bit early for a tinny, Dec,' Gareth joked.

Declan pointed. 'Above the door.'

Squinting, Gareth could see there was a security camera.

'Nice one. Let's go and have a chat, shall we?' Gareth suggested as they both crossed the road.

Declan stopped and looked up at the camera that was attached to the brickwork about six feet above the doorway. It looked like it was mounted to cover both the door and the pavement outside the window display.

Gareth looked across the road at the door to The Red Lion. 'I wonder how much of the road this camera covers,' he said, thinking out loud.

'Exactly,' Declan said.

Taking out his warrant card, Gareth entered and saw a large man in his early twenties with a dark, patchy beard.

'DI Williams and DS Flaherty, Beaumaris CID,' Gareth explained and then gestured outside. 'We were just looking at your CCTV camera.'

The bearded man rolled his eyes. 'Yeah. Head office put it up. We kept getting kids kicking in the window, taking bottles and running. It's meant to be a deterrent.'

'How's it working out?' Gareth asked.

'Better than I thought it would,' the bearded man admitted.

Declan looked at him. 'We're wondering how much of the road that camera takes in.'

The bearded man took two steps behind the counter and pointed to a monitor. 'Do you want to come and have a look?'

Gareth gave him a kind smile. 'Thanks, that would be great.'

The bearded man unlocked the counter and let them in so they could see a black monitor showed two CCTV feeds – one from inside the shop, and one from the camera outside.

Gareth moved closer and could immediately see that the CCTV camera from outside covered the whole road, the pavement opposite *and* the entrance door to The Red Lion. He shared an encouraging look with Declan.

Bingo!

'Have you got the CCTV from Saturday afternoon and evening?' Gareth asked hopefully.

The bearded man pulled a face. 'Sorry. We have to send the CCTV files up to Head Office every day. Then we delete them here.'

'Do you think they'll still have them?' Declan asked.

'Oh yeah,' the bearded man said. 'I think they keep them for a few weeks. If you want, I can contact Head Office and get them to send all the CCTV files for Saturday back to us. I'll just explain that you guys need to see them.'

Gareth was pleasantly surprised by the bearded man's offer of help.

'Thank you, that would be incredibly helpful,' Gareth said as he fished out a card and handed it to him. 'If you can give me a call as soon as they've sent the files, that would be great.'

CHAPTER 31

Sitting at her desk, Laura spotted a text on her phone. It was from Claudia Wright. It said no more than *Can we talk?* It wasn't the best of timing now that Beaumaris CID had been thrown into a homicide case, but Laura was keen to know if there had been any developments since their meeting earlier. She texted Claudia back and agreed that they could meet again. At this stage, Laura didn't want to do anything via phone, text or email as she had no idea if Pete, or anyone else from the MMP, was tracking her communications. And she certainly wasn't going to take any risks given the serious nature of what she knew.

Glancing around at the open-plan office, she could see the CID officers hard at work chasing leads, typing at computers, talking into phones. Despite the noise and bustle, the atmosphere was now very focused. An innocent eighteen-year-old boy had been murdered and thrown into the sea. They needed to do their best work for Callum's family and get justice by catching his killer.

Spotting Gareth at his desk, she got the distinct

impression that he was avoiding her. Maybe she was just being sensitive. The whole thing with Pete had made her increasingly paranoid, and her dreams in recent weeks seemed to continually involve her being chased by unknown people. However hard she ran, they were always within touching distance, and it wasn't uncommon for her to wake up in a cold sweat.

Getting up from her desk, she sidled across the office and looked in at Gareth. He was peering at his computer screen and typing furiously.

'Hey,' she said under her breath. She was feeling vulnerable and needed a bit of reassurance.

Gareth looked up and gave her a half-smile. Even that made her feel relief.

God, I really am a needy mess, aren't I?

'You okay?' he asked as he sat back in his padded office chair.

'Yeah, sort of,' she replied with a hand gesture to indicate she was a bit wobbly. 'Are *we* okay?' she asked.

Gareth surreptitiously reached out his hand and took hers. 'Of course,' he whispered. 'I was just a bit pissed off this morning. I wish you'd told me all that stuff. But none of it is your fault. And I'm happy to do whatever you need me to do to help you.'

Laura smiled and took a breath. It was just what she needed to hear.

'Thanks,' she said, giving his hand a squeeze.

Gareth got up and they both went out into the CID office as though they were no more than work colleagues.

'Any news from forensics on those fingerprints on the

bank notes?' Gareth said loudly.

Andrea shook her head and pulled a face. 'They're short-staffed down there. But I told them how urgent it is.'

The doors to the CID office opened and Declan came marching in holding a computer print-out.

'Boss,' Declan said in an urgent tone. 'I went down to chase forensics.'

'Okay,' Gareth replied as he leaned forward.

'The blood on Callum's trainer matches Tom Hegerty's DNA,' Declan said.

* * *

Gareth arrived at the Hegertys' home with Declan, Ben and two uniformed officers in case Tom decided to kick off. He gave the tatty front door an authoritative knock and took a step back.

On the journey, he had tried to piece together what might have happened. While making their way through Newborough Forest, Tom and Callum had possibly got into an argument, which had escalated into a fight. Callum could have punched Tom, splashing Tom's blood onto his trainer. Tom could then have chased Callum through the forest, towards the beach, with Callum losing his trainer and baseball cap on the way. The fight might have continued on the beach, with Tom eventually strangling and killing Callum before dragging his friend's body to the sea, pulling him in and letting the tide take him away. Tom could then have re-joined the others and pretended to be concerned as they looked for him. It was a decent hypothesis.

After a few seconds, Gareth knocked again and exchanged a look with Declan.

The front door then opened very slowly and Tom's face appeared.

'Shit!' His eyes widened in shock.

Tom went to slam the door in Gareth's face but he had pre-empted the possibility by putting his foot in the way. The door jammed and Tom turned and ran.

Pushing the door open, Gareth set off after him down the hallway and into the kitchen.

Glancing left, he saw an open door to a utility room and a door out into the back garden.

Gareth ran through both and immediately heard the sound of footsteps.

Turning, he caught sight of Tom charging towards a flimsy, five-foot-tall wooden fence. He then threw himself at the top, pulling himself up and over in one quick movement. The fence rattled noisily as he went.

Gareth sprinted after him and got to the fence a few seconds later. He pulled himself over clumsily and suddenly found himself behind Tom as they raced across the neighbour's garden.

A six-foot drystone wall was on the far side and Tom was soon up and over it, like the Parkour runners Gareth had seen on television.

'Bloody hell,' Gareth swore as he got to the wall. He wasn't going to make it over something that high without injuring himself, but with a groan of effort, he jumped, grabbing hold of the top edge. The stone cut into his fingers as, wedging a foot into a gap, he managed to push and pull himself to the top. The jump down on the other side seemed to jar every bone in his body.

Looking up, he saw Tom disappear over what looked to be the last fence before farmland.

An elderly neighbour nervously peered over at Gareth from her back door.

'It's okay, I'm a police officer,' he reassured her as he grabbed his Tetra radio and charged across the garden after Tom, who had vanished again.

Gareth clicked his radio on. 'Nine-three to Alpha four. Over,' he said between gasps.

Alpha four was the call sign for the uniformed officers.

'Nine-three, this is Alpha four. Over,' they replied.

'I am in pursuit of target suspect Tom Hegerty. He is heading west across the back gardens of Farm Lane. I have lost visual contact. Request back-up and for all exits from Farm Lane to be sealed off. Over.'

'Nine-three, received. Over.'

Sucking in breath, Gareth pounded towards the fence. This one was made of flush horizontal slats, making it virtually impossible to climb.

Without pausing for thought, Gareth grabbed hold of two slats with his left hand and two more with his right and pulled hard, pushing at the ground with both feet while simultaneously lifting himself. If he could just get a foothold on a third slat from the bottom...

His arms burned with lactic acid build-up but he refused to give in and he growled out loud as he pulled himself another foot up the fence. Throwing his leg over the top, he lost his balance slightly and fell over the other side before he'd had time to brace himself.

'Fuck!' he yelled loudly as a searing pain shot through his ankle.

Gareth scanned his surroundings for Tom's position.

Out of the corner of his eye, he could see the teen sprinting away across a field of knee-high grass.

'Bollocks.' Gareth put his weight onto his ankle and the piercing pain made him wince.

There was no way he could continue the chase.

Then, from out of nowhere, Declan appeared, sprinting full pelt across the field to intercept Tom.

Tom looked up and tried to side-step him but it was too late. Declan rugby-tackled Tom and wrestled him to the ground. Declan had clearly lost it, however, as he then punched Tom and started to berate him.

Ben and the uniformed officers had thankfully caught up, and they ran over quickly and managed to pull Declan off before it got really ugly.

Ben then pulled Tom's hands behind his back and cuffed him.

Limping gingerly, Gareth approached and saw Tom glaring at him.

'He punched me,' Tom snapped, looking at Declan, who was trying to steady himself. 'I'm going to report him.'

Ben pulled Tom to his feet. 'You were resisting arrest.'

Gareth locked eyes with him. 'Tom Hegerty, I'm arresting you on suspicion of the murder of Callum Newell.'

CHAPTER 32

'Interview conducted with Tom Hegerty, Monday, 10.20 p.m., Interview Room 2, Beaumaris Police Station. Present are Thomas Hegerty, Detective Inspector Gareth Williams, Duty Solicitor Patrick Clifford and myself, Detective Inspector Laura Hart.'

Laura glanced over. 'Tom, do you understand that you are still under caution?'

Despite his slight sneer, she could see that Tom was scared. She knew that he'd been in trouble with the police in Beaumaris before, but it had only been for minor offences in the past.

'Tom?' Laura said gently.

'What?' he snapped irritably.

'Do you understand you are still under caution?' Laura asked again slowly.

Clifford, the duty solicitor, leaned in and whispered something in his ear.

'Yes, of course,' Tom replied. 'But I haven't done anything.'

'Okay.' Gareth moved the files so that they were in

front of him. 'I would like to confirm that you are Thomas Anthony Hegerty?'

'Yeah,' he said with a smirk. 'Why are you asking me this? You know who I am.'

'It's just a formality, Tom,' Clifford informed him.

Laura looked at him with a calm expression. 'Tom, can you tell us what happened on Saturday afternoon when you, Callum, Osian and Ethan arrived at the Newborough Forest campsite?'

Tom frowned and shrugged. 'I don't know. We tried to put up the tents for a bit, which was a total fucking disaster. Then we decided to go down to the beach.'

Gareth leaned forward with a quizzical look. 'Aren't you forgetting something?'

'No,' Tom replied and then looked at Clifford as if to say, 'What's he talking about?'

'Is it correct that you and the others drank vodka and ate chocolate laced with magic mushrooms?' Gareth reminded him.

'Oh, that,' Tom snorted. 'Yeah, so what?'

Laura moved a strand of hair from her face and tucked it behind her ear. 'Afterwards, you decided to head for Newborough Beach by walking down through the forest. Is that also correct?'

'Yeah,' Tom replied with a nod.

'And how were you all feeling as you walked down through the forest?' Gareth enquired.

'At first, we were okay,' Tom explained. 'But after about ten or fifteen minutes we were all fucked.'

'You were hallucinating?' Laura asked to clarify.

'Yeah, we were all tripping.'

'And how was Callum at this point?' Gareth said.

Tom shrugged. 'He was off his head. We all were. Laughing, shouting, running about, you know? It was a laugh.'

Laura shifted forward in her seat. 'And did Callum seem any different to anyone else?'

'Do you mean was he more off his face than anyone else?' Tom asked casually.

Laura gave a small nod. 'Yes. That's exactly what I mean.'

'Not really. I mean, not that I noticed.'

'And you were all still together at this point?' Gareth said.

Tom rubbed his chin and mouth. 'Sort of. I mean we were running off and that. But yeah.'

'Can you remember the last time you saw Callum?'

Tom rolled his eyes. 'Yeah, I've told you and Osian's dad up at the campsite all this. And I made a statement.'

Gareth fixed Tom with a stare. 'Well, humour me, Tom, and tell me again,' he said coldly.

Considering that a close friend of his had been found murdered, Tom's complete lack of shock or grief was highly suspicious. He was acting as if the interview was nothing more than an annoying inconvenience.

'Callum was standing on that fallen tree that I showed you,' Tom said. 'He was dicking about and pretending to be a monkey. I carried on walking for a bit. Then, when I turned around, he'd vanished.'

Gareth took a few seconds, reached over to a folder and pulled out a photograph. 'For the purposes of the tape, I am showing the suspect Item Reference DKF4.' Gareth turned the image so that Tom could have a look. 'Tom, can you tell me what you can see in this picture?'

Tom leaned forward and peered at it. 'That's Callum's trainer. The one you and Osian's dad found just up from that tree.'

'Okay,' Gareth said, placing his finger on the image. 'Tom, can you see these dark spots on the toe of the trainer?'

'Yeah,' Tom said, looking confused.

'Would it surprise you to know that these are spots of blood?'

Tom shrugged. 'Okay.'

'Would it surprise you if I told you that these are spots of *your* blood?' Gareth said quietly.

'Eh?' Tom furrowed his brow. 'I don't understand.'

Laura leaned forward. 'Can you tell us how spots of your blood got onto Callum's trainer, Tom?'

For the first time, Tom looked genuinely rattled. His eyes roamed nervously around the interview room. 'No.' He blinked slowly before adding, 'Maybe it was from Friday night when I smashed my hand?' He turned his right hand to show the scabs across his knuckles where he had punched the wall.

Gareth shook his head. 'Callum was wearing a different pair of trainers on that night. We've checked the photos from the party.'

'Why did you and Callum get into a fight on Friday night?' Laura asked.

'I just made a joke about his sister,' Tom replied. 'He got a bit salty about it.'

'Did you have another fight with Callum on Saturday afternoon?'

'No,' Tom said, sounding nervous.

Laura waited for the tension to increase for a few seconds and then asked, 'Then why is your blood on the trainer Callum was wearing the day he disappeared?'

'I don't know, do I?' Tom now sounded desperate and confused.

Gareth gave him an empathetic look. 'Look, if you and Callum got into a fight on Saturday, you just need to tell us. Maybe it got out of hand?'

'No!' Tom snapped. 'We didn't get into a fight.'

Tom then leaned in and spoke quietly to Clifford, who nodded in agreement with what Tom was saying.

Clifford looked across the table at them. 'After consultation with my client, I am advising him to answer "no comment" to any more questions you might have today.'

CHAPTER 33

It was six a.m. the following morning. With his feet up on his desk, Gareth smoothed his hand over his scalp. It felt comforting as he tried to make sense of the jumble of thoughts that spun around his head. Not only was he trying to play out if Tom Hegerty really was guilty of Callum's murder, his mind also kept coming back to what Laura had told him about her investigation into Sam's murder and the corruption inside the MMP. He knew he needed to let go of his anger that she'd kept it from him.

A knock on the door broke his train of thought.

'Boss?' Ben said, holding a folder. His expression made it clear that he didn't want just a friendly chat about the recent Welsh rugby game.

'What have we got?' he asked, sitting up.

'Forensics have managed to match fingerprints on the money that we found hidden in Callum's bedroom,' Ben explained.

Gareth arched his eyebrow quizzically. 'And?'

Ben gave him a look. 'For starters, we've got a match for Tom Hegerty's prints.'

Tom Hegerty?

For a moment, Gareth's brain raced through various hypotheses. Why did Callum have three thousand pounds hidden under his bed that might have belonged to Tom? Was he hiding it for him... or from him?

'We've also got another set of prints,' Ben continued. 'They belong to a Stewart Tyler.'

'Stewart Tyler?' Gareth said with a frown. 'Why do I know that name?'

'Local, small-time dealer,' Ben reminded him. 'Police National Computer says that he's served three prison terms for dealing and he's been out on licence for the past six months.'

Gareth took a few seconds to digest it all. 'So, we've got money hidden under our victim's bed that looks like it belongs to a local drug dealer and is connected to Tom Hegerty.'

Ben looked at him. 'That's not all. We've also got Zoe Newell's prints on a few of the bills.'

Gareth was confused as he got up from his desk, trying to make sense of the evidence. 'We'll have to go and talk to Tom again.' They had had to release Tom last night as they didn't have enough evidence to hold him any longer. 'But I think I should go and talk to Zoe first.'

Declan arrived at the door at that moment, looking worried.

'Boss,' Declan said. 'Someone broke into the Newells' home this morning and ransacked the place.'

Gareth furrowed his brow. 'Where were the family?'

'Luckily they'd taken the dogs for a walk on the beach,' Declan answered.

* * *

As Gareth and Declan peered in from the doorway, they could see that Callum's bedroom had been totally turned over. His clothes were flung far and wide, as if they had been caught in a tornado-like whirlwind, and drawers from a pine chest had been pulled out and upended. His bed was flipped upside-down, and the duvet and mattress had been thrown across the room.

'Jesus,' Declan said under his breath as he and Gareth pulled on their blue forensic gloves and slowly stepped into the room.

'Someone was desperate to find something in here,' Gareth observed and then gave Declan a knowing look. 'Could be that money we found under his bed.'

'Makes sense,' Declan agreed.

Callum's A-level books lay strewn on the floor, some bent and torn. His games console had been smashed to pieces, its wires hanging loosely. Even the posters had been ripped from the wall.

Gareth looked around at the devastation. There was a strange stillness in the room, like the aftermath of a storm after it had passed through.

'We're going to need to get the SOCOs down here,' Gareth said quietly. He then looked at Declan. 'It feels personal though, doesn't it?'

Declan frowned. 'Sorry, boss?'

'If you're looking for something specific, like that money, you go through a room systematically,' Gareth explained. 'Whoever came in here ripped up books and tore posters from the walls. It's as if they were somehow angry with Callum, if that makes sense?'

'Yeah.' Declan nodded as he looked around. 'Especially as the rest of the house was untouched.'

Gareth gestured. 'Let's leave this to forensics.'

They left the room, walked along the landing and went down the stairs. The house smelled of stewed tea and cigarette smoke.

Gareth spotted the Family Liaison Officer in the kitchen making several mugs of tea.

'Where the hell was the FLO when all this was happening?' Gareth asked.

'She'd gone home to shower and get a change of clothes,' Declan explained.

'Maybe whoever did this was watching and waiting for her and the family to leave?' Gareth suggested.

'Too much of a coincidence for them not to have been,' Declan agreed.

Entering the living room, Gareth saw that Vicky and Zoe were sitting on the sofa together. They had both been crying and looked to be in shock.

Vicky looked over at Declan as she wiped her face. 'Why would anyone do this?' she asked in a distraught tone.

'We don't know, Vick,' Declan admitted. 'We think they might have been looking for the money that we found under Callum's bed.'

Gareth watched Zoe for a moment. She suddenly looked

very uncomfortable and it wasn't a mystery as to why. She had claimed to have no knowledge of the money when asked, but her prints were on some of the notes that had been found in Callum's bedroom during the initial search.

'She slept through it, thank God,' Vicky said and then looked at Zoe. 'I can't imagine what would have happened if you'd gone in there to confront them.'

Gareth was confused. The first reports had said that the house was empty at the time of the invasion.

'You were home when this happened, Zoe?' Declan asked, looking equally baffled.

Zoe nodded. She looked terrified.

Gareth furrowed his brow. 'Callum's bedroom has been turned upside-down and your bedroom is just down on the opposite side of the hall, is that right?' he asked.

'Yeah.' Zoe nodded as she clutched her mother's hand.

'But you didn't hear anything?' Gareth asked in a quizzical tone to let her know that this didn't make any sense.

Zoe pointed to her ears. 'I listen to podcasts to help me sleep, so I was wearing my noise-cancelling headphones. I can't hear anything when I've got them in.'

Gareth nodded. Even though it was a plausible explanation, he got the distinct feeling that Zoe was definitely hiding something. However, he didn't want to confront her about her fingerprints in front of her mother, so he would talk to her on her own.

'Zoe,' Gareth said as he got up from the armchair, 'can you come with me upstairs? If you're up to it, I'd like you to take a quick look at Callum's bedroom and tell me if there's anything significant missing from it.'

Zoe looked at Vicky, who looked a little confused, presumably thinking they should have asked her to look at Callum's bedroom instead. Then she gave Zoe a slight nod to indicate she should go with Gareth.

They retraced the steps to Callum's room and Gareth once again took note of the family photos that he'd seen before. Mark Newell had made sure that he was never close to Callum in any of the photos. It was very strange.

What is that all about? Gareth wondered for a second time.

As they went along the landing, they passed what Gareth assumed was Zoe's bedroom. He turned to look at her.

'Actually, Zoe, do you mind if we just go in here for a second?' Gareth said in a calm, affable tone as he gestured to the room. 'There's something I'd like to ask you about that I didn't want to bring up in front of your mum.'

Zoe blinked nervously. 'Erm, yeah. Okay.'

The room was neat and tidy. A tall poster of the singer Sam Fender hung over a cluttered dressing table where a plethora of make-up, brushes and perfumes were arranged. Under the window, a rack of vinyl records were organised by a turntable. The front record was *When We Fall Asleep* by Billie Eilish. Over by the bed was an amethyst crystal that glowed in a soft pink.

The curtains were closed against the sun, but light slid in through their thick blue fabric, throwing rectangles onto the floor and walls like a patchwork quilt. Tidy stacks of decorative pillows dressed each corner of the room, and a large flat-screen TV was mounted on one wall.

Gareth walked to a wicker chair over by the window and

sat down. He pointed to the bed and said quietly, 'Why don't you sit?' He could see that Zoe was getting increasingly nervous. 'Don't worry, you're not in trouble, Zoe.'

Zoe sat down with her shoulders hunched as she began to bite at the skin around her nails.

'Do you remember that we found some money hidden under Callum's bed?' he asked slowly.

Zoe nodded but didn't reply.

'And, if you remember, our forensic team took your DNA and fingerprints when they were here for an elimination sample from each of the family members,' Gareth said.

Zoe nodded. 'Yeah,' she whispered.

'Would it surprise you if I said we found your fingerprints on some of the bank notes in the money we found under Callum's bed?' Gareth asked in a calm tone.

There was silence.

'No... I...' Zoe's eyes roamed nervously around the room. 'I mean, I-I don't know,' she stammered.

Gareth looked at her but she was avoiding eye contact. He waited for a few seconds and then asked very gently, 'How do you think your fingerprints got onto those bank notes, Zoe?'

Zoe shrugged defensively. 'I don't know, do I?'

For a second, she looked at him and then away. She wasn't doing a very good job of disguising that she was hiding something.

He waited for a few more seconds as the tension in the room grew. Then he softly said, 'Zoe, you need to tell me why your fingerprints were on those bank notes. I know you were close to Callum, so I need you to tell me the truth so we can find out what happened to him.'

Zoe took an audible breath as she nodded, her eyes filled with tears. 'I gave the money to Callum to hide. I'm really sorry.'

'Okay,' Gareth said encouragingly. 'Can you tell me who the money belongs to?'

Zoe shook her head. She looked scared as she wiped her eyes and sniffed.

'Does the name Stewart Tyler mean anything to you?' Gareth asked.

She shook her head, looked down at her nails and began to bite them again.

'Zoe, look at me please,' Gareth said quietly. 'You're not in trouble. Does the money belong to Stewart Tyler?'

She nodded her head without looking up.

'And Stewart asked you to look after that money for him?'

'Yeah,' Zoe whispered.

'Okay. Why would he do that?' Gareth asked in a tone that implied no judgement.

Zoe began to sob. 'I can't tell you.'

'Zoe, we're going to find all this out one way or another, so you're better off just being honest with me,' Gareth explained. 'Are you in a relationship with Stewart?'

'No.' She shook her head. 'It's nothing like that.'

'Then what is it? Were you buying drugs from Stewart? We know that he's a seller.'

She shook her head.

'Okay. Were you selling drugs for him?'

Zoe nodded. She looked utterly ashamed and crestfallen.

'Just to friends and that,' she said, and then she broke down in tears again. 'I'm so sorry…'

'Why are Tom Hegerty's fingerprints on the bank notes?' Gareth asked.

Zoe shrugged. 'I don't know.'

'Come on, Zoe. You can't protect Tom after everything that's happened.'

There were a few seconds of silence.

Zoe took a deep breath and looked at him. 'Tom was helping me.'

'Tom was helping you sell drugs?' Gareth asked to clarify.

Zoe nodded and then she wiped more tears from her face.

Gareth was trying to piece together what Zoe was telling him. Callum had Tyler's drug money hidden in his bedroom. Was that why he was murdered?

'It's okay,' Gareth reassured her. 'What kind of drugs were you and Tom selling?'

Zoe closed her eyes. Her whole world was falling apart.

'Zoe? What kind of drugs?' Gareth asked. He needed to know if it was just a bit of weed, or Class A drugs as well.

'Weed. Ket. Flake,' Zoe whispered.

Class A. That's not good, he thought.

Gareth leaned forward. 'Why did Stewart need you to hold on to money and drugs for him?'

'He thought he was under surveillance from the police about a month ago,' Zoe replied very quietly. 'He said he thought his flat was gonna get raided so he needed someone to keep hold of his stash and his money for a while.'

'Someone who we wouldn't suspect of being involved with him, I take it?'

She nodded but continued to bite at her nails. 'Yeah.'

Gareth looked at her. 'Are there drugs in this house?'

She didn't respond.

'Zoe, are there drugs in the house?' he asked with a slightly more forceful tone.

'Yeah,' Zoe said.

'Where are they?'

'That's the thing. I don't know.' She looked at him with a pained expression. 'I gave the drugs and money to Callum to hide in his bedroom. Mum never goes in there so I knew she'd never find them.'

Gareth thought for a second and then frowned. 'We found the money in there, but where are the drugs?'

'I don't know,' Zoe said, sounding distraught. 'I don't know where Callum hid them.'

'I take it that it was Stewart Tyler who turned Callum's bedroom upside-down?' Gareth said as he began to piece the sequence of events together.

'Yeah. Stu turned up here earlier. He wanted the drugs and money back,' Zoe said.

'Stu?' Gareth said as a realisation hit him. 'Does Stewart Tyler work behind the bar in The Red Lion pub?'

'Yeah.' Zoe nodded.

'So, Stu and your dad are friends?' Gareth asked, remembering how Stu had covered for Mike Newell when they'd asked about his whereabouts at the time of Callum's disappearance and murder.

'Yeah,' Zoe replied. 'But my dad doesn't know about any of this.'

'Did Stu manage to find where Callum had hidden the drugs?'

Zoe shook her head. She looked frightened. 'No.'

'What did he say?'

'He said that I owed him the money and the drugs... or thirteen grand to cover his losses...' Zoe trailed off.

'Or what, Zoe?'

'Or he was going to hurt me.'

Gareth took a moment and then gave her a quizzical look. 'When did Stu first ask for everything back?'

Zoe's face fell as she took a nervous breath. 'About a week ago.'

Gareth frowned. 'A couple of days before Callum was killed?'

Zoe nodded. It was obvious to both of them where this line of questioning was about to go.

'You must have asked Callum where he had hidden it all?'

'Yeah,' she whispered as she looked at the floor.

'And what did Callum say?'

Zoe dissolved into sobs as she put her hands to her face.

'Zoe,' Gareth said gently, 'I need you to tell me exactly what Callum told you.'

After a few seconds, she looked up and wiped the tears from her puffy cheeks. 'He told me he wasn't going to help me deal drugs. And that he wasn't going to give the money or drugs back.'

'What did you say?'

'I went mental,' Zoe admitted. 'I told him they weren't mine and we'd both be in deep shit if he didn't give them back.'

'What did Callum say to that?'

Zoe shook her head. 'He said his mind was made up. He also said he was thinking of telling Osian's dad what was going on.'

Gareth ran his hand over his scalp. A motive for Callum's murder was becoming increasingly clear. 'What did you tell Stu?'

Zoe pursed her lips but didn't reply.

After a few seconds, Gareth leaned forward and looked at her. 'Zoe, did you tell Stewart Tyler what Callum had said to you?'

Zoe closed her eyes, nodded and then sobbed.

'What did Stu say?'

'He said that if Callum didn't hand them back, he'd kill him.'

CHAPTER 34

Two hours later, Gareth was outside The Red Lion pub with Declan and two uniformed police officers, in case things got out of hand. Gareth had secured an arrest warrant for Stewart Tyler based on what Zoe had told him. He also had a Section 18 Search Warrant.

The council tax records showed that Tyler lived in the flat above the pub and had done for the past six months. Declan gave an authoritative knock and stood back.

Gareth glanced up to the first floor and saw a light at a window switch off. Then another light. He glanced over at Declan.

'Someone's definitely in,' Gareth noted. 'Unless there's a ghost turning off all the lights.'

Declan rolled his eyes.

The sky above them was a growing mass of steel grey clouds that were slowly crawling across the sun like a dark, thick blanket. The street was still and quiet except for the distant unsettling moans of gulls.

Declan banged aggressively on the door again.

Nothing.

Gareth felt the cold splash of a raindrop on the bridge of his nose just as the wind moaned with a howl, which seemed to rise in pitch and intensity as it went on. An empty Coke can skittered along the pavement, rattling as the wind carried it into the road.

After a few more seconds of silence, Declan gave Gareth a knowing look and then gestured to the door. 'Want me to see if this will open?'

'Why not,' he said to Declan with a shrug. Their arrest and search warrant would cover a forced entry, given they now suspected Tyler of being involved in Callum's murder.

Taking a step back, Declan crashed against the wooden door and it flew open with a bang.

Gareth turned to the uniformed officers and signalled for them to all go inside.

Behind the door was a narrow staircase that led straight up to a dark red door at the top, which presumably led to Tyler's flat.

Jogging up the stairs, Gareth braced himself in case Tyler decided to do something stupid.

His pulse quickened as he opened the door to the flat and stopped for a moment to listen.

Nothing.

'Mr Tyler,' Gareth said loudly. 'It's DI Williams. I'd like you to show yourself.'

The flat was untidy and smelled of takeaway food and weed. The carpet was dark brown with an orange pattern and looked like it had been there since the seventies.

'Mr Tyler?' Declan called again.

Spreading out, they began to search each room.

Going into the living room, Gareth saw a table full of empty beer cans, a small bag of weed and an ashtray full of cigarette butts and splifs. The air was thick with the smell of marijuana, as if someone had been smoking weed in there only a matter of minutes ago.

Spotting a mug of tea on the arm of a large armchair, Gareth went over and touched it. It was still warm.

Declan appeared at the doorway. 'Nothing, boss.'

Gareth frowned and pointed to the tea and the ashtray. 'That tea is still warm so he's got to be in here somewhere.'

Striding out into the hallway, Gareth glanced around.

Where the hell is he?

Maybe there was a door leading to a fire-escape to the ground floor?

A male uniformed officer approached. 'Sir, we've checked every cupboard, wardrobe, everywhere. Nothing.'

Gareth gave a frustrated shrug. 'He can't have vanished into thin air.'

Scanning the hallway again, Gareth looked up and saw something on the ceiling – the square hatch to a loft.

'Think I might have the answer,' he said, pointing up. If Tyler had used a ladder to get up there, he must have somehow pulled it up with him as there was no sign of it in the hallway.

The uniformed officer disappeared and then came back with a chair from the kitchen. As he went to step on it, Gareth put his arm out.

'It's okay, Constable, I've got this,' he said as he stepped onto the chair and looked up at the hatch on the ceiling.

As the senior officer, he felt it was his responsibility to face whatever was hiding behind that door.

Reaching up, he pushed the hatch very slightly while taking a nervous gulp. Perched on top of the chair, he felt incredibly vulnerable, knowing that his odds weren't great if Tyler decided to attack him.

He slid the hatch up and across so that it moved into the loft.

Now what?

He didn't have the strength to pull himself up off the chair and all the way into the loft.

Then he had an idea.

'Mr Tyler,' Gareth said calmly. 'We know you're in there. I'm not about to try and climb up to get you, and I'm not about to send one of my officers up there either. So, what I'm going to do is bring in the Canine Unit and we're going to send up a great big German Shepherd to flush you out...' Gareth waited for a second and then added, 'Or you can just come down now and we can go to the station for a chat.'

Gareth stepped down from the chair, looked at Declan and the other officers and shrugged, whispering, 'Worth a try.'

After a few seconds of silence, there was a noise of movement.

Tyler appeared at the hatch, his face full of thunder. 'I'm coming down.'

CHAPTER 35

Laura was sitting at her desk looking down at her phone. She had arranged to meet Claudia Wright from *The Sunday Times* the following morning at Beaumaris Beach at 6.30 a.m. Laura wondered what Claudia had found, but she didn't want to pre-empt their meeting with her own theories.

Looking up, she saw Gareth approaching.

'We've got Tyler in custody,' he said. 'The duty solicitor is here so can you come and interview him with me? You know, in case we need to go all "good cop, bad cop" on him.'

'Of course,' Laura said, getting up from her desk and grabbing her jacket. They headed for the doors to CID. 'I'm guessing that you and Declan in an interview ends up as "bad cop, worse cop"?' she quipped.

Gareth smiled. 'Yeah, something like that.'

'You think Tyler murdered Callum?' Laura asked as they strode towards the interview room.

'I think he was definitely involved,' Gareth replied. 'Callum had thirteen grand's worth of drugs and money that he wouldn't hand back. And that's definitely motive.'

233

'What about Tom Hegerty?' Laura asked. 'He was there with Callum. And his prints are on the money. His blood is also on Callum's trainer. If Tom worked for Tyler, maybe the fight at the Sports Club was about Callum's refusal to hand back Tyler's stash. And maybe they argued about it again the following afternoon. Callum could have told Tom he was going to take what he knew to Declan, leading Tom to take matters into his own hands.'

Gareth nodded encouragingly. 'That certainly fits in terms of motive, means and opportunity, doesn't it?'

They got to the door and went into the interview room.

Laura and Gareth sat down on the opposite side of the table and arranged their files for a few moments before Laura leaned over and pressed the red button on the recording machine. There was a long electronic beep and then she began. 'Interview conducted with Stewart Tyler, Tuesday, ten a.m., Interview Room 1, Beaumaris Police Station. Present are Duty Solicitor Patrick Clifford, Detective Inspector Gareth Williams, and myself, Detective Inspector Laura Hart.'

Tyler gave Gareth a stare.

Laura raised her eyebrow. 'Stewart, do you understand that you are still under caution?'

Tyler then shifted his stare to Laura and gave a smirk, as though he had just heard a joke. 'No comment.'

Gareth shifted back in his seat and gave an audible sigh. 'Stu, I'd like to advise you that opting for a "no comment" interview isn't in your best interests here. The evidence against you is overwhelming and so some explanation is going to be needed.'

Tyler gestured to his solicitor and shrugged. 'That's what I've been advised to do.'

His annoying smirk was getting right up Laura's nose. 'Can you tell us where you were this morning?' she asked in a no-nonsense tone.

Tyler shook his head with mild amusement. 'No comment.'

Laura pointed to a document in front of her. 'We have an eyewitness that puts you at a property in Hazelmere Avenue at around 5.30 a.m. Is there anything you can tell us about that?'

'No comment.'

'Stewart, do you know a Zoe Newell?' Gareth enquired.

Tyler took a few seconds to answer, as if the question had surprised him. Maybe he had counted on Zoe keeping her mouth shut and not talking to the police. 'No comment.'

'Well, Zoe Newell says that you forced your way into her home this morning. You then proceeded to ransack a bedroom in that property looking for illegal drugs that you asked Zoe to look after for you several weeks ago. She also told us that you asked her to hide a substantial amount of money for you,' Gareth said calmly. 'What can you tell us about that?'

Tyler scratched his neck and jaw. 'No comment.'

Laura reached over for a folder and pulled out a photograph. 'For the purposes of the tape, I am showing the suspect Item Reference 292F.' She slid the photograph across the table for Tyler to look at. 'Can you please tell me what you can see in this photograph?'

Tyler locked eyes with her, looked amused and said, 'No comment.'

'Item Reference 292F is a photograph of a roll of bank notes amounting to three thousand pounds that was found hidden in the bedroom of Callum Newell.' Laura gestured to the photograph. 'Have you ever seen this roll of money before?'

Tyler leaned over to Clifford and they spoke in hushed voices for several seconds. He then said, 'No comment.'

Laura moved the photograph back. 'Would it surprise you if I told you that your fingerprints were found on several of these bank notes? Can you explain that for us?'

'No comment.'

Gareth leaned forward, placing his elbows on the table. 'Zoe Newell told me that she has been dealing drugs for you. Is that correct?'

'No comment.'

'And several weeks ago, you were convinced that you were under surveillance and that your flat was going to be raided by Anglesey police officers. You asked her to hide a substantial amount of drugs and money at her house for you. Zoe then gave the drugs and money to her brother, Callum, to hide in his bedroom. Is that correct?'

'No comment.'

Gareth scratched his nose, looking frustrated. He then glanced down at the signed statement Zoe had given him and Declan. 'About a week ago, you asked Zoe to return both the drugs and the money as you felt that you were no longer under surveillance. Is that correct?'

'No comment.'

'When Zoe asked her brother to return the drugs and money to her, he refused. He also said that he was thinking of talking to Detective Sergeant Declan Flaherty at Beaumaris CID,' Gareth said. 'Do you remember Zoe telling you this?'

'No comment.'

Gareth fixed him with a steely look. 'My guess is that you do remember because you were incredibly angry with Callum. In fact, you told Zoe that unless Callum returned the drugs and money, you would kill him. Do you remember saying that?'

For a few seconds, Tyler was silent as his eyes roamed around the room. 'No comment.'

Laura frowned. 'It was about three days after Zoe told you this, and you made that threat, that Callum Newell was murdered. Is there anything you'd like to say about that?'

Tyler fidgeted a little awkwardly in his seat. 'No comment.'

Gareth waited for a few seconds. 'Did you murder Callum Newell?'

'No comment,' Tyler said, but his voice was quieter and less confident.

'Can you tell us where you were on Saturday afternoon?' Gareth asked as he pulled a piece of paper from a folder. 'For the purposes of the tape, I'm showing the suspect Item Reference 394G. Can you please look at this and tell me what it is?'

For a few seconds, Tyler didn't respond. Then he huffed, took the piece of paper, looked at it and then tossed it back onto the table. 'No comment.'

'For the purposes of the tape, on the sheet of paper is the work rota for The Red Lion Public House. And it shows clearly that Mr Tyler wasn't working on Saturday afternoon,' Gareth explained and then pointed to the rota. 'If you look here, it says you started work at six p.m. Is that correct?'

'No comment.'

'Callum Newell went missing between one and two p.m. on Saturday afternoon,' Laura said. 'Can you tell us where you were at that time?'

Tyler looked uncomfortable. 'No comment.'

'Does the name Tom Hegerty mean anything to you?' Gareth asked.

Tyler reacted the same way he had when Zoe was mentioned – as if he wasn't expecting Tom's name to come up. He quickly composed himself. 'No comment.'

'You see, not only did we find yours and Zoe Newell's fingerprints on the money that was discovered in Callum's bedroom, we also found Tom Hegerty's,' Gareth said. 'Is there anything you can tell us about that?'

Tyler now looked agitated. 'No comment.'

'Did Tom Hegerty work for you, dealing drugs?'

'No comment,' Tyler said, his frustration clear.

'We know that you were very angry at Callum for keeping hold of your drugs and money,' Laura said. 'Did you ask Tom to confront or even attack Callum so that he would hand them back?'

'No!' Tyler snapped loudly.

'Did you personally follow Callum to Newborough Forest and confront him there? Maybe things got out of hand and you took it too far and killed him?' Gareth said.

Without warning, Tyler stood up and glared at them. 'No fucking way. You are way off.'

The duty solicitor glanced disapprovingly at his client.

Laura said in a calm voice, 'Why don't you sit back down, Stewart?'

CHAPTER 36

Sitting on his bed, Osian took a deep breath. The emotion of Callum's death kept overwhelming him. He would forget for a few minutes and then the terrible realisation that his friend was dead came flooding back. His eyes filled with tears again and he wiped them away with his pillowcase. How could it be that he was never going to see his friend again? It just didn't feel real.

He and Callum had known each other since primary school. They had got drunk on cheap cider in the local park together when they were fourteen. They had both snogged Libby Peters at the same party. They had gone to Leeds Festival two years ago, smoked a spliff and jumped around to Stormzy and AJ Tracy.

Osian blew out his cheeks and closed his eyes. The last few days had felt like some terrible nightmare. It was something that happened to other people, wasn't it? He and Callum had recently talked about their hopes and plans for going to university. Callum had been up to Oxford to look around. He thought he might study for a degree in Philosophy, Politics and Economics.

The door to Osian's bedroom opened slowly and his mum and dad looked in. As soon as they saw that Osian had been crying, they came over, sat on his bed and his mum gave him a hug.

'Just thought I'd see how you're doing?' Sue said softly.

Osian nodded. He didn't know how to respond or what to say. 'How is Callum's mum?'

'She's devastated, mate. We all are, aren't we?' Declan replied as Sue nodded and put her hand to Osian's face to comfort him.

Osian looked at her, gave a slight nod and then frowned over at his dad. 'Ethan texted me to say that Tom had been arrested. Is that right?'

Sue pulled a face.

'I can't really talk about it. Sorry,' Declan admitted.

Osian was perplexed by confirmation of the news. 'You think Tom had something to do with what happened to Callum?'

His dad didn't respond for a few seconds. 'We don't know. Why? Is there anything about Saturday that you haven't told us?'

Osian shook his head but knew he needed to tell his dad what he'd seen at Tom's house the day before. It might just be gossip but it might be important.

'No, but there is something else,' he admitted.

'Okay,' Declan said with a slight tone of apprehension.

'I went around to see Tom yesterday. You know, to see how he was,' Osian said. 'I saw him and Zoe in her car outside his house.'

'What were they doing?' Declan asked.

'Tom was smoking a spliff. And I could see that Zoe was upset,' Osian explained and then stopped for a moment. 'And then they kissed.'

'Kissed?' Sue looked confused. 'You mean like…?'

'Yeah,' Osian replied, nodding.

'You didn't know there was anything between Zoe and Tom then?' Sue asked.

'No. Of course not,' Osian said, then paused for a moment. 'But I did suspect there might be something going on.'

'Do you think that's what Tom and Callum were fighting about on Friday night?' Declan asked.

'I don't know,' Osian admitted with a shrug. 'I couldn't hear what started it. Tom just said he'd made some inappropriate comment.'

Declan raised an eyebrow. 'Do you think Callum would have been angry if he'd found out something was going on between Zoe and Tom?'

'I don't know.' Osian paused for a second to think. 'It would be weird, but I don't know if they'd get into a big fight about it.'

Sue put a reassuring hand on Osian's shoulder. 'I'm gonna finish up tea while you chat to your dad.'

Osian watched her go and sensed that his dad was about to talk to him about something serious.

Declan gave him a look. 'Did you ever hear about Tom or Zoe dealing drugs?'

'What?' Osian spluttered in shock. 'God, no. Tom smoked a bit of weed. And I've never seen or heard Zoe have anything to do with drugs. Why? Were they?'

242

'I'm not sure. But this stays between us, okay?' Declan said. 'You can't even tell Ethan.'

'God, I won't tell Ethan anything,' Osian said.

'Ever hear Tom talking about a man named Stewart – or Stu – Tyler?' Declan asked.

Osian thought for a moment. The name registered. 'I think Tom said something about a *Stu* on Friday night. I thought he might be Zoe's boyfriend or something. But that's the only time I've ever heard the name.'

'Okay,' Declan said. 'And there's nothing else?'

Osian looked at him and shook his head.

CHAPTER 37

It was nearly six a.m. by the time Laura had got to Beaumaris Beach for her early morning swim. Rosie had decided to have a lie-in for once and Laura was grateful as she had arranged to meet Claudia at 6.30 a.m. Laura glanced at her waterproof watch to check she still had plenty of time for a swim. She knew that the rush of the cold sea would keep her mind sharp and focused when they met.

The wet sand was smooth and cold under her feet, like tiny pebbles smoothed by the sea. A quick hop, skip and dive and Laura was in. She felt nothing but the blissful sensation of the icy water as it passed over each square centimetre of her body, from her scalp to her bare toes. The freezing temperature seeped into her skin, stinging her with a million pinpricks, in turn numbing every inch of her nerves until she felt nothing. It was such a refreshing, exhilarating rush.

For a few minutes she lay back with her eyes closed. The sound of the waves crested and fell in a graceful, soothing rhythm, never changing its beat or melody. The rhythmic cadence calmed her and gave her some semblance of satisfaction that she had found a way to balance herself again between land and water. She smiled, knowing that, if only for these few moments, she could hold on to this feeling without any uncertainty or fear coming forward to disturb her serenity.

Laura's mind drifted back to when she was learning how to float on her back in swimming lessons as a child. She remembered walking along the side of the main swimming pool at Beaumaris and looking down to the bottom of the deep end. It terrified her. She would only have been five or six. She recalled the terrible thought that if she fell in she would sink to the bottom and drown. But she got her confidence over the next few weeks with Mrs Cole, her smiley swimming teacher. And she remembered how proud she had been when she managed to swim a whole length of that pool and Mrs Cole had presented her with her twenty-five-metre swimming badge and certificate.

Laura turned and dived beneath the water, feeling the freedom of just floating in the silence and darkness. The shock of the cold had now gone, replaced by an inner warmth. She turned and looked up, seeing the growing light of the day reflected on the water's surface, like coloured glass. She felt alive. She felt whole. Her past, present and future were all rolled into this moment. Then she returned to the surface with a gasp and stood on the sand beneath her.

Glancing at her watch again, she saw it was time to get out, get dry and dressed and then wander up to the car park to meet Claudia. Making her way to where Elvis was lying in the sand, the chilly sting of the cold air rippled along the wet skin of her bare arms. It was invigoratingly cold, and so piercing that it made her shudder until she could wrap the huge towel around herself.

Putting on a thick hoodie, joggers, trainers and woolly hat, she reached down for the flask of hot tea that she always brought with her. She sat down on a rock and took a mouthful. It tasted incredible after being in the sea.

Elvis sat up and looked at her with his big chestnut eyes. She patted his head. 'It's not a bad view is it, eh?' she said to him as she looked across the Menai Strait to the Welsh mainland, where the dark, cloud-topped mountains of Snowdonia scarred the orange horizon.

Laura clipped on Elvis' lead and headed up the beach towards where she had arranged to meet Claudia.

Two minutes later, she saw Claudia's car parked in roughly the same place as their last meeting. Claudia flashed her headlights and Laura gave a half-wave to acknowledge that she'd seen her. She tied Elvis to the railings and wandered over, checking both ways to make sure no one had seen her.

'Hi there,' Claudia said as Laura got into the car and sat on the passenger seat. 'I took the liberty of getting you a coffee once I knew you'd be insane enough to go for a swim out there.' Claudia gestured to the two takeaway cups that sat in the holder between the seats.

'That's great,' Laura said with a smile as she took one and had a swig. 'When I first heard that people swam in the sea off Beaumaris all year round, I thought they must be mad. And I never thought I'd ever do it.'

Claudia raised an eyebrow. 'Please don't tell me you go in there without a wetsuit in the depths of winter.'

Laura laughed. 'All year round. I've even been in there when it's been snowing.'

Claudia snorted. 'I know it's meant to be very good for you, but I think I'll stick to a hot bath, a good book and a weekly Pilates class.'

'It really helped me when I first moved back here,' Laura admitted. 'After what happened to Sam, I suffered from terrible anxiety and panic attacks. I was eventually diagnosed with PTSD. But the swimming has virtually stopped all that. My daughter's had a very rough time in recent months and I've even got her coming a couple of times a week.'

'Good for you,' Claudia said with a genuinely supportive tone.

There was a natural lull in the conversation as they both sipped their coffees.

'You said that you'd found something?' Laura asked.

'Yes,' Claudia said as she reached onto the backseat and pulled over a smart-looking laptop case. She took out her laptop and turned it on. 'I've now spoken to the journalist who first picked up on the story of corrupt police officers in the MMP working with a powerful OCG in the city in 2018. It seems that he was looking at some of the officers that you told me about.'

Laura arched an eyebrow quizzically. 'But they never ran the story?'

'They couldn't get anyone to go on record. Everyone connected to that particular OCG was too scared to say anything so, despite some evidence and their suspicions, they could never run the story.'

'Have you got details?' Laura asked, intrigued by the

fact that journalists had been convinced of corruption in the MMP at the time of Sam's death.

'Yes,' Claudia replied with a nod as she opened up some files on her computer. 'Do you know this man?'

Laura peered at the image of a thick-set man in a tracksuit with a shaved head and bulldog features. She knew exactly who he was. 'Danny Wright. He's a leading member of the Fallowfield Hill Gang in South Manchester.'

'Okay, well that tallies with our research from back then,' Claudia said.

'In the lead-up to the operation at Brannings Warehouse, we'd been working with the North West Regional Organised Crime Unit. We arrested two leading members of the Fallowfield Hill Gang – Lee Jennings and Tyrone Amis – for a drive-by shooting at the funeral of a member of the Doddington Gang,' Laura explained, and then she pointed to the photo. 'That put Danny Wright pretty much in charge. And then we found a link between Wright and Superintendent Ian Butterfield through a holding company called Clayton Vale Holdings. It should be in all the stuff that I gave you.'

Claudia nodded. 'The link is Jack Taylor, whose daughter was married to Butterfield.'

'Exactly,' Laura said.

Claudia gave her a dark look. 'I found a photograph that I want to show you, which I think is going to confirm all your suspicions.' She clicked to open another photograph.

The image had been taken with a telephoto lens and showed four people chatting at a table in the corner of a greasy-spoon café.

Laura immediately recognised Ian Butterfield and Louise McDonald sitting together on one side.

Her heart sank when she saw the man sitting opposite.

It was Pete.

Looking at the date of the photo, she saw that it was taken three months after Sam's death and two months after Louise McDonald's funeral.

'Unfortunately that is DCI Pete Marsons sitting with Ian Butterfield and Louise McDonald,' she said quietly.

'Do you know this man?' Claudia asked, pointing to the final person at the table. 'It's a bit blurred but I wondered if you recognised him?'

Laura's eyes rested on the man sitting next to Pete, and though the image was unclear, it didn't take her long.

'Yeah, that's Area Commander Paul Atkins.' Laura looked at Claudia feeling real fear. 'That is, he was Area Commander in 2018. He's now Chief Constable of Greater Manchester Police and therefore the most powerful police officer in the city.'

CHAPTER 38

Later that afternoon, Gareth and Laura were sitting in the main meeting room on the ground floor of Beaumaris nick. Even though they were convinced that Tom Hegerty and Stewart Tyler were involved in Callum's murder, they needed to talk to the Crown Prosecution Service to see how to proceed.

'I'm afraid it's circumstantial with Hegerty,' said Victoria Charles, the CPS lawyer. She was forty years old, with a slim build and an oval face with thin eyebrows that arched dramatically over her dark eyes. Her black hair always looked perfect, like it was cut from onyx and sealed into place, and dressed in a smart charcoal suit, Victoria's business-like manner immediately gave the impression that she was in charge.

Gareth pulled a face. He had suspected that Victoria and the CPS were going to turn them down at this stage.

'We're still waiting for a possible DNA sample from blood found on one of our victim's teeth. It's only trace, which is why it's taking so long,' Laura explained. 'I assume that if that DNA matches either Hegerty or Tyler, we might be able to consider charging them with Callum's murder?'

Victoria nodded. 'I think a DNA match could give us a direct and provable link between the victim and suspect, but I don't know if it'll be enough.' Victoria moved a tress of hair back from her face. 'With Stewart Tyler, you only have Zoe Newell's testimony plus the fingerprints, and a decent defence would drive a train through her on the witness stand. And the fingerprints on the bank notes is circumstantial. The same with Tom Hegerty. You've got some circumstantial evidence and Zoe's testimony. Plus Zoe is young and emotionally vulnerable. What if she decides to retract her statement? The whole case would be scuppered.'

Gareth gave a sigh. He'd known they needed more but it was still frustrating to hear it out loud.

Victoria nodded, grabbed her files and stood.

'Thanks for coming in,' Laura said.

'Not a problem,' Victoria said with a slightly forced smile.

There was a knock at the door. It was Declan.

Gareth knew that it had to be urgent if he had felt the need to interrupt their meeting with a CPS lawyer.

'Sorry, boss,' Declan said, looking shaken. 'Have you got a minute?'

'Actually we were just finishing,' Gareth replied and looked over at Victoria. 'We'll be in touch.'

As Laura escorted Victoria out, Gareth ushered Declan into his office and closed the door behind them.

'Are you all right, Dec?' Gareth asked, seeing now that he looked upset.

'We've just had word from a uniformed patrol,' Declan explained with a frown. 'They got a call out to the Newells' home and they've found a woman who is unresponsive. They… they think she might be dead.'

'Who is it?' Gareth asked, alarmed.

'It's Vick.' Declan said it as though he just couldn't believe it. 'It's Vicky Newell.'

CHAPTER 39

Laura and Andrea screeched to a halt outside the Newells' home, their tyres kicking up gravel as the blues and twos blared out a warning. The neighbours had already gathered on the pavement, talking in hushed tones as they tried to pry information from uniformed officers who had sealed off the house with evidence tape. As Laura and Andrea approached, they could see several marked police units parked across the road, stopping all traffic from entering. An ambulance was parked a little further away with two paramedics talking quietly. Laura knew they would have done all they could.

A SOCO wearing the full Tyvek suit stepped out of the forensic van, packing away evidence into its back doors. With each step closer to the young officer manning the cordon, Laura could feel the tension growing in her stomach.

They made their way towards Gareth and Declan, who were waiting for them with grim expressions. All four then headed for the house.

A young female officer – twenties, hair scraped back, pale – was supervising the cordon and keeping the neighbours away.

Gareth got out his warrant card. He didn't recognise the young officer.

'DI Williams, Beaumaris CID,' he said. 'What have we got, Constable?'

She looked down at her notepad. 'Husband, a Mr Mike Newell, came home from work and found his wife lying unconscious on the living room floor. He rang 999.'

'And you were the first officer at the scene?' Laura asked.

'Yes, ma'am.'

'Where exactly did you find the victim?' Declan asked.

'Lying in the middle of the carpet,' the constable replied.

'Any sign of forced entry?' Gareth enquired.

'No, sir.'

Declan narrowed his eyes. 'Where's Mike now?'

'He's with the FLO in the garden,' the constable explained.

Laura frowned. 'What about their daughter, Zoe?'

The constable shrugged. 'No, sorry. There was no one else at the property when I arrived,' she explained.

Laura frowned and exchanged looks with the others. Was that something they needed to be concerned about? She looked over at Gareth. 'I'll talk to the FLO. See if she knows where Zoe is. I'll also get her number, see if we can reach her on her mobile.'

'Thanks, Laura,' Gareth said. He then turned to the constable. 'If you can start running a scene log, please? And no one comes onto the crime scene without my say-so.'

'Yes, sir.' The constable looked a bit overwhelmed. Laura

didn't blame her. She was young and this might well be the first time she had ever attended a murder scene. Laura remembered it had taken her days to get over her first one.

Laura moved a little closer to her and said under her breath with a kind look, 'It does get easier, I promise you. You're going to be fine.'

The constable nodded as if Laura's words had given her some comfort before pulling up the police tape so Gareth, Declan, Laura and Andrea could enter the house.

At the front door, they showed their warrant cards and a SOCO handed them each a full Tyvek forensic suit. They smelled of chemicals and rustled noisily.

Snapping on her blue latex gloves, Laura looked at Declan. She knew that he and Vicky were very close.

'Declan, do you want to wait outside?' she suggested with a concerned, gentle tone.

Declan stopped in his tracks for a moment, as if he was seriously considering what she had said. Then he shook his head. 'No. It's fine. I want to see her.'

Gareth gestured for them all to go inside and they found several SOCOs dusting surfaces and examining the carpet for forensic evidence. There were already steel stepping plates across the carpets in the hallway leading into the rest of the house.

For a moment, Laura's eyes were drawn up to the studio photographs of the Newell family that adorned the wall up the stairs. It was devastating to think what had happened to them in the past few days. Two of them were no longer alive.

Laura made her way through to the living room and saw a crouched SOCO taking photographs of Vicky Newell's body lying on the floor. Something about the expression that remained on Vicky's face suggested her death had been violent.

Laura nodded to North Wales' chief pathologist, Professor Helen Lane, who was crouched over Vicky's body and using a torch while examining her.

'What have we got, Helen?' Laura asked.

Lane looked up at her. 'Morning, Laura.'

Laura crouched down to look at Vicky. Her skin still had the colouring of life rather than the pale, greyish hue that came several hours after death.

With red marks and small lacerations around Vicky's neck, Laura knew immediately she had been strangled – and she guessed it had been done manually, based on the lack of ligature marks.

Vicky's blue eyes were still open wide, but the pupils had become a clouded void where life no longer existed.

Glancing up, Laura could see Declan's distress as he looked at his childhood friend.

'Sorry,' Declan muttered as he turned away and headed towards the front door. Despite his many years as a CID detective, it was clearly all too much for him.

'Cause of death looks like asphyxiation,' Lane said and then pointed to Vicky's neck. 'And my guess is that she was strangled manually,' she added, confirming Laura's unvoiced assumption.

'Time of death?' Gareth asked.

Lane took a moment to think. 'Maybe an hour or two before her husband says he arrived home. Around two or three p.m., most likely.'

Laura thought about how this unpleasant development changed things. Had Vicky's murder thrown into doubt their theory that Callum had been murdered because he had refused to hand back drugs and money to Stewart Tyler? Or had Vicky somehow become embroiled in that dispute too?

Laura gave Lane a quizzical look. 'Could it be the same killer as our previous victim, Callum Newell?'

Lane shrugged. 'Hard to say with absolute certainty. But given that they are mother and son, and – as far as we know until the postmortem confirms things – killed in exactly the same way, I'd say that the overwhelming evidence is that both murders were carried out by the same person.'

Andrea arrived in the living room. 'Boss, there are signs of a forced entry at the rear of the property. A glass panel in the back door is smashed. Looks like the keys had been left in the door, so that might be how the killer got in.'

Laura nodded. 'Which would rule out Mike Newell?'

'Possibly,' Gareth said thoughtfully. 'Unless he wanted to make it look like someone broke in, in order to cover his tracks.'

'Maybe,' Laura said, but based on what she knew of the man, she didn't know if Mike had the intelligence to think of that.

'When can you do a preliminary PM?' Gareth asked.

'If you want me to fast-track it, Gareth,' Lane said, 'by the end of the day.'

'That would be great. Thanks, Helen,' he replied.

'I'd better go and see how Declan is,' Laura said, still feeling a little worried for her colleague.

Suddenly, there was a terrible screaming from outside.

A woman's voice was wailing, 'NO! NO!'

Moving quickly out of the living room, Laura made her way out of the hallway. As she peered out, she saw Zoe Newell on the driveway struggling with the FLO.

'I want to see her!' Zoe screamed.

'You can't go in there, Zoe,' the FLO said gently, trying to hold her back.

Laura pulled down her mask and approached them just as Zoe pushed the FLO to one side with an aggressive shove and stormed up the drive.

Oh God, this isn't good.

'You can't stop me from seeing her,' Zoe sobbed. 'She's my mum.'

Laura put up her hands in a placating gesture and made eye contact with the teen. 'You can't go in there, Zoe. It's an active crime scene, so we can't let you.'

'I don't care!' Zoe thundered.

Two male uniformed officers were marching towards them but Laura gave them a furtive glance as if to say *I've got this*.

She put her hands on Zoe's shoulders to prevent her from going any further but Zoe just pushed her away and moved as though she was going to carry on towards the house no matter who tried to stop her.

'Zoe, look at me,' Laura said firmly. 'You don't want to see your mum like that. I promise you.'

Zoe stopped in her tracks and looked at her. 'But she's all on her own in there,' Zoe cried. 'I want to be with her.'

'I know. Of course you do,' Laura said, putting a reassuring hand on her shoulder. 'We're going to look after her, okay? And when she's at the hospital later, you can come and be with her for as long as you need to.'

Laura wasn't sure if that was going to be possible – it might have to wait until morning – but she didn't want two burly police officers wrestling Zoe away or having to put her in cuffs.

Zoe blinked and looked at Laura. 'I can go and be with her later?'

'Yes.' Laura nodded with a kind expression. 'Of course you can. And I'll make sure that someone is with her the whole time until you arrive. Okay?'

Zoe's eyes flitted around and then she nodded. 'Yeah.' Then her eyes filled with tears again. 'What happened?'

'I really don't know, Zoe,' Laura explained. 'But we will find out what happened to her and we'll get justice for both her and your brother.'

Zoe nodded slowly but then dissolved into the grief and pain that was overwhelming her.

Laura put her arms around her as she sobbed uncontrollably.

CHAPTER 40

Having changed out of his forensic suit, Gareth looked around for Declan to make sure he was okay. Declan had been close to the Newell family for decades, so it wasn't surprising he had been completely stunned by the events of the past few days. It was all too close to home.

As he scanned the area outside, Gareth tried to piece together what the implications of Vicky's murder were and whether or not they fitted with any of their hypotheses about Callum's death. Were Stewart Tyler or Tom Hegerty involved? Had Vicky become embroiled in the dispute between Callum, Zoe and Tyler? Did she know something that made her a threat to Tyler? A significant part of Gareth doubted that theory because something about it didn't feel quite right. To target Vicky Newell in her home was premeditated.

Similarly, Tyler was a low-level drug dealer so it was a bit of a stretch to believe that he would have deliberately murdered Callum over what was a relatively small amount of drugs and money – but it *was* possible that things had got out of hand during a confrontation in Newborough Forest.

Declan was sitting on the front garden wall, staring down at the ground.

Gareth approached. Even though Declan was his right-hand man in Beaumaris CID, Gareth wasn't sure if it was appropriate to run his theories past him quite yet, not when he was still trying to process Vicky's death.

'Hey,' Gareth said quietly. 'Why don't you go home for a bit, eh?'

Declan looked up. 'No. I want to catch the bastard that did this.'

Gareth sat next to him on the garden wall. SOCOs were scuttling to and from the house with boxes of forensic evidence that were then carefully stashed in the back of a van that had 'POLICE FORENSIC UNIT' printed on its side.

His attention was then drawn to another van that had been let through the cordon and was driving towards the house. It was the dark grey coroner's van that had 'Private Ambulance' on its side. Once the SOCOs had finished, it would take Vicky's body from the house to the hospital for a preliminary postmortem.

'I can't believe she's gone,' Declan said sadly as they looked at the van.

'I'm so sorry,' Gareth said quietly. 'I know how close you were.'

Declan looked at him. 'Vick's parents were killed in a car accident when she was only fourteen. She went to live with her grandparents who were kicking on a bit and I spent a lot of time with her. She talked to me about how she was feeling.'

Gareth gave him an understanding nod. 'Don't worry, we're going to find out who did this to Vicky and Callum. I promise you.'

'You think this is Stewart Tyler?' Declan asked with a frown.

'I don't know,' Gareth admitted. 'Why don't you go back to CID? I don't think it's doing you any good hanging around here, is it?'

Declan nodded in agreement and got up from the wall. 'Thanks, boss. I'll see you back there.'

Gareth watched Declan as he walked away and then realised that he needed to go and speak to Mike Newell, who he assumed was still sitting in the back garden with the FLO.

The sky above had seemingly stretched out into a sheet of dark grey above him, mirroring the mood in the Newells' home. In the near distance, the landscape was decorated with purple heather, the land flat and unyielding – exactly how he needed to approach this next conversation.

Walking down the side passageway of the house, Gareth came out into a neat garden where clothes were hanging from brightly coloured pegs on a small line on the far side.

He spotted Mike sitting at a garden table. He had a cigarette in between his fingers and an open can of Stella in front of him. The FLO was sitting opposite but looked a little lost by the turn of events. Gareth didn't blame her. The FLO had probably got to know Vicky quite well in recent days as she helped her deal with Callum's murder. To now discover that Vicky had been killed too would have shocked most people.

'Mr Newell?' Gareth said quietly as he went over.

'It's Mike,' he mumbled as he reached for the beer and drained the last of it.

'I'm so sorry for your loss,' Gareth said.

Mike fixed him with a confused stare. 'What the hell is going on?' he said, his voice full of emotion as he shook his head in disbelief.

'We're going to find out who did this to Vicky and Callum,' Gareth reassured him, although there was a part of him that still wondered if Mike had anything to do with their deaths. 'Can you tell me what happened?'

Sitting back, Mike took a long drag of his cigarette, looking crestfallen. 'Really? I've been through all this with her,' he said with a groan, pointing to the FLO.

'Can you give us a minute?' he asked her. She probably needed some time to get her head together anyway.

'Of course, sir,' she said as she made herself scarce.

Mike leaned down to the stone patio and pulled another can of Stella out of the pack by his feet.

'Mike,' Gareth said as he leaned forward. 'It would really help me if you could tell me what happened today.'

Mike shrugged and swigged a few gulps from the can. 'I went into work. I haven't been in this week – obviously. I just wanted to get out of the house for a bit anyway. You know?'

Gareth nodded empathetically. He wanted to lull Mike into a false sense of security that he was only talking to him as a witness and not a suspect. They already knew that

Mike was a functioning alcoholic with a short temper and a tendency to bully and even violence.

'What time did you leave this morning?' Gareth asked.

He thought for a second. 'About ten a.m.'

'And who was in the house when you left?'

'Vicky was up,' Mike said. 'I assumed that Zoe was still in bed. Ever since what happened to Callum, she's been in bed a lot.' He blinked and then took another long swig of beer. Gareth needed to get as much information out of him as he could before Mike got completely pissed.

Gareth looked at him with a blank expression, hiding what he really thought of the man. 'And you returned here at what time?' he asked in a routine tone.

'Just after four,' Mike said. 'The four o'clock news had just been on Radio 2.'

'And the front door was locked?' Gareth asked to clarify.

'Yes and no. I used my yale key to get in but the Chubb lock wasn't on.'

Gareth scratched his jaw and looked over at him. 'And you found Vicky on the floor of the living room?'

'Yeah.' Mike nodded slowly as he took another cigarette from the packet and popped it into his mouth. As he took out a lighter, Gareth could see that his hands were shaking enough to make lighting the cigarette difficult. He didn't know if it was from the shock of finding his wife dead or due to the stress of having murdered his wife – there was no way of telling.

'Do you want a hand with that?' Gareth asked.

Mike nodded but looked embarrassed as he handed over the lighter. Gareth clicked it and shielded the flame as Mike lit the cigarette, took a deep drag and then blew out a long plume of smoke.

'And then you rang 999?' Gareth asked.

Mike's expression changed slightly. 'No,' he whispered, 'I went to Vicky to see if she was all right. But she was cold and she wasn't breathing. I tried to see if I could find a pulse on her neck or her wrist but there was nothing.'

Mike then reached up with his hand to wipe away the tears from his eyes as he sniffed. If he was guilty of Vicky's murder, he was doing a very good job of playing the role of the grieving husband.

CHAPTER 41

Laura was sitting on the open back of the ambulance next to Zoe, who was covered in an aluminium blanket and sipping hot, sweet tea. She was still in shock and very shaky.

'Do you want me to hold that?' Laura asked as she noticed that Zoe was trembling so much that her tea was coming over the side of the mug.

'Thank you,' she whispered as she handed it to Laura. She looked like she was in a trance.

For a few seconds, Laura squinted up at the sunshine that was dappling its warmth through the leaves of the beech tree that loomed above them. Normally, she would have enjoyed the feeling, but it just didn't feel appropriate, given the events of the day.

Laura had spent the last ten minutes trying to establish where Zoe had been while taking into account her very fragile state. Zoe said she had popped out when her mother had told her that they'd run out of milk, bread and a couple of other things. While at the supermarket, Zoe had run into an old friend and they had grabbed a coffee at the Beaumaris Tea Rooms, which was just next door.

Laura took a breath and looked at Zoe. She needed to get details from her as quickly as possible.

'Can you remember what time you left to go to the shop?' she asked very gently.

Zoe didn't respond for a second or two. She was lost in her trauma and grief.

'Zoe?'

She blinked and looked at her. 'Sorry, did you say something?'

'Can you remember what time you left to go to the shop?'

'Erm… just before one, I think,' Zoe said, her voice still shaky.

Laura gave her a sympathetic look. 'I am going to need your friend's name and number at some point.'

'Of course.' Zoe nodded as she reached for her tea and Laura handed it back to her.

'We've spoken to both Stewart Tyler and Tom Hegerty,' Laura said softly.

'Tom?' Zoe asked with a frown.

'It's okay, Zoe. We know that you and Tom have some kind of a relationship.'

'No, we don't,' Zoe protested a bit too adamantly.

'Come on, Zoe.' Laura gave her a look. 'You don't need to lie about this.'

Zoe looked down with a shrug. She'd been caught out.

'How long have you and Tom been seeing each other?' Laura asked.

'A few months.'

'Is it serious?'

'Sort of,' Zoe admitted.

Laura looked at her with a grave expression. 'We know that you and Tom were doing some very minor dealing for Stewart Tyler. Is there any reason you can think of that he or Tom would harm your mum?'

'No.' Zoe looked confused. 'Tom's not like that,' she said defensively.

'What about Stewart Tyler?'

'I don't know.' Zoe thought for a few seconds. 'Maybe. He's a bloody psycho and everyone's scared of him. But I can't think of any reason why he'd want to hurt Mum.' Zoe shook her head as the enormity of what had happened seemed to overwhelm her. 'What am I going to do?' she sobbed.

Laura put a reassuring hand on her shoulder. 'I'm so sorry, Zoe... You and your dad are going to need a lot of help and support in the next few weeks.'

'My dad?' Zoe asked with a look of utter disgust. 'You're joking, aren't you?'

Laura frowned. 'Your dad has lost his wife and son,' she pointed out as kindly as she could.

'He doesn't care.' Zoe looked at her and shook her head. 'He never cared about any of us. He's a nasty, violent, drunken wanker.'

'There must have been some good times,' Laura offered.

'No, there weren't.' Zoe fixed her with an emphatic stare. 'He's vile. And he's going to have to live with the fact that his wife and son hated him. Especially after this morning.'

Laura gave her a quizzical look. 'What happened this morning?'

'The usual shit,' Zoe said with a shrug. 'Mum and Dad rowing. Slamming doors.'

'Did you hear what they were rowing about?' Laura asked, her interest piqued. Could this have had anything to do with what happened to Vicky?

'Dad was accusing Mum of having an affair. But that's par for the course,' Zoe explained. 'He's paranoid.'

Laura frowned. 'I'm sorry to ask, but *was* she having an affair?'

Zoe took a moment to respond. 'No. No, she wasn't.'

Something in Zoe's response suggested she wasn't telling the truth.

'Are you sure about that?' Laura asked delicately.

Zoe put her head in her hands. 'I just don't want to talk about that.'

Laura knew that it wasn't the time to pursue this any further. However, if Vicky Newell was having an affair with someone, who was it? And if Mike suspected, did that mean he might have killed her out of jealousy?

CHAPTER 42

It was an hour later and those CID officers who weren't involved in the door-to-door enquiries in the houses adjacent to the Newells' home had just arrived back into the CID office.

Gareth was in his office taking a few moments to digest the terrible news about Vicky Newell, while trying to remain fully focused on running the investigation. He blew out his cheeks with an audible sigh.

Come on, Gareth, you got this, he said to himself.

His eyes rested on the photograph of his brother, Rob, standing with his wife, Aleida, and their children, Charlie and Fran. They were high up a mountain of some kind, the Hong Kong skyline stretched out behind them.

It was in moments like this that Gareth wondered if he would trade in everything in his own life for Rob's six-figure salary, the penthouse overlooking Hong Kong harbour, the wife, the kids. He didn't know. Or at least, he didn't want to admit that maybe he would… It was all very well claiming to have the satisfaction of being a serving police officer and helping others in their darkest moments, but there were also moments when Gareth longed for an easier, softer and more selfish existence. Did that make him a bad person? He didn't know, and he didn't want to pull at that thread too hard.

Taking a deep breath, Gareth loosened his tie, got up out of his chair and marched out towards the scene boards, which had now been updated to include the information they had so far on Vicky's murder.

For a moment, he looked over at Vicky's photo, which now sat central to a new scene board. She was smiling at the camera, cocktail in hand. A beaming beautiful smile of happiness.

Jesus, what the hell happened to you and your son? he wondered.

Scribbled in black pen to the right of the photo were the bare facts. A person's life narrowed down to a couple of stark details.

Vicky Mary Newell – D.O.B. 12 May 1976
Cause of death – asphyxiation?

'Right,' Gareth said with new resolve as he turned to look at the detectives in the room. Looking at Vicky's photo had not only made him feel a little sad, but also determined to get her justice. 'From the evidence we have so far, Mike is our prime suspect here. He is the one who found Vicky, or so he claims. We also know from Zoe that he and Vicky rowed this morning. Let's comb through the statements from the door-to-door as soon as they're in. Maybe one of the neighbours saw Mike leaving or returning to the house.'

He looked at Laura. 'How did Zoe respond when you asked her if Vicky was having an affair?'

'She denied it,' Laura replied, 'but she was definitely hiding something.'

'Vicky wasn't having an affair,' Declan said quietly.

'How do you know that?' Gareth asked tactfully.

'She told me everything. And I mean everything,' Declan said sadly. 'She was like a sister to me. And she would have told me if there was someone else.'

Gareth wasn't sure that was necessarily true. Would someone like Vicky confide in a male friend like Declan that she was cheating on her husband?

'Okay,' Gareth said, deciding it was best to move on for now. Tyler had been released on bail, pending an appearance at a magistrate's court the following day. 'We also need to go and find Stewart Tyler and Tom Hegerty. Find out where they were this afternoon. If we think they could have been involved in Callum's murder, then from what the PM and the pathologist have said, one of them could also have been responsible for Vicky Newell's murder.'

Gareth looked out at the assembled CID team. He could sense the palpable sense of shock that two members of the same family had been murdered within days of each other. Both Vicky and Callum had been part of Declan's life, too, which made it feel more personal than most crimes.

Declan grabbed his jacket. His shock seemed to have been replaced by an intense focus. 'I'll go now.'

Gareth could see Declan was fired up. 'I think it's best you stay here, Dec. No offence, but this investigation is very close to home and understandably incredibly difficult for you. If Tyler or Hegerty say anything that implicates them in the murders, I want it to be to an officer that's less personally involved.'

'Fine.' Declan nodded and sat down reluctantly.

Andrea frowned. 'What's the motive for Tyler or Hegerty to attack Vicky Newell? I can't see the connection, boss.'

'I don't know yet,' Gareth admitted. 'But there is a very clear motive for Callum to be targeted. And given that Vicky was his mum, we have to think they're involved somehow.'

'Maybe Vicky found out that Zoe was dealing with Tom for Tyler?' Laura suggested.

'She didn't know anything about the money we found hidden under Callum's bed,' Gareth said, thinking out loud.

Laura shrugged. 'She could have been covering for Zoe.'

'Even though Callum was missing at that point?' Ben pointed out.

Declan sat forward on his chair. 'Who else has motive to kill them both? We know that Callum's murder is likely to be connected to Tyler and Hegerty. We just have to find out why they might then target Vicky,' he insisted.

Gareth thought for a few seconds. 'Okay, let's go back to basics. We focus less on the why and concentrate on getting every piece of evidence we can lay our hands on. Ben, can you talk to Traffic? Pull up any CCTV or ANPR cameras on the roads around the Newells' home.' He then looked over at Andrea. 'Anything come in from forensics yet?'

Andrea pointed to the phone on her desk. 'Just had a call, boss. They've managed somehow to get trace DNA from the speck of blood on Callum's teeth. They should be able to analyse that, and then run it through the database.'

Declan frowned. 'Why are they so sure that that blood isn't Callum's?'

'Professor Lane found no signs of cuts or wounds inside Callum's mouth,' Laura explained. 'Plus the blood was focused just on the jagged part of his tooth, which is why she thinks it came from Callum's biting his attacker.'

Declan nodded but didn't seem convinced.

'We've got both Tyler and Hegerty's DNA on the national database now, haven't we?' Gareth asked to confirm.

'Yes, boss,' Andrea replied with a nod. 'Hegerty's DNA was done as part of the elimination sample at the weekend. And Tyler's DNA is on there from his prior arrests and convictions.'

'Good,' Gareth said. Getting the DNA could be the breakthrough they needed. 'Obviously there's going to be a delay in getting any forensics from the latest crime scene.' He looked over at Ben. 'Anything on that phone number we found on Callum's call history?'

'Definitely a burner phone, boss,' Ben explained. 'I've checked the serial number and it was bought at the Tesco's in town. At the moment, we don't know when, but they're going to run the serial number through their records to see if the customer paid with a debit card or credit card. If they were smart enough to pay cash, then there won't be any record.'

'Okay, fair enough,' Gareth said.

'I've tried to call the burner phone number and it's still switched on and ringing,' Ben explained. 'I can see if Digital Forensics can get a trace on its location.'

'Yes, that would be good,' Gareth said. 'And maybe next

time you ring that number, record the call just in case the owner makes a mistake and answers it. The voice might give us a clue as to who it belongs to.'

'Yes, boss.'

The phone rang on a nearby desk and Andrea answered it.

'Something else, boss,' Ben continued with a serious expression. 'Digital Forensics are also looking at Vicky's phone. They've sent me a preliminary list of all the numbers Vicky called and received calls from in the past week.'

'And?' Gareth prompted him.

'That burner phone number called Vicky's phone nine times in the last week,' Ben explained.

'Okay, let's keep on at the supermarket to check their records as a matter of urgency.'

If both victims had received multiple calls in the lead-up to their murders, then finding the owner of the phone was a key step to discovering who their killer was.

'Laura and Andrea,' Gareth said, changing tack. 'Can you go over to the mortuary and see what Professor Lane has found on the preliminary PM? Then go and question Tyler about his whereabouts this afternoon. Bring him in if he's evasive.'

Andrea nodded. 'Boss.'

'Ben, any news about the CCTV from that off-licence that's opposite The Red Lion? We asked for it two days ago,' Gareth said.

Ben signalled to his computer and nodded. 'It came in about an hour ago and I've been trawling through it.'

'Anything interesting?' Gareth asked.

'Yes,' Ben replied. 'I'll show you.'

Gareth walked over to view the CCTV footage on Ben's computer monitor.

As Ben clicked a button to play the footage, Gareth noted the time and date code in the bottom right-hand of the screen. 'Okay, so this is the footage from twelve p.m. on Saturday. As you can see, Mike Newell arrives and goes into The Red Lion.' Gareth watched the figure get out of a car, come along the pavement and go inside the pub. It was clearly Mike.

'So, Newell wasn't lying to us,' Gareth said. 'And he has an alibi for the time of Callum's murder?'

'No,' Ben said, shaking his head as he pulled up another CCTV clip. 'Because at one p.m., this happens.'

Gareth peered at the screen. At precisely 13.00, Mike Newell comes out of the pub with a mobile phone to his ear, walks over to his car, gets in and drives away.

'So, he was lying to us,' Gareth said. 'Let's get a full ANPR and Traffic check on Mike Newell's car for the whole of last Saturday.'

'I've already requested it, boss,' Ben said. 'Should be here in an hour or two.'

'Good work, Ben,' Gareth said as he looked at the screen again. 'Where the hell was he going at one p.m.?'

Ben gave Gareth a dark look. 'Newborough Forest?' he suggested.

CHAPTER 43

Laura and Andrea pushed the button to get the lift to the basement of Glan Clwyd Hospital, where the mortuary was located.

As they waited for the lift to arrive, Laura noticed Andrea's slight apprehension. It wasn't the first time she'd noticed it.

'I take it you're not a fan of lifts then?' Laura remarked.

'That obvious, is it?' Andrea shrugged, looking a little embarrassed. 'Feels a bit stupid, given that we've just been to a murder scene.'

'Not at all,' Laura said. 'My mother had terrible claustrophobia. Lifts, enclosed spaces, flying… She even insisted on getting an aisle seat if we ever went to the cinema or the theatre.'

'Yeah, I'm a bit like that as well,' Andrea admitted.

The lift arrived and the metallic doors opened with a clunk.

'We can get the stairs down, if you want?' Laura suggested.

'No, it's fine. It's only one floor,' Andrea said, getting in. 'I went to London a few months ago and we got the lift up the Shard to the viewing deck on the seventy-second floor. That took ages so I didn't really enjoy that much.'

There was a beat as the lift doors closed.

Andrea turned to Laura with a frown. 'Do you think that someone is targeting the whole Newell family for some reason that we haven't even thought of yet?'

'Possibly,' Laura admitted. She hadn't yet managed to fully process what had happened to Vicky and how it might be linked to Callum. 'Let's see what the PM gives us for starters.'

The lift arrived at the basement and they got out and marched across the smooth flooring of the corridor. A few seconds later, they came through the double doors into the hospital morgue. Laura got an instant hit of the artificial, acrid smell of preservatives that were always thick in the air here.

Spotting Lovell on the other side of the morgue, Laura and Andrea weaved their way through the stainless steel covered boards that were tilted at an angle with drains on either end, then the gurneys for lifting bodies and the workbenches.

Lovell was standing over the body of Vicky Newell. He pulled down his surgical mask when he saw them.

'This is a first for me,' he said sadly. 'Don't think I've ever had to look at a parent and child who have been murdered within days of each other. I can't imagine how the rest of the family are coping.'

Laura looked at him. It was strange to hear a pathologist

make such an emotive comment. Usually, they were incredibly reserved and clinical in their work.

'They're being supported, but obviously they're devastated,' she acknowledged.

'Anything you can tell us at this stage would be great,' Andrea said.

'I'm afraid I've only had her here for twenty minutes,' Lovell admitted.

'That's fine,' Laura said. 'We're just looking for the headline notes to start with.'

Lovell reached up, took the spotlight and put it over Vicky's head. He then pointed to the bruising around the neck, which was now more pronounced than it had been at the crime scene.

'Cause of death is identical to that of her son,' Lovell explained. 'Asphyxiation due to manual strangulation.' He then pointed to a lightbox on the wall. 'If you come over here, there's something important I need to show you.'

Laura and Andrea exchanged a look and followed Lovell over to the lightbox where two photographs had been illuminated.

Both images showed a human neck with bruising patterns around the throat.

'So, this is your female victim here on the left,' Lovell said, pointing to the image. 'And this here, is her son's injuries to his neck.'

Laura frowned. 'They look similar.'

'They're not similar.' Lovell shook his head. 'No, they're *identical*. I've measured the circumference of these bruises from the fingers and they match exactly. So, if you were in any doubt, I can now confirm that the same person killed them both.'

'Okay,' Laura said. It was a relief to have that confirmed. 'That's very helpful.'

'And there's something else,' Lovell stated, looking at them as he gestured to the body. 'Your victim had sexual intercourse just before she was killed.'

Andrea looked confused. 'She was raped?'

'No,' Lovell replied. 'There are no bruises to suggest that the sex was anything but consensual.' Lovell looked at them. 'From what I can see, it happened no more than an hour before she was murdered.'

CHAPTER 44

It was just after seven p.m. by the time Laura and Andrea walked into The Red Lion pub in search of Stewart Tyler. The pub was dank, cheap-looking and smelled of stale beer and bargain bar food. An old man stood over by the fruit machine with his weary dog sitting at his feet.

There were loud cheers and laughter from a group of men at a corner table. There were about a dozen of them and they ranged from twenties to forties. Dressed smartly in shirts, trousers and lace-up shoes, Laura guessed they were just off work.

Becoming aware of the detectives' presence, a few of the men looked over.

'Oi oi, here come the strippers,' a man with a shaved head shouted and they all dissolved into laughter.

'Bloody hell,' another said. 'I'm not paying for those two slags to take off their clothes.'

Laura could see Andrea bristling with anger.

'Just leave it,' Laura said to her under her breath. 'They want to get a reaction.'

Heading for the bar, Laura spotted Stewart Tyler chatting to one of the men from the group at the far side of the bar.

Laura and Andrea got out their warrant cards and showed them, much to the amusement of some of the men. Others looked a little more concerned that the women they'd verbally abused were police officers.

Tyler turned towards them and his face twisted in anger.

'Are you fucking joking me?' Tyler sneered at them. 'You've only just let me out. What do you want now?'

'Can you tell us where you were this afternoon?' Laura asked calmly.

'What's it to you?' Tyler said as his nostrils flared and his whole body tensed. He looked like he was going to hit one of them.

Christ, he's a right piece of work, Laura thought.

Andrea fixed him with an icy stare. 'Just answer the question.'

Tyler looked at Laura. 'Oh it talks, does it?' Then he looked at Andrea, moving his eyes up and down to give her the once-over. 'Let anyone in the police these days, don't they?'

Laura assumed that Tyler was referring to the fact that Andrea was mixed race. Taking a breath to calm herself, Laura wasn't going to let Tyler see that he had got to her in any way.

'Vicky Newell was found murdered this afternoon,' Laura explained calmly. 'So, either you tell us where you were between one and four p.m., or I'm going to cuff you and take you back to Beaumaris nick for a little chat.'

There were comments and laughter from the group of men.

Tyler made eye contact with Laura, giving her an icy stare. 'I was in here. I've been here since I opened up at 10.30 a.m.'

'Can you prove that?' Andrea asked, unable to disguise the contempt on her face.

Tyler smirked and looked at Andrea. 'Can you prove I wasn't?'

Andrea raised an eyebrow. 'I don't need to.' She took the cuffs from her belt. 'You're going to need to come with me.'

Tyler gestured to the men sitting at the table. 'The lads will tell you. I've been in here with them all afternoon.'

The man with the shaved head looked over. 'Yeah, why don't you leave him alone and go and nick some real criminals, darling?'

Laura gave him an amused look. 'He was in here with all of you all afternoon?' she asked with more than a hint of suspicion.

'Yeah, he was,' said another man.

There were general nods and mumbles to back up Tyler's alibi.

The man with the shaved head got up, holding out his phone as he walked towards them. 'Here you go, copper,' he said in a disparaging tone. 'Here's a photograph of us sitting here with Stu. And I posted it online at two p.m. this afternoon.' He grinned at her. 'That proof enough for you?'

Shit!

Laura didn't respond for a few seconds as some of the men laughed.

'Yes,' Laura said with a forced smile. 'That's very helpful. Thank you.'

She walked over to the table where the men were sitting. A few minutes earlier, she had spotted that not only was the table covered in empty pint glasses, mobile phones and wallets, there were also at least five sets of car keys.

Laura smiled and gestured to the table. 'I hope none of you are going to be driving today if you've been drinking?'

'Of course not,' the man who'd elected himself group spokesperson said sarcastically.

Some of the others shared knowing grins as they mockingly shook their heads.

'Glad to hear it,' Laura replied with an exaggerated smile. 'Because I'm going to station a patrol car out in the car park here. And if any of you try to drive, I'm going to have one of my officers breathalyse you. Have a nice evening, lads.'

Laura could see the reaction of some of the men who clearly had been planning on driving.

'For fuck's sake,' one of them muttered angrily.

She turned on her heels and headed for the doors with Andrea.

'Nice one, boss,' Andrea said under her breath.

'Well, hopefully that will put a dampener on their day,' Laura said as she opened the doors and they went outside. 'It does mean that Tyler couldn't have murdered Vicky though. And that rules him out of Callum's murder too, if we trust Lovell's analysis – which we obviously do.'

Laura glanced at Andrea and they shared a look of frustration.

CHAPTER 45

Osian cycled up to the stone steps that led to St Mary's Church in Beaumaris, then leaned his bike against the dark red brick wall that encircled the perimeter of the church grounds and the graveyard.

Having heard the news about Callum's mum, Osian needed to get out of the house. How could both Callum and his mum have been murdered? It didn't make any sense. Who would do a thing like that? Even though he didn't like Zoe much – she was beautiful, but seemed a bit patronising and up herself – he couldn't help but feel bad for her. He couldn't imagine what she was going through. He wondered if Callum's dad, Mike, was somehow involved. He seemed like a man who was on the verge of exploding in anger at any moment. But why would he want to kill his own son and wife?

Entering the graveyard, Osian looked for Ethan. They had messaged each other as soon as the news broke that Vicky had been killed. It wasn't until they'd already agreed to meet up that Ethan had mentioned that he was with

Tom, which made Osian feel a little uncomfortable, given what he'd seen and the conversation he'd had with his dad. However, he'd known both Ethan and Tom all his life and they were the only ones that knew how he was feeling.

Making his way through the graves, his feet crunched noisily on the twisting gravel pathway. Dark green moss and lichens covered many of the older gravestones that flanked the path and he noticed how the headstones were all different shapes and sizes. The lettering on them had been worn away by the wind, rain and time itself, so that many were now illegible under their thick layers of moss.

Up ahead was a huge, towering monument of a tomb that resembled an altar, with deep indentations marking out rows of names. Its granite face was carved into grooves with seaweed-like tuffs of lichen creeping outwards from the seams. Huge flowers wrapped around the base like climbing vines and extended upwards towards the sky. Stepping closer, he saw battery-powered candles had been placed at its base.

'Took your time, la,' said a voice.

He turned to see Tom.

'Hi, Tom,' Osian said, trying to put his discomfort to one side.

Ethan appeared and gave a wave.

'I've been with this loser all day,' Tom joked.

Osian forced a smile. 'What have you been doing?'

'Not much.' Ethan shrugged. 'Just watching Sidemen prank videos on YouTube.'

'To be honest, I can't concentrate on anything at the moment,' Tom admitted.

Osian gave them a dark look. 'I can't believe what's happened to Vicky, can you?'

They both shook their heads sadly.

'Do you think someone is trying to kill everyone in their family or something?' Ethan asked.

Tom gave him a playful punch on the shoulder. 'Don't be a twat, Ethan.'

'Sorry.' Ethan looked embarrassed. 'I just don't understand, that's all.'

Osian looked at him. 'I don't think anyone understands it, mate.'

They all sat down on the stone steps that led from one part of the graveyard to another.

Tom picked up some gravel and started to lob individual stones into a drain cover.

Osian heard the sound of footsteps on the path.

They all turned to see two figures approaching.

It was his dad and Gareth. Given that there was a killer on the loose, his dad had insisted that Osian text him wherever he went, so he'd texted him to say he was meeting Ethan and Tom.

Osian had no idea they were going to turn up and felt a little embarrassed.

'For fuck's sake,' Tom muttered. He glared at Osian. 'Did you tell them we were here?'

Osian scowled back at him. 'I didn't know they were going to turn up, did I?'

'All right, lads?' Declan said. 'I assume you've heard the terrible news about Callum's mum?'

They all nodded with serious expressions.

'How are you doing, Tom?' Gareth asked.

'Fine,' Tom answered defensively.

'Can you tell me where you were this afternoon?' Gareth said. 'About two, three o'clock?'

'Why?' Tom growled and then frowned. 'I didn't have anything to do with what happened to Callum's mum.'

'Just answer the bloody question, Tom,' Declan snapped angrily.

'He was at my house,' Ethan explained timidly.

'Tom was at your house this afternoon?' Gareth said with more than a hint of scepticism.

'I stayed over last night, actually,' Tom said with a sneer. 'We were up playing Call of Duty until about three a.m. So, we were both asleep until mid-afternoon.'

Gareth frowned. 'Can anyone verify that?'

'He can,' Tom said, pointing to Ethan.

'Ethan?' Gareth asked with a serious tone.

Ethan nodded. 'He was at my house, Mr Williams.'

Declan raised an eyebrow. 'Anyone else in the house this afternoon that can vouch for the fact that Tom was there?'

'His mum made us a late lunch,' Tom replied.

Declan looked at Ethan. 'And she'll verify that, will she, Ethan?'

Ethan nodded but looked scared.

'Right, lads,' Gareth said. 'We'll be on our way. But you've been through a lot. All of you have. So, if you need anything, me and Osian's dad are here.'

Ethan nodded. 'Thanks, Mr Williams.'

Osian watched as his dad and Gareth walked away and

disappeared around the corner of the church. He looked over and saw that Tom was staring at him.

'Come on, Ethan,' Tom said, tapping Ethan's shoulder. 'Let's get out of here, eh?'

Ethan looked awkward but nodded as they got up.

'See ya, Osian,' Ethan mumbled as he and Tom walked the other way back through the graveyard.

Picking up some gravel, Osian could feel the confusion, anger and rejection welling inside him. He launched the handful at a nearby gravestone and watched the stones bounce off and fall into the grass.

CHAPTER 46

It was seven a.m. the next morning. Standing in the canteen, Laura took the two coffees from under the machine, put lids on them and looked around. She needed some kind of chocolate or biscuit. She was aware of all the stuff she'd read about sugar, slow-release carbs and how she should really eat some fruit. But she thought, *Fuck that. I want a coffee and a chocolate brownie. I'm hardly a bloody smack addict, am I?*

Andrea approached and Laura handed her the black Americano. 'Here you go.'

'Ta. How much do I owe you, boss?' she asked.

'On me,' Laura replied with a smile and then gestured to an array of biscuits and chocolate bars. 'I'm getting a brownie. Do you want one?'

'Sounds good to me,' Andrea said brightly.

'What's going on?' Laura asked, sensing that Andrea had something to tell her.

'Tom Hegerty has a watertight alibi for the time of Vicky Newell's murder,' she replied. 'Ethan's parents have confirmed that he was at their house all day yesterday.'

'Bollocks,' Laura sighed as she moved towards the till and paid for the coffees and brownies. 'That's both our prime suspects for Callum's murder with alibis for yesterday.'

Andrea frowned. 'I was convinced it was Tyler. Who else has motive to kill them both?'

'Mike Newell?' Laura suggested, thinking out loud.

'You think he had sex with her and then killed her?' Andrea asked.

Laura took a few seconds to respond. 'I just don't know. From what we know, Mike and Vicky weren't exactly a happily married couple.'

Laura's phone buzzed and she saw it was a text from Pete. Her stomach tightened.

'I'll catch you up,' Laura said to Andrea, indicating that she needed to look at her phone and she would see her in CID.

As Andrea left the canteen, Laura opened the text message.

Hiya. How are you doing? Kids okay? Just wondering if you've ever come across a woman called Claudia Wright?

Also, there's a couple of things that I've discovered that I need to update you on. I'd prefer to do it face to face. I know you're in the middle of this case, but I'm happy to come over, even if it's for a coffee, cake and a chat. My treat!

Let me know how you're fixed.

Love, as always, Pete xx

Laura felt her stomach tighten with nerves. How had Pete managed to get hold of Claudia's name? Did he know that Claudia was digging around into what had been going on at the MMP? Surely she would have been careful enough not to alert officers of the story she was investigating. And why did Pete want to come over to talk to her in person? It made Laura feel incredibly uneasy.

She took her phone and texted Pete back.

Hiya, all good here. Same old, same old. Who's Claudia Wright? Never heard of her.

We've now got two murders here so things are pretty crazy. I'll text you in the next few weeks with a time we can meet.

Cake? Sounds good to me.

Love, Laura xx

Taking a deep breath, Laura knew that she needed to alert Claudia that Pete might be on to her. It made her nervous to think that the investigation might have been flagged up already. Was it possible that what Claudia was doing could be linked back to her?

Resolving to put it to the back of her mind until she had a free moment to reach out to Claudia, Laura swigged her coffee and headed out of the canteen.

Wandering along the corridor, she passed through reception and saw the duty sergeant, Alan Symes, give her a wave.

'DI Hart,' he called over.

Laura liked Symes. He was in his sixties and was a proper

'old school' copper. If you wanted to know anything that was going on in Beaumaris nick, you just needed to ask him.

'Morning, Alan,' Laura said with a kind smile as she went over.

Symes smiled at her. 'Ah, you've bought me a chocolate brownie for my breakfast. Very kind,' he joked.

Laura laughed as she gestured to her coffee and brownie. 'I'm surviving on a strict diet of caffeine and sugar at the moment.'

Symes raised an eyebrow knowingly. 'Yeah, sounds like it's all hands to the pumps up there in CID.'

'How can I help?' Laura asked, wondering why Symes had called her over.

'A woman came in about twenty minutes ago,' he said as he looked down at his notes. 'A Mrs Higgs. She says she lives opposite Vicky Newell's house but she was out when officers were doing the door-to-door. She claims that she saw something yesterday afternoon around the time of the murder, so I've put her in Interview Room 3.'

CHAPTER 47

Anne Higgs was in her sixties and wore a bright blue twinset over grey slacks. The soft colour of her ensemble framed the subtly dyed blonde-grey hair that fell to just below her ears. Round-faced and smiling, she wore her years well and looked like an elderly Audrey Hepburn. Her make-up was tasteful and understated, nicely complementing her pearl earrings and pendant on a silver chain.

Gareth and Laura sat opposite her in Interview Room 3.

'Thank you so much for coming in to talk to us, Mrs Higgs,' Laura said with a kind smile.

'Oh, it's Anne, please,' she replied, shaking her head. 'The only person who calls me Mrs Higgs these days is my doctor. And he's about twelve.'

Gareth smiled, took out his pen and looked over at her. 'And you live in the house directly opposite the Newells' home?'

'That's right,' she said. 'Number 54. My husband and I moved in in 1972.'

'And did your husband come in with you this morning?' Gareth enquired.

'No, he passed away five years ago, dear,' Anne explained. 'Dementia. Horrible disease. Cruel.'

'I'm sorry to hear that,' Gareth said with an empathetic expression.

'I just can't believe what's happened to Vicky,' Anne said with a bewildered look. 'After what happened to poor Callum too.'

'Were you close to the Newell family?' Laura asked.

'Not really,' Anne admitted. 'We were just good neighbours. You know, wave to each other. Have a quick chat. That sort of thing.'

'And you said you were out when our officers knocked on the door?' Gareth asked.

'That's right,' Anne said with a nod. 'I couldn't believe what was going on by the time I came home from the supermarket. Police cars everywhere. And then Henry from next door told me that he thought Vicky had been attacked and killed. When I saw the BBC news talking about it last night I thought I'd better come and see you.'

'Can you tell us what you saw?' Gareth asked.

'I was just getting ready to go out around two p.m.,' Anne explained. 'And I looked out of my kitchen window, which looks across the road, and saw a man standing on their driveway.'

'On the Newells' driveway?' Gareth said to clarify.

'Yes,' Anne replied. 'He looked a bit confused, so I went out and asked him if he was looking for someone.'

Laura shifted forward on her seat. This sounded significant. 'And how was this man acting?'

'I don't know,' Anne said. 'A bit shifty, if I'm honest.'

Gareth ran his hand over his scalp and frowned. 'Did the man seem like he'd been inside the house?'

'I don't think so,' Anne stated. 'But I can't be sure.'

'Could you tell us what happened then?' Laura said.

'Well, I asked him if he was looking for someone,' Anne said. 'He said that he'd come to see Vicky. I noticed that both the cars were missing from the drive so I told him that maybe they were out. But I did offer to tell her that he'd called round if he gave me his name.'

Gareth frowned. 'Okay. And what did he say to that?'

'He said that it didn't matter, or was it that it wasn't important?' Anne replied. 'I think he said that he'd drop back later, but he was mumbling by that point. He seemed to be in a rush to get away.'

'And then he left?' Laura said.

'That's right,' Anne said. 'He walked off quickly, heading down to the main road.'

'Did you see if he got into a car?'

'I'm sorry, I didn't.' Anne shook her head. 'I was going out shopping so I went back inside to get my bag.'

Gareth stopped writing and glanced over. 'Can you describe this man for us?'

'Oh yes,' Anne said, raising an eyebrow. 'He was unusual looking. Hair in a ponytail and a big beard. And he was wearing a kind of smock. He looked like a hippy – you know, the ones you see in the films from the sixties.'

Gareth shot a look at Laura.

Anne had just described David Coren.

* * *

Half an hour later, Gareth and Laura were driving along the coast out towards Lon Capel and David Coren's home. Laura buzzed down the window and surveyed the beach. Apart from a man throwing a stick for his black Labrador, it was completely deserted.

'There's something I've been wanting to talk to you about,' Gareth said hesitantly.

'Oh God,' Laura said, rolling her eyes. 'Have you found another eccentric place for us to get married?'

'No,' Gareth laughed and then looked offended. 'Cribinau is not eccentric. It's romantic.'

'If you're Jacques Cousteau,' Laura joked. 'What is it?'

'I'm just trying to get my head around all the stuff you told me the other morning,' Gareth admitted. 'What did the OCG have over Louise McDonald that would force her to do all that?'

'They had photos of her snorting cocaine and in a threesome,' Laura explained.

'Jesus,' Gareth sighed. 'And you think Pete might have killed her?'

'I think he organised it,' Laura replied. 'This car came out of nowhere and ran her over. A hit-and-run. No one knew she was there except me and Pete.'

'Right...' Gareth said, clearly trying to process what she was telling him.

'I also think that Pete might know that I've been talking to a journalist,' she admitted.

297

'Jessu, Laura.' Gareth shook his head. 'Just tread carefully, okay?'

Laura nodded. It was still so hard to think that Pete had anything to do with Louise's death or Sam's murder.

Over in the distance, she took in the view of Bangor on the Welsh mainland. The rays of sunlight reflected off the buildings. When she was younger, Laura had always dreamed of living in Bangor. To her, it had been the exciting, slightly mysterious city on the other side of the Menai Bridge. It had a university, a cathedral and the huge Victorian Garth pier. Once she moved to Manchester, Bangor seemed somewhat parochial in comparison.

After a few minutes of comfortable silence, Gareth said, 'If we've ruled out Tyler and Hegerty, then maybe the whole drug thing has been a red herring all along.'

It broke Laura's train of thought. She closed the window as she tried to take in what Gareth had said and get her head back into DI mode. 'Looks that way,' she said after a few seconds. 'There's no doubt that Tyler was set on doing Callum harm. It's just that someone else got to him first. Are we going back to thinking that David Coren is our prime suspect?'

'The explanation about having Callum's mobile phone has always seemed flimsy,' Gareth stated. 'And by his own admission he was definitely on Newborough Beach on Saturday afternoon. He also had a questionable relationship with Callum, and was spotted leaving the Newells' home around the time of Vicky's murder.'

Laura raised an eyebrow. 'You've given him means and opportunity. But we don't have a motive.'

'Do you think that Zoe was lying about her mother having an affair?'

'She was definitely covering up something,' Laura replied.

'Despite what Declan says, I don't think Vicky would have confided in him that she was cheating on Mike.'

Laura raised an eyebrow. 'So if you think she definitely was having an affair, who do you think she was having it with?'

'Maybe she was having an affair with David Coren. Think about it: Callum finds out and threatens to tell his father, so Coren goes to confront him on Saturday but things get out of hand and he ends up killing him,' Gareth explained, thinking out loud. 'Vicky suspects that Coren is somehow mixed up in Callum's death, so Coren goes to talk to her. They have sex but afterwards she confronts him with her suspicions and he kills her too.'

Laura nodded. 'Okay. That does sound plausible,' she admitted as they turned left and headed up the road towards David Coren's house. 'I'm not convinced that Callum would threaten to tell his dad anything though.'

'True,' Gareth said. 'Let's see what we can get out of Coren for starters.'

Laura peered out at the uniform houses that belonged to The Fair Men community. The hanging sculptures. A wrought-iron 'Tree Of Life' that swung in the breeze. The window blinds were all closed.

'This place gives me the creeps,' Laura said quietly.

A white-bearded old man wearing a straw hat, waistcoat and white shirt shuffled along with the help of a cane. He looked up at them as they passed but wore a completely blank expression.

'You think they're all in on it?' Gareth asked.

'All covering for Coren, you mean?' Laura asked to clarify.

'Yeah,' Gareth replied. 'I don't know much about The Fair Men, but if it's some kind of cult, and Coren is their leader, it stands to reason that they'll protect him.'

'It's like that film where they're all pagan, live on a Scottish island and believe in human sacrifice,' Laura said.

'*The Wicker Man*?' Gareth asked.

'That's the one,' Laura said.

Gareth gave her a dark but amused look. 'We'd better be careful because in that one they end up burning the detective from the mainland to death.'

'Great,' Laura said sardonically as they parked up outside Coren's house.

Getting out, Laura could hear the eerie twinkling of wind chimes and the screech of gulls above.

They walked up the garden path. To the right was a large wooden sculpture of a man's head. He was wearing a hood and in place of his mouth was a huge hole that gave the impression that he was screaming.

What a charming little statue, she thought sardonically.

Gareth knocked at the door.

Silence.

Laura went across to peer through the downstairs window but the blinds had been shut and she couldn't see anything. However, she could hear strange folk music from inside.

'Someone's definitely in,' she said, looking over at Gareth.

The door opened and Coren looked out at them. For some reason, it was as if he was expecting them.

'Sorry,' Coren said in an almost jovial tone. 'We're making preparations for our May Day festivities. It's the biggest celebration in our calendar.'

'We've got a couple of questions,' Gareth said casually. 'Do you mind if we come in?'

'Not at all, not at all,' Coren said, gesturing for them to come inside. There was clearly no resentment from his arrest a few days ago.

They walked into the hallway and then followed him into the living room.

Coren sat down on a patterned chair and looked at them. 'Have you managed to find out what happened to Callum?'

'We can't really discuss the investigation,' Gareth explained. 'But we are following several lines of enquiry.'

'I see,' Coren responded and then shook his head. 'It still doesn't feel real. I just don't understand who would want to harm Callum.'

If Coren had murdered Vicky Newell yesterday afternoon, he was doing a very good job of hiding any anxiety or guilt. Maybe he was a psychopath and felt nothing about what he had done.

Laura looked at him. 'Could you tell us when you last saw Vicky Newell?'

Coren frowned and scratched his beard. 'I've only met Callum's mother once or twice. And that was a few months ago. Long before Callum's death.'

Laura nodded nonchalantly. 'Was that at their home?'

'No,' Coren replied. 'I've never been to their home.'

Laura gave Gareth a surreptitious look. *Well, we know that's a lie for starters.*

Gareth sat forward on the sofa that he and Laura were sitting on. 'Could you tell us where you were yesterday afternoon around two p.m.?'

Coren couldn't hide his sudden discomfort as his eyes roamed nervously around the room.

'Erm, let me think,' he said, clearly stalling to give himself time to think. 'I'm pretty sure I was here. I was here all day.'

Got you!

Laura took a few seconds to allow the tension in the room to build and then she frowned at him. 'You don't seem sure, David. If you'd been here all day yesterday then you must know where you were at two p.m.?'

'Yes, of course,' Coren said, but he was getting flustered. 'My head is always a bit of a muddle in the lead-up to May Day.'

Laura fixed him with a quizzical stare. 'And if you were here, then you couldn't have been standing outside the Newells' house in Beaumaris at that time, is that correct?'

'No,' Coren said with a nervous laugh. 'Why would I be there?'

'I don't know,' Gareth replied. 'Can you think of any reason why you might have been there?'

'Sorry... I'm... I'm getting terribly confused here,' Coren stammered.

'It's okay, David. I'll explain it to you,' Laura said. 'We

302

have an eyewitness that saw you on the driveway of the Newells' house at two p.m. yesterday afternoon.'

'Really?' Coren said, trying to sound astounded.

'Come on, David,' Gareth said in a friendly tone. 'We know you were there. We just don't know why you've spent the past few minutes lying to us about it.'

Coren took a moment to compose himself. 'No, you're right. I was there.'

No shit, Sherlock, Laura thought.

Gareth looked at him. 'Can you tell us why?'

'I wanted to pass on my condolences to the family. Well, to Callum's mother and sister at least,' Coren explained. 'I wanted to let them know that our community would be there if they needed anyone.'

'What did they say?' Laura asked.

Coren blinked nervously and then looked at her. He was clearly rattled. 'Erm, no one was in.'

'You didn't go inside the house?' Gareth enquired.

'No,' Coren replied cautiously. 'I don't understand why you're asking me all this.'

'You see, now I'm confused, David,' Gareth said in a mock friendly tone. 'Why did you lie to us if all you did was go and knock on the Newells' front door and no one answered?'

'I don't know,' Coren muttered.

Laura gave him a quizzical look. 'It seems to be a considerate and caring thing to have done, doesn't it? Why would you need to lie about that?'

'I suppose I just panicked,' Coren explained, looking very uneasy.

303

'If you didn't do anything wrong, then why did you panic and lie to us?' Gareth asked with a more uncompromising tone.

'I was scared I might get arrested again,' Coren admitted.

'You just need to tell us the truth, David,' Laura said gently. 'You knocked at the door. Vicky Newell answered the door and you went in, didn't you?'

'No.' Coren shook his head.

'And you argued about something, didn't you?'

'No.'

Gareth fixed Coren with a stare. 'Were you having an affair with Vicky Newell?'

Coren looked shocked. 'No, of course not.'

'David, look at me,' Gareth said in a severe tone. 'Did you murder Vicky Newell yesterday afternoon?'

The colour drained from Coren's face. 'Vicky's dead?'

'Come on, David,' Laura said quietly. 'We know you were there. We have an eyewitness. If you and Vicky were arguing about something and things just got out of hand, you need to tell us. Now is your chance.'

'Oh my God.' Coren was shaking.

Gareth looked over at Laura. Coren was at breaking point.

'David,' Laura said in a friendly tone, 'you can tell us what happened.'

'I didn't kill her,' Coren whispered. 'I promise you, I didn't kill her.'

Gareth got up from the sofa. 'Okay. We're going to take you down to the station now for further questioning. And if you would like to have a solicitor present, then we can arrange that for you. Do you understand?'

Coren didn't respond, just buried his face in his hands.

CHAPTER 48

By lunchtime, Gareth was in full flow in the CID office. Rolling up his sleeves, he could feel the adrenaline coursing through his veins. David Coren was now their prime suspect and sitting in a holding cell down in the custody suite on the ground floor.

He turned to the scene board as the other detectives looked on. 'Okay. If David Coren is our man, we need to establish motive, means and opportunity.'

Declan, who was sitting at his desk in front of his computer, looked over. 'Maybe I got it wrong. Maybe Coren really was having an affair with Vicky. She'd told me many times how much she hated Mike and she always had a bit of thing for old hippies. So, Coren befriended Callum and became a father figure to him. Vicky sees the positive effect that Coren has had on Callum over the months. Coren then becomes a shoulder to cry on as she pours her heart out to him about her marriage and husband.'

Gareth frowned at Declan's change of mind. 'Are you

sure? You were adamant that she would have told you if she was seeing someone.'

Declan took a few seconds to answer, as if something had occurred to him and he wanted to first think it through. 'To be fair, before all this, I would say that she'd seemed happier than she had done in months, even years.' He shook his head. 'Christ, I even joked to her that she seemed more cheerful and that it must be her *fancy man* that she was knocking off with. I didn't even think…' Declan looked troubled.

Gareth had suggested on several occasions that Declan might be too close to the investigation and that he could take some kind of compassionate leave. But he'd insisted that he owed it to the memory of Vicky and Callum to find out who killed them and get them justice. Seeing his depth of feeling, Gareth realised it would be cruel to take that away from him.

'So, we go with the theory that Coren had started to have an affair with Vicky a few months ago?' Laura said. 'Are we really saying that Callum found out and threatened to reveal what was going on? If you think about it, Callum admired Coren and hated his own father. You'd think that Callum would be pleased that his mother was seeing a man like Coren.'

Declan interjected. 'I don't think it works like that. If Callum was protective of his mother, he might be angry that they were having an affair. Or maybe he thought that Coren had only befriended him to cosy up to Vicky. That would be hard to take.'

Gareth nodded. It was a good point.

'Coren was on the beach at the time that Callum was attacked and killed. And he was on the driveway at the time of Vicky's murder. That seems to be way too much of a coincidence, doesn't it?' Andrea suggested.

'It does,' Declan agreed.

'Boss.' Ben waved to get Gareth's attention. 'We've got that burner phone number that kept ringing both Callum and Vicky's mobile phones in the lead-up to their murders. Could it belong to Coren?'

'Possibly. Any news back on the customer data?' Gareth asked.

'Not yet.' Ben shook his head. 'I'll keep chasing it.'

As Gareth walked back to the scene board his phone buzzed. He looked down and saw that it was an internal number in the station.

'DI Williams,' he said, answering it.

'Sir, it's the forensic lab here,' said a male voice. 'We have the analysis on the material that was found burned in the oil drum. We could only find canvas in our analysis. My guess is that it was an old tent or something like that.'

Gareth narrowed his eyes. It wasn't helpful news, given they were trying to build a case against David Coren. 'Definitely no clothing in there?'

'No, sir,' the man replied. 'However, Dr Salmon would like you to come here and look at some of the DNA results from the blood we found on your first victim.'

'Thanks, I'll be there in five minutes,' Gareth said, hoping that this would be the breakthrough they'd been waiting for. He ended the call and looked at the CID team. 'Forensics have got the DNA from the blood in Callum's mouth. If it's a match to Coren's, then we've got him.'

CHAPTER 49

Gareth and Laura entered the forensic wing of Beaumaris nick and headed for the lab to their left. It was brightly illuminated with several rows of forensic equipment – microscopes, fume hoods, chromatographs and spectrometers – as well as vials and test tubes of brightly coloured liquids.

A lab technician in a full forensic suit, mask, and gloves approached them at the doorway. 'Can I help?' she asked.

'DI Williams and DI Hart,' Gareth explained. 'I've just had a call that you'd found something in a DNA sample?'

'Yes.' The lab technician nodded as she handed them forensic gloves and masks to put on. 'I'll take you over.'

They followed her over to see the chief lab technician, Nicola Salmon, whom Laura had met a few times since arriving at Beaumaris nick.

'DI Hart, DI Williams,' Nicola said from behind her mask. She was holding a test tube and looking at a computer screen with a coloured graph on it.

'What have you got for us, Nicola?' Gareth asked.

'We've got the trace DNA that we managed to take from

your first victim's tooth,' Nicola explained. 'After several attempts, we've now managed to get a DNA profile that we can use.'

Laura exchanged a look with Gareth. It was very good news.

'Okay,' Gareth said, sounding encouraged. 'And?'

Nicola turned and pointed to a large computer screen that showed the image of the DNA profile. 'So, this is the DNA profile of the sample we obtained from your first victim. It's virtually complete. We usually base our profile on twenty-four genetic markers, each of which contains what we call an STR, a "short tandem repeat". It's basically a section of the DNA that repeats itself.'

Laura couldn't help but feel a little confused as to where and how this was relevant.

Nicola looked at them both and said, 'Bear with me, because this is the bit where it gets interesting.' She pointed to the screen. 'So, most markers show two peaks, which you can see here, and these markers produce a unique series of forty-eight numbers. In this instance, we were only able to establish thirty-six numbers, which is pretty good, given what we were working with.' Helen clicked a button and another DNA profile appeared on the screen. 'This is your victim's DNA results.' She pointed at the screen. 'Here you can see the same patterns.'

Laura peered closely at the screen. 'Is it me, or do these DNA profiles look exactly the same?'

'Well spotted,' Nicola said a little too cheerily for a murder investigation. 'So, this image is the DNA we took from the blood on the tooth of your victim placed over the

DNA of your victim.' She pointed at the screen again. 'You can see how the peaks are virtually identical.'

Laura started to jump ahead and guess what Nicola was about to say. 'It's familial DNA.'

Nicola nodded. 'Correct again. We don't have a full profile so I can't match the killer's DNA against the elimination samples, for instance, but what I can tell you is that the person who attacked your first victim is genetically linked to that victim.'

Gareth's eyes widened. 'Parent?'

Nicola shrugged. 'Most likely.'

CHAPTER 50

Laura leaned forward and pressed the red button on the recording equipment. They had picked up Mike Newell an hour earlier and brought him back to Beaumaris nick. He had said nothing on the journey but he was clearly a broken man.

'Interview conducted with Michael Newell, Thursday, two p.m., Interview Room 2, Beaumaris Police Station. Present are Michael Newell, Detective Inspector Gareth Williams, Duty Solicitor Patrick Clifford and myself, Detective Inspector Laura Hart.'

Mike gave Laura a look of dejected despondence. She assumed that he knew the game was up and he was now looking at spending most of his life in prison.

Laura raised her eyebrow. 'Mike, do you understand that you are still charged with two counts of murder?'

'Yes.'

Gareth shifted forward on his seat and looked over. 'Mike, can you tell us where you were on Saturday afternoon?'

Mike sniffed and then mumbled, 'No comment.'

Gareth shot a frustrated look at Laura. It didn't look like Mike was going to attempt to explain himself in any way.

Gareth opened a file and pulled some notes in front of him. 'You told detectives that you were in The Red Lion public house on Saturday afternoon and evening. Is that correct?'

'No comment.'

Gareth took his laptop, opened it and then clicked on an MPEG file. 'For the purposes of the tape, I'm showing the suspect Item Reference 382C.' Gareth turned the laptop so Mike could see it. He then played the CCTV footage that Ben had discovered. 'Mike, can you tell us what you can see on the screen?'

Mike shifted awkwardly in his seat and then glanced over at the laptop with a despondent expression. 'No comment.'

'Item Reference 382C is CCTV footage that shows the entrance of The Red Lion Public house. It also shows you leaving there at one p.m. precisely. Can you tell us where you were going?'

'No comment.'

'If I play this second clip from the same CCTV camera, can you tell me what you can see?'

Mike gave a sigh. 'No comment.'

'For the purposes of the tape, the CCTV footage shows the suspect returning to The Red Lion Public house just after four p.m. Can you tell us where you had been for those three hours, Mike?'

'No comment.'

'Your son went missing at approximately 1.30 p.m. on Saturday afternoon in Newborough Forest. Did you drive from The Red Lion public house to Newborough and attack your son Callum?'

Mike closed his eyes and shook his head. 'No comment.'

'I'll put this another way. If you had a perfectly good reason for why you weren't in The Red Lion public house between one p.m. and four p.m., then why didn't you tell us?' Gareth asked. 'In fact, the only reason to lie about your whereabouts during those times would be because you were doing something that you didn't want us to know about. What might that be, Mike?'

'No comment.'

'Because if you were visiting someone or going to the supermarket, you could just tell us right now and that would clarify where you were.'

Mike didn't say anything.

Laura reached over to a file and pulled out a document. 'For the purposes of the tape, I am showing the suspect Item Reference 983F. This is a DNA profile of a blood sample that we found inside Callum Newell's mouth.' Laura turned the DNA profile for Mike to look at. 'Can you have a look at this for me, Mike.'

He gave the document a cursory glance and then looked away.

'The DNA profile that was created from that blood sample is familial. Do you know what that means, Mike?' Laura asked.

He was now staring at the floor. 'No comment.'

'It means that the blood found inside Callum's mouth was from someone genetically linked to him. A parent or a sibling,' Laura explained. 'And we can rule both Callum's mother and sister out as they were at home at the time he was attacked. That leaves you. So, can you explain to us how your blood ended up inside Callum's mouth at the time of his murder?'

Mike looked upset. 'No comment.'

'What did you think of David Coren's relationship with Callum?' Laura asked. 'It must have been hard to see your son form such a close relationship with a father figure like David Coren. How did that make you feel?'

'No comment.'

'And then Callum threatened to leave the family home to go and live with the religious cult that David Coren runs in Lon Capel,' Laura said. 'That must have made you very angry, Mike?'

'No comment.'

Laura took the DNA document back and said, 'In fact, didn't you say that you would prefer that Callum was dead rather than seeing him go and live with David Coren and his community?'

Mike nervously scratched his nose but remained silent.

'If you could answer the question please, Mike?'

Mike looked over at her. 'No comment.'

'Did Callum tell you that he was going to leave? And did you go to Newborough Forest on Saturday to confront him about that?'

'No comment.'

'And did you end up killing him?'

Mike rubbed his jaw and sighed. 'No comment.'

There were a few seconds of silence.

Gareth grabbed another folder. 'How would you

characterise your marriage to Vicky, Mike?'

'No comment.'

'We understand that you believed that Vicky was having an affair, is that correct?' Gareth asked.

Mike leaned forward on his chair but continued to stare at the ground. 'No comment.'

Gareth frowned. 'Did you think that Vicky was having an affair with David Coren?'

Mike actively bristled at the question as he interlaced his fingers. 'No comment.'

'It must have been pretty hard for you. First David Coren takes your son away from you. Then he starts sleeping with your wife. You must have been very angry about all that?'

'No comment.'

'You were heard arguing with Vicky the morning before she was murdered and an eyewitness said you accused her of having an affair,' Gareth stated. 'Did you pretend to go out that morning and then wait to see who was coming to the house?'

'No comment.'

'Did you see David Coren arrive at your home? We have an eyewitness that saw him there,' Gareth explained.

'No comment.'

'Did you wait for David Coren and your wife to have sex, and then for him to leave, before going back into your house? Did you then strangle Vicky in a fit of jealous rage before pretending that you had discovered her dead?'

Mike closed his eyes and shook his head. He was getting emotional.

Laura looked over. 'Come on, Mike. No one would blame you. You've just seen a man go into your home. You know he's having sex with your wife. Then you see him leave. Maybe you went in to confront Vicky with what you'd seen. Maybe you had an argument and things just got out of hand. Is that what happened, Mike?'

'No comment.'

Gareth sat back in his chair. They weren't getting anywhere.

Gareth looked over at Mike and Clifford. 'I think that's all the questions we have at the moment.' He glanced at his watch. 'Interview suspended at two-thirty-three.'

CHAPTER 51

Two hours later, Mike Newell was standing in front of the custody sergeant with his hands handcuffed in front of him. Gareth and Laura were standing either side. At that moment, the evidence against him was overwhelming. The DNA evidence was damning and Newell had lied about his whereabouts on Saturday afternoon at the time of Callum's murder.

The custody sergeant looked across at Newell and said, 'Michael Edward Newell, you are charged with the murder of both Callum Newell and Victoria Newell contrary to common law. Do you have anything to say?'

Newell stared at the floor and shook his head.

A uniformed police officer led Newell out of the back entrance and down some steel steps into the rear car park. The rain had now stopped but the sky was still a dismal grey.

Due to lack of availability of custody cells, Newell was going to be transferred to a holding cell over at Rhosneigr Police Station. Laura and Gareth would continue their interview with him there when his legal representative had arrived. They would also carry out a thorough examination to see if Newell had anything that resembled a bite mark.

Laura and Gareth followed him outside to the waiting police car.

Suddenly, Newell smashed the uniformed officer in the face with his handcuffed fists and sprinted away across the car park towards the exit.

'Oh shit!' Laura yelled.

'Bollocks,' Gareth growled as they both broke into a run.

The officer groaned and sat up on the ground nursing a bloody nose.

'You okay, mate?' Gareth shouted as he ran past him.

The officer nodded and said, 'Yeah, just don't let him escape.'

Laura and Gareth sprinted after Newell.

'He can't get very far,' Gareth said. 'He's wearing bloody handcuffs.'

'You'd be surprised,' said Laura.

As they sped through the car park and reached the entrance, Gareth grabbed his leg in extreme pain. 'Oh fuck!'

Laura stopped in her tracks. 'What is it?'

'It's my ankle from the other day,' Gareth said, wincing and holding his leg.

'Don't worry, I've got this,' Laura said, already breathless.

Gareth gave her a look. 'Be careful and don't do anything stupid. I'll call for back-up, so keep your radio on.'

Laura nodded and dashed away.

As she came out of the car park exit, she spotted Newell running ahead towards the main roundabout. Several pedestrians moved out of his way as he yelled at them. She was furious that Newell had managed to escape so easily.

Setting off in pursuit, Laura was trying to work out where he was going and how he thought he was going to get away. Maybe he just didn't care anymore? Had nothing left to lose?

There was the sound of an irate driver pumping their horn as Newell darted through the traffic. Up ahead was the multi-storey car park on Prince Street.

Oh bollocks, he's going in there

She watched as Newell ran past the automatic barrier at the car park entrance and then disappeared around the corner.

Thirty seconds later, Laura arrived at the car park's ground floor. Sucking in breath, she stopped running and began to walk briskly. Her chest was burning and her shoes were now rubbing the back of her feet.

Jesus, I thought I was actually pretty fit.

As she made her way inside, she continued trying to get her breath back as she noticed the drop in temperature from the outside. The cold car park smelled of motor oil and urine.

Moving through the space, Laura gazed up at the low concrete roof and the long line of parked cars. The click of her shoes echoed noisily around the concrete walls.

Where the bloody hell has he gone?

Laura clicked her Tetra radio. 'Six three to Control. Over.'

'This is Control, go ahead six three.'

'I'm pursuing suspect Mike Newell who has escaped from custody. Suspect is now in the Prince Street multi-storey car park, Beaumaris, but I have lost visual contact. Request back-up. Over,' she said as her breathing began to return to normal.

'Six three, received. Will advise, stand by. Over.'

Laura stopped, listened, and heard movement over by the door to the stairs. She jogged towards where she had heard the noise and saw that the door that led to the stairwell was open. As she went in, the stench of urine became overwhelming, and there were two syringes on the floor.

Lovely.

She began to walk up the stone steps and then heard, from higher up, the sound of someone running.

Why the hell is he going up to the top floor?

Picking up the pace, Laura reached out and held onto the black handrail to keep her balance. Her head was swimming from the effort of chasing him.

The sound of movement and of doors opening came echoing from above.

'Mike! Just stop. You're not going to get away,' Laura yelled, her voice reverberating around the stairwell.

She couldn't deny she was beginning to feel uneasy. Maybe he had no intention of getting away. Perhaps he just couldn't face a long, emotionally painful trial followed by twenty-five years in prison.

She started to take the steps two at a time, gasping for breath again as she went. The muscles in her thighs began to burn but she wasn't about to let her suspect throw himself off the top of a multi-storey car park.

The staircase ended suddenly and there was a door out to the top floor of the car park, which was open air. As she opened it, a swirling gust of wind blew against her.

She clicked her radio. 'Six three to Control, I have pursued the suspect to the top floor of the Prince Street multi-storey but still have no visual. Over.'

'Control to three six, received. Back-up is en route. ETA five minutes. Over.'

There was a noise from the far side of the car park.

Laura could see Newell climbing up onto a narrow perimeter wall.

Oh shit!

'Mike! Stop there. Please. I want you to talk to me!' she yelled.

As he glanced back at her, Newell continued climbing up onto the wall as best he could with his hands cuffed. It didn't look like he wanted to talk.

Laura ran towards him, and she could feel the wind charging boisterously through the parked cars. It howled and groaned as it swirled around her.

Getting to his feet, Newell glared at Laura. 'Leave me alone!' he shouted as he balanced precariously on top of the wall.

'Just stop whatever it is you're thinking of doing,' Laura yelled at him over the noise of the wind.

Moving closer, Laura could now see the road below. It was about a seventy or eighty-foot drop. *He's not going to survive that.*

'Stay there!' Newell roared.

Laura slowed her approach. 'Okay, what about Zoe?'

Newell shook his head. 'She hates me.'

Laura shook her head and said, 'Don't you think she's been through enough though?'

322

Newell gave an ironic laugh. '*I've* been through enough. They all hated me. Of course I knew that Vicky was having an affair.'

'Is that why you killed her?'

Newell looked at her. 'I don't know what happened to us. We used to be happy.'

'We can talk about that when you come down from there,' Laura said. 'This isn't the answer to anything, is it?'

'Do you really think I want to sit in a court with my daughter looking at me with a face full of hate? And then sit in prison for twenty-five years?' Newell shouted at her.

Laura moved closer. 'I don't understand why you killed Callum.'

Newell shook his head. 'I didn't kill him.'

'But we know that you did,' Laura said gently. 'Just talk to me.'

'Why should I? So you can wrap up your case nice and neatly? I don't think so.' Newell's voice was filled with anger and resentment.

Laura approached him cautiously and reached out. 'Come on, Mike. Just take my hand and come down. Please.'

Newell shook his head. 'No, I don't think so. I've got a three-second fall down there and then peace. That's a lot more appealing than what you're offering.'

Laura leapt forward, grabbed the front of his jacket and pulled, trying to get her hands underneath his arms.

'What the hell are you doing?' Newell cried out as he struggled with her.

With an almighty heave, she tried to pull him off the wall, and for a second, they locked eyes.

But then Newell gave her a sharp shove in the face, lost his balance, and fell backwards and out of sight.

As Laura struggled to her feet, she heard a piercing scream.

Glancing over the ledge, she could see Newell's body lying at an awkward angle on the pavement below, passers-by staring in horror.

CHAPTER 52

The next morning, Osian got up very early. The enormity of losing his best friend, coupled with the violent deaths of Vicky and Mike Newell, felt too overwhelming for him to sleep. The world suddenly seemed to be a frightening and unpredictable place.

'Try it again, mate!' his dad shouted.

Osian and his dad had been in the park kicking and throwing a rugby ball around for about half an hour. Even though Osian was finding it difficult to concentrate, he knew that he had to do something to take his mind off what had happened.

Osian nodded, took the ball and thundered a kick high into the air. 'There you go!' he yelled.

'Here we go indeed,' his dad said as he looked up and prepared to catch the ball. Instead, the ball bounced off his chest and fell onto the grass. 'Bollocks.'

Osian laughed at him. It was a relief to feel something other than anxiety, fear or grief.

Scooping up the ball in his arms, his dad wandered over with a self-effacing smile.

'And that's why I never played rugby to the standard you do,' Declan said. He looked at his watch. 'Listen, mate, I've got to get a shower and get in to work now. But you let me know if you need anything.'

'I'll come back with you,' Osian said.

'Good lad,' Declan said, ruffling his hair. 'I know this isn't easy, but you're going to get through it. We all are. It just takes time.'

Osian frowned. 'I just don't understand why he killed them.'

'We're not sure yet,' Declan admitted. 'There's going to be a full coroner's inquiry into everything.' Declan looked at him. 'You know there's a memorial service for Callum and Vicky at St Mary's later this afternoon?'

'Yeah, I saw that online,' he replied.

'You think you'll be up to going?' Declan asked.

'Are you going?' Osian asked.

Decan gave him a reassuring look. 'Of course I am, mate.'

'Okay,' Osian said. 'I'll come with you then.'

CHAPTER 53

Laura turned over in bed and saw that Gareth was sitting up, looking at his phone.

'Morning,' she said and then groaned as she stretched.

'No swim?' he said, his eyes glued to the screen.

'The alarm went off and I just thought, *I need more sleep*,' Laura admitted.

Gareth turned and put a reassuring hand to her face. 'Not surprising after yesterday.'

Propping up some pillows, Laura sat up. 'The last week has been pretty horrible.'

Gareth gestured to his phone and pulled a face. 'The papers are having a field day.'

'I've already spoken to my Federation rep,' Laura admitted uneasily. 'We're meeting tomorrow so she can advise me, as I know the Independent Office for Police Conduct will be doing a full and thorough investigation into the death to make sure that there was no culpability on my part. I know these kinds of investigations are pretty standard in events like this; it's another stress in my life that I could do without,' she confessed.

'You'll be fine,' Gareth reassured her. 'In fact, you tried to save his life.'

'Yeah, but the last time I spoke to officers from the IOPC, they made me feel guilty before they'd even heard me out,' Laura groaned.

Gareth nodded. 'I know, but they're just doing their job. And you didn't do anything wrong.' He clicked on his phone and showed her the screen. 'So, more importantly, St Cwyfan's Church. What do you think?'

Laura smiled as she looked at the sunset photo of the church.

'Fair play, that does look nice,' she said.

'Nice?' Gareth said, arching an eyebrow. 'It's stunning and incredibly romantic.'

'Okay, okay,' Laura laughed. 'It's dead romantic.'

Gareth gave her a playful dig in the ribs. 'Dead romantic? Jesus! Have you ever realised that the traditional gender roles of wedding planning have been completely reversed in our case?'

'Yes. Obviously,' Laura said with a grin. 'Hey, I like it that you're doing all the legwork.'

'Oh, I bet you do,' he snorted. 'But if you could be a little more enthused please, Mrs?'

Laura looked at him for a moment and suddenly realised that she hadn't looked at him properly for days.

Their eyes locked for a few seconds.

'God, I'm lucky to have you,' she said.

Gareth gave her a sexy smirk. 'Yeah, you really are.'

She pulled him towards her. 'Come here.' She kissed him hard on the mouth as he rolled on top of her.

CHAPTER 54

'Morning, everyone,' Gareth said as he walked to the centre of the CID office. After the events of the previous night, the atmosphere was strange among the team. 'As most of you know, Mike Newell took his own life at the Prince's Street multi-storey car park yesterday afternoon. Although he didn't make a full confession, I think that in conjunction with the evidence we already have and Laura's account of what he said to her, we can conclude that Mike Newell murdered both his son, Callum, and his wife, Vicky. I have a meeting with the CPS booked in for tomorrow. I think it's likely that they will decide to issue a charging decision. Once that is done, North Wales Police will make a public statement.' Gareth looked at the CID team. 'Look, guys, I know this isn't what we wanted. And I know how frustrating it is that Mike Newell isn't going to trial to face the consequences of what he did. But we do owe it to Zoe Newell and other members of the family to uncover every scrap of evidence when it comes to the murders of Callum and Vicky.'

Declan, who was sitting at his desk, nodded sadly.

'Laura?' Gareth prompted.

Laura got up to address the CID team. 'From the DNA evidence, we know that Callum was murdered by a very close relative. We can rule out Vicky, and Zoe was in the family home at the time of his murder. Plus we have no motive for Zoe to kill either her brother or her mother.' Laura sipped from her bottle of water. 'So, that only leaves Mike. Before he took his own life, Mike admitted to me that he knew that Vicky was having an affair behind his back, so we can assume that this was what prompted him to murder her.'

Ben looked over with a frown. 'Do we know who she was having an affair with?'

Laura went to the scene board and pointed to a photo. 'Our theory is that Vicky was having an affair with David Coren, the two of them having met through Callum's friendship with Coren. We suspect that Mike discovered the affair but didn't confront Vicky with what he knew until he had evidence. For this reason, he waited for Coren to arrive to see Vicky on Wednesday afternoon – when she believed Mike to be at work – and then, once Coren had left, Mike went into the house and killed Vicky in a jealous rage.'

'Thank you, Laura,' Gareth said as she sat back down. 'I want to thank everyone for all your hard work on this case up until this point,' he said, changing directions. 'And I know that Declan is very grateful as this one was so close to home for him.'

Declan nodded.

'I now need each of you to finish off your lines of investigation, type up any witness statements, tie up loose ends… the usual stuff,' Gareth said. 'There will be a memorial service at St Mary's this afternoon for those of you who feel you want to attend. For now, I'll be in my office if you need anything.'

CHAPTER 55

It was late afternoon and Laura and Gareth had arrived at St Mary's Church in Beaumaris for the memorial service for Vicky and Callum Newell. There would be separate funerals for both of them in the coming weeks.

Laura and Gareth had got there half an hour early so that Gareth could visit the graves of his *nain* and *taid*, who were buried at St Mary's. He had told her the stories of going fishing with his *taid* on the coast at Moelfre. How they had stood close to the rocks as the tide rushed past and caught everything from sea bass to grey mullet and mackerel. Then they had taken it home for Gareth's *nain* to cook with vegetables from their garden. It sounded idyllic to Laura.

They began to make their way across the graveyard towards the entrance to the church. Even though Laura walked slowly and carefully crossed over the low wall of the graveyard, her trousers still snagged on a sharp edge of stone. She watched Gareth ahead of her, his cautious steps avoiding the ivy leaves laid out like ropes.

Laura savoured the stillness of the afternoon. Even though the spectre of Pete and the corruption at the MMP still hung over her, she had managed to put it to one side and resolved not to tackle it until the following week.

The spring air was heavy with a sweet aroma that she inhaled deeply. A cuckoo call echoed in the distance, and she paused to take it in. All she could see around her in the graveyard were faded grey monuments gradually fading into the light. In the near distance was the octagonal church, the ivy beginning to climb up its walls in a way that reminded her of how tombstones eventually become one with nature. The sky above was a bright blue and empty of clouds.

As she continued, she felt that every step was springy from the ivy bedding beneath her feet. She took in the details of the leaves that hung at waist height from a nearby tree – the veins running along their edges and tapering into tiny points looked almost like lace.

She finally joined the gravel footpath and followed it to the corner of the church itself.

Outside the church entrance, dozens of mourners dressed in black had assembled. Some were talking quietly in huddles. Others were filing inside in subdued solemnity.

Gareth waited for her and they walked together towards the enormous oak doors that led to the nave.

Declan and Sue were just inside the doors, standing to one side with Osian. They all looked suitably sombre.

'Hi, Declan,' Laura said with an empathetic expression. She could see that his eyes were glassy, as though he had been drinking. She didn't blame him after all he'd been through.

'Sue, this is Detective Inspector Hart,' Declan said very quietly.

Laura leaned forward and shook Sue's hand. 'It's Laura.'

Despite being dressed in black, Sue looked immaculately turned out in a designer black coat. 'I'm sorry we're meeting in such tragic circumstances,' she said with a sombre expression.

'Me too,' Laura said politely.

'Nice to see you, Osian,' Gareth said as he gave Osian a reassuring pat on the arm. 'We'll see you all after the service.'

Gareth and Laura turned and made their way to a nearby pew and sat down.

'Is it me or did Declan smell of booze?' Gareth whispered.

Laura nodded. 'Yeah. His eyes were a bit glazed. But it's not surprising.'

Out of the corner of her eye, Laura spotted Zoe sitting at the front with some relatives. She wore a haunted expression.

Laura hadn't managed to speak to Zoe since Mike's death and thought she should try to after the service.

***

An hour later, the service was over and relatives and friends had made their way out of the church. Some had left while others chatted quietly in the churchyard.

The service had been poignant and moving.

'Sonnet' by The Verve had been played as it was Vicky's favourite song and Laura could see the effect the music had had on various people in the church, including Declan. Then at the end, the track 'Is There Somebody Who Can Watch

You' by The 1975, Callum's favourite song, had been played and many of the teenagers from the local school had wept and held each other.

Laura and Gareth stood to one side.

'That was tough going,' Laura admitted under her breath.

'Yeah,' Gareth agreed quietly.

Declan approached. His face was red and blotchy from where he had been crying – and he definitely smelled of alcohol now.

'Some of us are going for a drink at the George and Dragon,' Declan said. 'If you fancy coming along?'

Gareth nodded. 'Yes, mate. We'll see you there.'

As Declan wandered away, Laura looked at Gareth and pulled a face. 'I'm not sure me going to the pub is the best idea.'

Gareth raised an eyebrow quizzically. 'Because?'

'I was on that rooftop with Mike Newell,' Laura explained. 'And when people are emotional and drunk, they say stupid things. I'd prefer not to get involved in any of that.'

'Yeah, now that you've mentioned it…' Gareth agreed. 'I'll go on my own. I probably need to keep an eye on Declan anyway as he's a bit all over the place. See you back at the house, okay?'

'Thanks,' Laura said.

Gareth leaned in and kissed her on the cheek. 'See you later.'

'You're not meant to kiss me in public, you loon,' she whispered.

'Yeah, well, once we get married we're not going to be

able hide it, are we?' he pointed out with a smile.

'You're getting very brave,' she teased him.

As Gareth wandered away to join Declan, Laura saw Zoe looking her way. Their eyes met.

Zoe gave her a nod of acknowledgement and it was enough to persuade Laura to go and talk to her.

'Hi, Zoe,' Laura said as she approached. 'I'm so sorry…'

'Thanks.' Zoe nodded thoughtfully. 'You were there, weren't you? When my dad killed himself?'

'Yes,' Laura said very quietly.

'I'm glad he's dead,' Zoe said. She didn't sound angry, or upset, just matter of fact. 'It makes it easier to deal with the loss of Callum and Mum if he's dead.' Zoe looked directly at Laura. 'Does that make any sense?'

'Yes,' Laura said with an understanding expression. Even though she'd had her own loss and grief, she couldn't possibly understand what Zoe had been through in the last week. And that made it impossible for her to judge the way she was feeling.

'Does that make me some kind of horrible psycho?' Zoe asked.

'No,' Laura replied with a slight shake of her head. 'Not at all. Your world has been turned upside-down, Zoe.' She instinctively reached out and touched Zoe's shoulder. 'For what it's worth, if there's anything I can do in the future, please let me know.'

'Thank you.'

CHAPTER 56

Gareth pulled the car up outside Declan's house, got out and went to the passenger door. At the same time, Osian climbed out from the back of the car.

'If you can give me a hand to get your dad inside,' Gareth said as he opened the passenger door.

'Of course,' Osian replied.

Declan had drunk far too much in the pub. He had swung between tears, reminiscing and jokes. Gareth didn't blame him. Everyone connected to the Newell family had been to hell and back in the past few days. Gareth had left Sue drinking in the pub and promised her that he'd get Declan and Osian home.

'Here we go, mate,' Gareth said as he helped Declan climb out of the car and try and get his balance.

Declan looked around, confused. 'What are we doing here? I don't want to be feckin' here. I want to go back in the pub.' He slurred the final few words.

Gareth supported Declan and tried to guide him to the

front door. 'Yeah, I'm not sure that's a great idea, Dec. I think you might need a bit of rest.'

'A bit of a rest,' Declan mumbled. 'Yes! That's a very good idea.'

Osian took his keys and opened the front door.

'I love your mother, Osian, you do know that?' Declan mumbled.

As Gareth helped Declan through the front door, he looked at Osian, who was obviously concerned by his father's drunken state. 'Just ignore him. He's drunk too much.'

'I've seen him drunk before,' Osian admitted. 'But I've never seen him like this.'

Gareth edged Declan towards the stairs. 'Yeah, well, he's been through a lot in the past week. You all have.' Gareth gestured upstairs. 'I'll take him up to the bedroom, shall I?'

Osian nodded. 'Do you want me to help?'

'No, it's fine,' Gareth reassured him. 'I'll be down in a second.'

Taking the stairs one at a time, Gareth and Declan eventually got to the top.

'Here we go.'

'Have I ever told you that you're a beautiful man, Gareth?' Declan said, his breath reeking of alcohol.

'Thanks,' Gareth said as he saw a room with a double bed. 'I'm just going to pop you in here, okay. Then you can sleep it off.'

'Sleep it off,' Declan mumbled. 'Yes, that's a feckin grand idea. Where's Sue?'

'She's still in the pub,' Gareth replied.

'Right you are.'

Once Gareth got them both next to the bed, he let Declan fall backwards onto it. 'There we go.'

Reaching down, he unlaced Declan's black shoes and placed them on the carpet.

He then lifted Declan and managed to get his suit jacket off, which he hung over the back of the chair. Declan was already snoring on the bed by the time he was done.

Wow, he's going to have a sore head tomorrow.

Gareth went along the landing, down the stairs and into the living room, where Osian was watching a football game.

'Your dad's fast asleep on the bed,' Gareth reassured him. He gestured to the television. 'Wrong-shaped ball, mate.'

'Yeah,' Osian said with a forced smile. Gareth could see that he was upset.

'Tell you what,' Gareth said, 'I've got to pop into work for a bit, but I come past here on the way home, so I'll drop in and just check on your dad. How's that?'

Osian looked relieved. 'Yeah, that would be great.'

'See you later,' Gareth said as he turned and headed for the front door.

CHAPTER 57

Striding through the double doors that led into the CID office, Gareth saw it was now virtually empty, aside from a couple of officers over in the far corner, who were part of the skeleton team that worked overnight in case anything major turned up.

Gareth saw that Andrea was over by the scene boards. Now that they knew who had killed Vicky and Callum Newell, the scene boards could be dismantled and the evidence stored away.

'You on the late shift?' Gareth asked Andrea as he looked at his watch.

'No, boss,' she replied as she put photos into a box.

'Then get yourself home,' Gareth said with a kind smile.

Andrea gestured to the scene board. 'I'll just finish this off.'

'Andrea?' Gareth said, raising his eyebrows with an amused expression.

'Boss?'

'That's an order.' Gareth knew how hard the team had

worked this past week. They all needed a rest.

Andrea smiled. 'Thank you.'

Ben came into the CID office with a concerned expression. 'I've been trying to call you, boss.'

Taking his phone, Gareth saw the series of missed calls. He had been too preoccupied with getting Declan sorted to notice.

'Is there a problem?' Gareth asked as he took off his jacket and headed for his office. He hoped it wasn't anything important. He was too tired to deal with anything other than tidying up a bit of paperwork. Then he'd swing by to check on Declan, pick up a bottle of wine on the way home and snuggle up to Laura in front of a movie.

'There might be,' Ben replied hesitantly. 'In fact, there might be a couple.'

Gareth stopped in his tracks. He didn't like the sound of Ben's worried tone.

'Go on,' Gareth said.

'We had a phone call from the mortuary,' Ben explained. 'They've searched Mike Newell's body but they can't find any evidence of a bite mark or even a wound.'

'Okay,' Gareth said, wondering if there might be some kind of explanation for that. 'What's the other problem?'

Ben pointed over to his computer. 'I need to show you something because it just doesn't add up.'

'Which isn't something that I want to hear,' Gareth groaned.

Ben ignored him and clicked on some CCTV files on his screen. 'Do you remember that when we got that CCTV footage from the off-licence that's opposite The Red Lion

341

pub, you asked me to talk to traffic and pull all ANPR and CCTV footage of Mike Newell's car?'

Gareth nodded but he was starting to feel uneasy about where Ben was going with all of this. 'Yes.'

'Okay,' Ben said as he used the mouse to pull down a thumbnail of an ANPR camera's footage. 'So, we got a hit for Newell's car on this ANPR camera going over the Menai Bridge at 1.30 p.m. on Saturday.'

'Do we have a return time for him coming back over the bridge?' Gareth asked tentatively. This wasn't good. If Mike had driven over to the Welsh mainland, he couldn't have been in Newborough when Callum was murdered.

Ben nodded with a dark expression. 'He doesn't come back until 3.30 p.m.'

Shit.

'Which means that he wasn't even on Anglesey when Callum went missing,' Gareth said, thinking out loud as his stomach tightened. 'Why the hell did he lie to us then?'

Ben looked at him. 'I think I know why, boss. I spoke to a traffic officer based at Deeside. Here,' Ben said, pointing on a map to where Wales bordered England at the end of the A5.

'Why did you do that?' Gareth asked.

'Because an ANPR camera showed Newell joining the A5 once he'd gone over the bridge,' Ben explained, 'And I took a punt that he would have used the A5 to head for England.'

'Okay, where are we going with all this?' Gareth asked, starting to feel anxious.

'The officer in Deeside ran Newell's plate through the

ANPR for Saturday afternoon,' Ben explained, 'and found Newell driving into this B&Q car park close to the industrial estate.'

Ben played the CCTV footage, which showed Newell's car pulling into the customer car park and parking next to a white Range Rover.

'And then this happens,' Ben said, pointing to the screen.

The footage showed Newell getting out of the car and talking to a man wearing a baseball cap in the passenger seat of the Range Rover. They then clearly exchanged packages and Newell fist-bumped the man before getting back into his car and driving away.

'Shit.' Gareth growled. 'Newell couldn't tell us where he was on Saturday afternoon because he had driven seventy miles to do a drug deal.'

Ben pointed to the screen again. 'And we know from the CCTV that he arrived back to The Red Lion at four p.m.'

'Mike Newell was buying the drugs for Stewart Tyler,' Gareth said as it clicked into place. He gave Ben a dark look. 'And now we know for certain that Mike Newell couldn't have killed Callum on Saturday afternoon.'

'No, boss,' Ben said with a sombre expression.

'Which means that he didn't murder Vicky either,' Gareth said under his breath. His head was spinning with the ramifications of all this. 'I don't understand.'

And then the penny dropped.

'The trace DNA could have been for a parent *or*… a sibling,' Gareth continued.

'Which means it has to be Zoe Newell, doesn't it?' Ben asked.

343

Gareth took a few seconds to process it, but he knew Ben was right. By a process of deduction, Zoe was guilty.

'If Zoe gave Callum drugs and money to hide and he refused to hand them back, then maybe she followed him to Newborough, confronted him and it got out of hand,' Gareth said, thinking out loud. 'And then Vicky discovered not only that Zoe was dealing drugs, but also that she was responsible for Callum's death. So Zoe killed her too.'

Ben nodded. 'That's all possible.'

'Jesus,' Gareth sighed. 'What a shitshow. I'm going to need to talk to Zoe right now.'

Ben looked at the screen and scribbled down a phone number. He handed it to Gareth.

'What's this?' Gareth asked.

'This is the number of the burner phone that rang both Callum and Vicky in the lead-up to their deaths,' Ben explained. 'I've tried calling it a couple of times in the hope that someone will pick it up. If you're going to see Zoe, it might be worth giving it a ring while you're there?'

'Definitely worth a try,' Gareth admitted. He patted Ben's shoulder. 'Good work, Ben.'

CHAPTER 58

Walking down the stairs in Declan's house, Gareth went into the living room where Osian was still watching television. He slumped down into the armchair, feeling heavy with the knowledge that in about fifteen minutes he was going to have to go and confront Zoe with everything that he knew.

'I've checked on your dad,' Gareth said. 'He's sleeping like a baby.'

'A big, drunk Irish baby,' Osian joked.

Gareth laughed. 'Yeah. He's that all right.' He gave Osian a meaningful look. 'You sure you're going to be okay here?'

'Yeah, no problem,' Osian reassured him. 'Mum's in a taxi on her way home now. She's getting fish and chips.'

'Good.'

Something on the television caught Gareth's eye – a character walking down the street, looking at a piece of paper and dialling a number into a mobile phone.

Maybe he would try the burner phone number one more time.

If Zoe answered it, then he would know it was her before he even arrived.

'Okay, Osian,' Gareth said as he gave him a reassuring pat on the shoulder. 'I'm going to get going now. But you know how to contact me if you need anything.'

'Yeah, thanks,' Osian said, but he looked tired and lost.

Gareth went out into the hallway, took out his phone and the piece of paper that Ben had given him.

Opening the front door, he dialled the number into the phone, hoping that the owner of the burner would pick up this one time.

He put his phone onto speaker as he closed the front door and the burner phone started to ring as he went down the steps towards his car.

But then he heard something.

What the hell is that?

Straining his ear, he realised it was a phone ringing somewhere nearby.

He looked down at his mobile phone, aghast, and turned off the speaker function.

Gareth froze as his blood ran cold.

Oh my God.

The burner phone was ringing from somewhere inside Declan's house.

I don't understand, he thought, now feeling sick with worry.

Banging on the front door, he waited for Osian to answer.

A second later, Osian opened the door and gave him a quizzical look.

'Can you hear that ringing?' Gareth asked him as he moved back into the house.

Osian nodded with a frown. 'Yes. I heard it as you went out.'

Gareth stopped, putting his hand up to signal for quiet.

His heart was thumping against his chest like a drum.

Why the hell was the burner phone in Declan's house? It didn't make any sense.

'I think it's coming from the kitchen,' Osian said, as he gestured along the hallway.

Gareth nodded and made his way down to the kitchen.

The ringing sound was loud and metallic.

Looking up, Gareth saw a blue metallic biscuit tin half hidden on top of a cupboard.

Stretching up on tip-toe, Gareth grabbed the tin, which was vibrating.

He pulled it down, put it on the counter, opened it and saw the black burner phone.

'Jesus,' Gareth sighed, his mind now racing in total panic.

'What is it?' Osian asked, looking over his shoulder.

'Just wait there,' Gareth said as he turned off his own mobile phone and the ringing stopped. His stomach was tight and twisted.

'I'm just going up to see your dad,' Gareth said.

'I thought you just checked on him?' Osian asked, sounding confused.

Gareth strode out of the kitchen, down the hallway and jogged up the stairs.

As he got to the top, he could hear a noise.

Someone was having a shower.

Gareth burst into the bedroom where he'd seen Declan five minutes earlier, fast asleep on the bed.

Declan was gone and his clothes were on the floor.

He must be in the en-suite shower.

Walking across the bedroom, Gareth turned the handle to the bathroom door.

It opened.

He went in and saw Declan's shadow through the perspex in the shower.

Grabbing the sliding perspex door, Gareth pulled it back and glared at Declan.

'Jesus!' Declan yelped as he nearly jumped out of his skin. 'What are you doing?'

Gareth's eyes roamed from Declan's shocked face down to his chest.

Then over to the top of his right arm.

Oh God…

There it was.

A bright red-black bruise and the indentations of a bite mark just above his bicep.

Gareth's eyes locked with Declan's as he turned off the shower.

Silence.

'I'm sorry,' Declan whispered.

'You'd better start talking,' Gareth said, now overwhelmed by fear and anger.

'I'm so sorry,' Declan said, his face contorted with pain.

Gareth took two steps back as Declan moved out of the shower and grabbed a towel.

'I don't understand,' Gareth said, shaking his head and trying to piece together how Declan could possibly be guilty of Callum and Vicky's murders.

Declan was shaking as he put his hand to his face. 'I didn't mean it. None of it.'

Gareth took a breath to steady himself. 'You killed them?'

Declan's eyes filled with tears. 'Yes.'

Gareth shook his head. 'Why?' he asked, feeling distraught.

There were a few seconds as Declan closed his eyes, trying to compose himself. Finally, he looked at Gareth.

'Callum was mine,' Declan whispered. 'He was my son.'

'What?' Gareth gasped, his eyes widening.

'Me and Vicky,' Declan said as he wiped the tears from his eyes, 'we'd had this on-off thing for years. She got pregnant with Callum and everyone assumed it was Mike's.'

'Did Mike know?'

'He suspected but never said anything.'

'Why did you kill them, Declan?' Gareth demanded.

'I just…' He stopped.

'Declan!'

'A few weeks ago, Callum found Vick's diaries up in the attic when he went up there to get some camping stuff,' Declan explained. 'They'd been in a locked box but the padlock had rusted away. Callum read them and went mental.'

'What, so you just killed him?' Gareth snapped angrily.

Declan shook his head, his face contorted in sorrow. 'No, of course not! He wanted me and Vicky to come clean to everyone. It didn't matter to him that it would destroy our families. After dropping the boys off, I went back to Newborough on the Saturday afternoon, to try and plead with him to keep it quiet. I thought he was going to tell Osian. We got into an argument and he punched me. I chased him down the beach and… I don't know what happened.'

'You don't know what happened?' Gareth growled. 'You murdered him. How can you not know what happened?'

Declan shook his head. 'We were fighting on the beach. He told me that it made him feel sick that I was his father. He said he'd always felt sorry for me because I was pathetic and stupid. And now he had those genes inside him. I put my hands around his neck. I was telling him to be quiet. And I was shaking him. And then he just stopped breathing.'

Gareth looked at him with total incomprehension. 'Jesus, Declan. What have you done?'

'I'm so sorry…'

'What happened with Vicky?'

'She guessed that I'd killed Callum. She'd found the diaries and knew Callum had read them. She put two and two together and suspected that Callum had confronted me with what he knew. She was going to tell you everything.'

Gareth narrowed his eyes in disgust. 'What, so you went round and killed her too?'

'No,' Declan whispered as he wept and his whole body shook. 'I went to talk to her.'

'You had sex with her!' Gareth growled.

'It just happened,' Declan said. 'But then she told me to

go. She told me that she'd never really loved me and I got angry. And then I just lost it.'

There were a few seconds of terrible silence as Gareth tried to take in everything that Declan had told him.

'Get dressed,' Gareth said, feeling completely broken. 'And then I'll take you in.'

CHAPTER 59

It was Friday evening and Laura had been pottering around at home for a couple of hours. For a moment, she wondered where Gareth had got to. He was probably still keeping an eye on Declan or trying to get him home from the pub in one piece.

Clicking the kettle on, she then had another thought and spun round to turn it off. Instead, she opened the fridge, grabbed a new, cold bottle of Sauvignon Blanc, took off the top and poured herself a large glass. She took a long swig and felt an overwhelming sense of relief that it was the end of the week and that the case had come to its conclusion. A horrible, devastating conclusion, granted.

Grabbing her phone, she made a decision to text Pete and stall him for a while. However, as she looked at her phone, she saw three missed calls from Claudia Wright. She had called thirty minutes earlier, when Laura had been busy sweeping the patio and rearranging some pots in the garden.

She looked at the messages but Claudia hadn't left a voicemail message. Maybe she just wanted to touch base?

However, there was something about the multiple missed calls that made her feel uneasy.

Laura rang Claudia's number but it went to voicemail.

'Hi, Claudia. It's Laura. I've got a couple of missed calls from you?' she said. 'Obviously I don't want to go into any details on the phone but if you do need to speak to me I should be around for most of the weekend. Okay, take care.' She ended the call but felt anxious.

Right, now to Pete.

For a moment, she felt overwhelmed again by all that she had discovered about Pete in the past week. The Newell case had been so absorbing that there had been moments when Laura had forgotten all about Pete's corruption. But then in quieter moments, it all came rushing back to her like a thundering express train.

She started to send him a text.

Hi Pete,
Not feeling great. As you've probably seen, the Newell case here has been very difficult so I'm going to lock myself away this weekend and get some rest.
Hope all is good with you?
I'll give you a call when I'm back up and running.
Much love, Laura xx

Laura took another long swig of wine. It had started to numb her head and take away some of her underlying anxiety.

'What's for tea?' asked a voice.

It was Jake. He was holding his phone.

'God knows.' Laura laughed.

Jake gave her a frown.

Laura stepped forward and hugged him. 'You can have something very beige from the freezer, or we can get takeaway.' She lifted up her glass of wine. 'Well, it will have to be a delivery actually.'

'Takeaway?' Jake said as he hugged her back. 'Nice one.'

Laura stepped back and gave him a knowing look. 'By the way, who's Hannah?'

Jake shrugged. 'I don't know.'

Laura gave an amused frown. 'Isn't there a Hannah in your class?'

'Oh, that Hannah,' Jake said nonchalantly.

'Is she a friend of yours?'

Jake gave her a disgusted look. 'No.'

'Mum, are you actually quizzing Jake about Hannah?' Rosie said as she came bouncing in.

'No,' Laura replied with a defensive smirk.

'Mum said we can get takeaway!' Jake yelled.

Rosie gave Jake a playful poke in the ribs. 'Don't change the subject, *bro*.'

'What?' Jake asked innocently.

There was a knock on the door. Laura knew it wasn't Gareth, as he had keys.

Laura felt her pulse quicken and her stomach tightened as she began to wonder if it was Pete on one of his surprise visits.

'Do you want me to get it?' Rosie asked.

'No, it's all right, darling,' Laura said, taking a breath. 'It's probably just a delivery that needs to be signed for.'

Walking along the hallway, she could see a dark figure on the doorstep.

Shit!

Taking a nervous gulp, her hand went to the door and she opened it and saw… Gareth.

'Sorry,' he said apologetically, seeing how flustered she was. 'Left my keys on my desk.'

Laura let out her breath in relief. 'Bloody hell. I thought you were Pete, that's all.'

'This whole thing is making you paranoid,' Gareth said, but he looked incredibly distracted.

Before she could ask him what was up, there was the noise of footsteps running up the hallway and Jake appeared beside her.

'If we get an Indian from Simla, Gareth could drive and collect it?' Jake said excitedly.

Laura pulled a face. 'Shall we let him get through the door and sit down first?'

With a smile on her face, Laura looked at Gareth. She was looking forward to spending the evening with him.

'Let's start again,' she said. 'Hello, darling.'

'Hi,' Gareth mumbled. He looked drawn, exhausted and completely bewildered.

'You okay?' Laura asked, now worried.

He shook his head sadly. 'No, not really.'

'How was the pub?'

'Can we go somewhere? There's something I need to tell you,' Gareth said quietly.

Laura's stomach tightened.

'I'm starving,' Jake said.

She looked at Jake as her pulse quickened again. 'I just need to quickly talk to Gareth about something first.'

'Okay. I'll go and get the Simla order ready,' Jake chirped and disappeared.

For a nerve-racking few seconds, Laura and Gareth walked along the hallway and into the untidy study.

Laura closed the door and they sat down.

'You're scaring me, Gareth,' she said, aware that her voice was very shaky.

'It's Declan,' Gareth said, taking a deep breath.

'Is he all right?' Laura demanded.

Silence.

'What's happened?'

'I don't know where to start with it,' Gareth said, shaking his head. He looked at her with a furrowed brow. 'Declan was Callum's father.'

'What?' Laura said, wondering if she'd misheard him.

'Declan was Callum's father,' Gareth repeated darkly. 'And Callum found out and confronted Declan with it.'

Laura was racing away with what Gareth was telling her.

'You're not saying that Declan had anything to do with Callum or Vicky's deaths?' Laura asked, terrified of the answer.

Gareth took a beat to respond.

'Yes. I'm sorry.' He looked at her. 'He killed them both.'

CHAPTER 60

The first rays of dawn began to paint the cloudless sky a pale pink and tangerine, but the air was strangely still.

Gareth was standing on the far side of Beaumaris nick car park, hands thrust into his pockets and the collar on his jacket pulled up. It might have been spring, but the mornings were still nippy until the sun was overhead. He jangled the loose change in his pocket nervously.

Gareth had received a call at five a.m. to tell him that Declan was going to be moved from Beaumaris to HMP Rhoswen on the Welsh mainland. He would stay on remand there, housed on the Vulnerable Prisoners wing – alongside sex offenders, sources and witnesses, police officers and prison officers – until he could be taken in front of a judge. It would be at a crown court, given the severity of his crimes.

Gareth and Laura had slept badly. In fact, at four a.m. they had decided to stop trying and ate toast and drank tea in bed while trying to get their heads around all that had happened. Were they to blame for not detecting Declan's guilt sooner? Would Vicky Newell still be alive if they had?

357

Were the CID team culpable for her death? These were all questions that the senior leadership of North Wales Police and the IOPC would be asking in the coming months. And, no doubt, when the media got hold of the story, it would be a major news event.

Neither Gareth nor Laura could believe that they'd managed to get the investigation so wrong. Declan had been there all along, hiding in plain sight.

Gareth watched as a prison van with *HMP Rhoswen* printed on its side turned into the car park and drove over to the rear entrance of the police station. A moment later, the large steel door that led to the custody suite swung open and a figure appeared dressed in the regulation grey sweatshirt and jogging bottoms.

Declan was handcuffed to a uniformed police officer.

Jesus, how is this actually happening? Gareth wondered to himself. It didn't seem real that his friend and colleague had committed two murders and was now going to spend most of his life in prison.

Declan glanced over in Gareth's direction and their eyes locked for a moment.

They looked at each other in silence, no words left to be said.

And then a prison officer took Declan by the arm and led him inside the van and shut the doors behind him.

Gareth just didn't know how he felt other than slightly numb. And bewildered.

The prison van pulled away, crossed the car park and left.

Gareth watched it go.

Then he saw something out of the corner of his eye.

A figure was standing next to a bike over by the road where the entrance to the car park was located.

It was Osian.

Gareth gave him an uncertain wave.

Then he saw that Osian was sobbing.

He wiped his face with the sleeve of his hoodie, jumped on his bike and cycled away.

CHAPTER 61

It was dawn and Laura looked out over towards the horizon – where the ridges of Snowdonia met the flamingo sky. Up to the right there was still the faint outline of a crescent moon. It was stunning, but after the events of the previous evening, the day was already tinged with immense sadness. The news about Declan had been shattering.

'Shall I let him off?' Rosie asked as Elvis strained at the lead.

'Yeah,' Laura replied, slightly lost in her thoughts. 'There's no one down here.'

A second later, Elvis was thundering across the flat sands of Beaumaris Beach.

Laura took a moment and closed her eyes, taking in the steady rhythm of the waves and moans of wind that carried with it the smell of seaweed. She needed to clear her head of all the racing thoughts.

'Come on, loser!' Rosie laughed as she sprinted down the beach towards the water's edge.

Laura pulled off her hoodie and looked around. To her left stretched an endless expanse of windswept coast up to the north. She particularly liked that part of the island in the winter. The harsh grey rocks and V-shaped ravines where the freezing sea would smash with terrifying power.

There was a scream as Rosie plunged into the sea. A moment later, she burst through the surface with a resounding 'whoop'.

'Mum?' Rosie called.

'I'm coming, I'm coming,' Laura muttered as she padded over the wet sand, feeling it squish between her toes. She slipped off her slides and walked into the icy water. It cascaded up her ankles and then to mid-thigh, while soft ribbons of oarweed gently curled around her feet.

Even though the sea was only lapping at her waist, it still felt fiercely cold. For some reason, she wasn't feeling as brave today as she usually did. She paused for a moment on one foot and looked across the Strait's three miles of sea, which stretched across to the Welsh mainland.

Come on, Laura, just bloody get on with it! her inner voice growled at her. *Oh bollocks*, it added as she jumped and dived into the icy water. All semblance of warmth was blasted from her body and for a few moments she fought against the piercing chill before she emerged above the surface again.

Laura gasped. 'Fuck me, that's better!'

'Language please, Mother!' Rosie joked with mock offence.

Laura laughed.

The water had taken away all her pain, frustration and grief in seconds, and brought back life; she was reborn.

Ten minutes later, Laura and Rosie were walking back up the beach to their bags, where they dried themselves and put on warm clothes.

'Come on, Elvis,' Rosie said as she put on his lead. 'Good boy.'

They turned and made their way up the beach towards the main road.

'I'm going to make some bread today,' Laura announced. 'I'll go and get the ingredients after we've had breakfast.'

Rosie gave her a look.

'What?' Laura asked.

'The last time you made bread, it wasn't exactly a triumph, Mum,' Rosie replied. 'No offence.'

'Well, I am offended,' Laura said with a smile. 'My sourdough?'

'I nearly broke a tooth on it,' Rosie joked.

'Sod off.'

Before Laura could say anything else, she saw a figure standing by a car up on the main road.

It was Pete.

Her stomach tightened immediately with anxiety.

Oh shit! What the hell is he doing here?

'Isn't that Uncle Pete up there?' Rosie asked, pointing in his direction.

'Yeah, it is,' Laura said, trying to make light of a situation that was making her feel increasingly uneasy.

Pete waved at them with a beaming smile. 'Hey!'

'What are you doing here?' Laura asked in as friendly tone as she could muster.

Pete pointed to the car – a sleek black Audi convertible. 'I was picking up this beauty from a bloke up in Holyhead. I thought it would be rude not to drop in.'

'Great,' Rosie said with a smile. 'Nice car.'

'Thanks.' Pete looked at Laura. 'Fancy coming for a quick spin before we go back to yours?'

Laura gestured to Rosie and Elvis.

'It's all right, Mum. You go,' Rosie reassured her. 'I'll see you guys back home in a bit.'

Laura watched Rosie turn right and then head away.

'Everything all right?' Laura asked Pete, her pulse now racing.

'Yeah. Fine,' Pete replied with a cheesy grin. 'Especially now I've got this boy toy.'

'Actually, you know what, I think I'll walk,' Laura said, trying to make a joke but panicking. 'I'm still a bit damp from my swim.'

'Come on,' Pete said. 'I'm not taking no for answer.' He tossed her the keys, which she instinctively caught. 'Tell you what, why don't you give it a spin? Goes like the bloody clappers.'

There seemed to be no other option but to get into the car.

'Okay,' Laura said uncertainly as she went to the driver's door and opened it. 'But I don't want to be too long.'

'It's fine,' Pete said as he got in. 'Down the coast to Menai and back. Twenty minutes.'

Laura started the engine but she was feeling very tense as she pulled away.

'There you go,' Pete laughed. 'I'll put the top down in a minute.'

Laura drove them out of Beaumaris and along the main coastal road down to Menai.

Pete looked over at her. 'I've got something to show you,' he said as he opened the glove compartment.

'Okay,' Laura said uncertainly. She had no idea what he was talking about.

As she looked over, to her horror she saw that Pete was holding a Glock 17 handgun.

'I think it's time that me and you went somewhere for a little chat, don't you?' he said coldly.

Laura gasped. 'What the hell are you doing, Pete?'

'Just drive the car, Laura,' Pete snapped.

'Where are we going?'

'I thought you and I, and your friend Claudia, could have a chat and clear up a few things. It won't take long.'

Laura frowned. 'Where is she?'

Pete gestured to the back of the car.

At that moment, there was a metallic thud. Someone was inside the boot of the car.

AUTHOR NOTE

This book is very much a work of fiction. It's nothing more than a story that is the product of my imagination. It is set in Anglesey, a beautiful island off North Wales that is steeped in history and folklore spanning over two thousand years. It is therefore worth mentioning that I have made liberal use of artistic licence. Some names, places and even myths have been changed or adapted to enhance the pace and substance of the story. There are roads, pubs, garages and other amenities that don't necessarily exist on the real island of Anglesey.

It's important for me to convey how warm, friendly and helpful the inhabitants of Anglesey have always been on my numerous research visits. The island itself is stunning and I hope that my descriptions of its landscape and geography have done it some justice.

If you enjoyed *The Drowning Isle* and would like to be the first to know about my upcoming novels, any promotions and my writing, you can join my newsletter. Visit https://tinyurl.com/TDISM to sign up. Just for signing up, you'll also receive a FREE copy of the prequel to my DI Ruth Hunter Series. Just so you know, your data is private and confidential and it will never be passed on to a third party. I'll only be in touch about books news, and if you want to unsubscribe, you can do so at any time.

ACKNOWLEDGEMENTS

Thank you to everyone who has worked so hard to make this book happen. The incredible team at Avon who are an absolute dream to work with. Sarah Bauer and Helen Huthwaite for their patience, guidance and superb notes. The other lovely people at Avon – Elisha Lundin, Gabriella Drinkald and Maddy Dunne-Kirby, as well as Toby James in the art team, who produced such a fantastic cover; Sammy Luton in the sales team; and Emily Chan in production, without whom this book wouldn't exist.

To my superb agent, Millie Hoskins, at United Agents. Dave Gaughran for his ongoing advice and working his magic behind the scenes.

Finally, my mum, Pam, and dad, Dave for their overwhelming enthusiasm. And, of course, my stronger, better half, Nicola, whose initial reaction and notes on my work I trust implicitly.

If you loved *The Drowning Isle*, why not go back to the beginning of the Anglesey series?

Will there be blood in the water?

The first book in Simon McCleave's gripping crime thriller series.

Available in all good bookshops now.

Some secrets should stay buried for ever…

The second book in Simon McCleave's pulse-pounding crime thriller series.

Available in all good bookshops now.

Three bodies on the beach.
One killer on the loose.

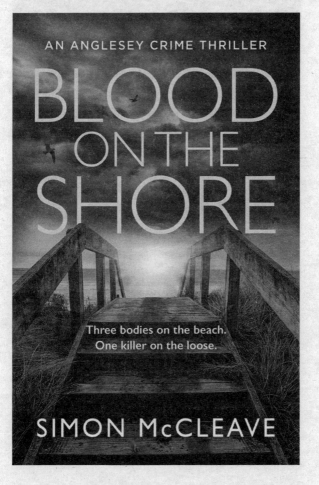

AN ANGLESEY CRIME THRILLER

BLOOD
ON THE
SHORE

Three bodies on the beach.
One killer on the loose.

SIMON McCLEAVE

The third book in Simon McCleave's atmospheric
crime thriller series.

Available in all good bookshops now.

Your FREE book is waiting for you now!

Get your FREE copy of the prequel to the DI Ruth Hunter
Series NOW!

Visit:
https://tinyurl.com/TDISM
and join Simon's VIP Email Club.